Praise for
The Guest Book Trilogy
Book Two
The Girls in Cabin Number Three

"Annie meets a new guest who slowly begins to unravel secrets from her own family's past in the second part of The Guest Book Trilogy: The Girls in Cabin Number Three. This book takes up where The Man in Cabin Number Five left off, with plenty of intrigue in an idyllic mountain locale." Susan Denley, former Associate Features Editor, Los Angeles Times

The Man in Cabin Number Five

"For those looking for a complex, engaging novel you won't be able to put down, this book is for you." – Review by Book Excellence (www. bookexcellence.com)

"Your book came yesterday, stayed up half the night reading it, and finished this morning. I guess you can figure out I LOVED it and can't wait for the next book. You spun an incredible tale, and I fell in love with all the characters.

"I felt I was right in the middle of the book with Annie and seeing everything through her eyes.

"Thank you for such a great read."

Deanne Dillenbeck

"Masterfully written. An entertaining work that will keep the reader hooked until the end. Congratulations on an exceptional book." Readers' Favorite.

Also by Chrysteen Braun

The Man in Cabin Number Five,
Book One of the Guest Book Trilogy

Coming Soon:

The Starlet in Cabin Number Seven
Book three of the Guest Book Trilogy

And

Family Portrait

THE GUEST BOOK TRILOGY  BOOK TWO

THE GIRLS IN CABIN NUMBER THREE

Keep Reading!
Chrysteen

A NOVEL

CHRYSTEEN BRAUN

Design and distribution by Bublish, Inc.

ISBN: 978-1-647046-34-7 (eBook)
ISBN: 978-1-647046-32-3 (paperback)
ISBN: 978-1-647046-33-0 (hardcover)

For Larry, with love;
always the wind beneath my wings.

PROLOGUE

This afternoon, they brought three new girls up from Los Angeles. The one with shoulder-length brown hair, large brown eyes and painted red lips was called Ida Mae. Violet, a redhead, held on to her young son's arm as he pulled at her to go see the horses hitched to a nearby wagon. With red curly hair himself, he was probably five or six. I didn't hear the name of the third girl at first, but Violet called out to her to help restrain her son as she tried to keep from dropping her suitcase. Her name was Norma. She was pretty, too, with bleached blonde hair and beautiful blue eyes. They were all very slender, including the boy, and I made a mental note to make sure they had enough to eat. I'd learned most men liked their women seductive and well-proportioned.

I stood at the front door of Bracken Fern Manor, their new home, and watched for a few minutes while the men unloaded the rest of their belongings, then stepped out from the shade, covered my eyes from the bright sun, and went to greet them. A quick cool breeze whipped Norma's hat off and Violet's son quickly forgot about the horses and ran to pick it up.

My name was Elizabeth, and in those days, they called us "working girls."

Elizabeth Davis, 1930

BOOK TWO

Another Year has Passed

I'm almost eighty-one now, and I can count on one hand those I have left; at least, those I truly care about. Of course, I still have my husband and his daughter. And I have to count her children, but I'm talking about family and old friends. Sometimes, all I can think about is death.

It was over fifty years ago when my sister died.

I always cry at weddings and funerals, and this was no exception, although I believe my tears were more for my parents than for my sister. After all, she was gone; her struggle with alcohol was finally over. *At peace now*, as everyone liked to say, as their way of expressing their condolences.

I tried to call up other memories of that day so many years ago, but I only recall taking my mother's hand and squeezing it.

My dear friend Sarah was eighty when she died last year. She was back on the East Coast, and at least we'd had a chance to talk just before her heart attack. She was always the one I could go to when I needed a friend; I was the same for her, no matter where we lived. I could pick up the phone to call her and she'd say, "I was just thinking about you!"

I flew back for her funeral. She'd moved there when her third husband, an engineer, was transferred for work, and stayed after his death.

Her daughter Annalise was there with her children, all of them dressed in black, and they sat in the front row and wept.

Thoughts of our childhood came rushing back to me as I sat in the small chapel. I recalled when we shaved our legs for the first time and thought we were so clever. I know an involuntary smile came to my face, but I didn't care.

"Get in here and clean this tub," my mother called to me when we were done. We never thought to wipe away the blood from the nicks on our legs and the hair we'd left behind.

For years, I'd sneak Sarah a Christmas present when her mother was in one of her anti-holiday moods; something like a new book that could be hidden under her bed. One year, I really tempted fate; I bought her a "Best Friends" necklace with two halves of a heart. I wore mine every day, visible for all to see. She wore hers, but under her blouse.

And now a friend of my husband's has died. He lost his wife several years ago, and I think he was simply lonely. Some men lose their will to live when they lose their wives, and he was one of them. We made a point to include him in any weekend trips we planned, and we always had him over for the holidays. He unfailingly put on a bright face, but I could tell he was just a shell of the man my husband had called a friend for so many years.

His daughters made all the funeral arrangements. They cremated him. They had boards on easels filled with photos, just like I'd had for my eightieth birthday. His were glimpses from his youth, his wedding, his children, and, of course, his classic car. The service wasn't too religious, which was fine by me. The pastor referred to him by the right name, which was helpful; I'd actually been to funerals where the deceased's name had been mispronounced. Of course, everyone pretended they hadn't noticed when they later said, "What a lovely service."

My husband offered to buy his car, a beautiful 1964 Rolls-Royce Silver Cloud III, and the girls gave him a fabulous Colt handgun collection they didn't want to deal with. It was on the Sunday after he picked up the car and guns that I came back from the grocery store and found him sitting at the dining room table surrounded by boxes of guns and a pad of paper.

"I'm cataloging these," he offered. "I really need to do the same for mine."

"Yes, you do," I commented. "And take photographs of them, too."

No one took real photos any more. They used their cell phones and stored everything on them or on their computers on the cloud. I barely trusted the computer to not crash, much less store valuable information on it.

I tried to set my aches and pains aside and get back to work on my books. I'd finished the first one about the cabins I bought in the mountains so many years ago, and the secret one held. And now I was working on the second one. It was the 80s then, and I was only thirty and had little fear. If I believed what a friend once told me, that I'd live to my mid-eighties, then I knew I had plenty of time left to work on the puzzle that was my life.

Today, with my own mortality looming around me everywhere, I hoped I'd live long enough to finish the next two books.

Part One

Springtime in the Mountains

CHAPTER ONE

It was 1981 and springtime in Lake Arrowhead, California, and there was still some snow on the ground in areas where the sun hadn't melted it. Berms were now covered in dirt, and small grainy volcanic rock lined the roads up the mountain, looking dingy, needing a fresh layer of snow to be pretty again.

Daffodils and tulips that had been planted over the years popped up along the roads into town. Every once in a while, it was obvious which ones had multiplied on their own, for they spread naturally in random clumps. Clusters of them emerged from the small gardens in front of each of the cabins too, and soon I'd finish filling in with spots of other annual color.

I'd purchased the B&B, actually a series of seven cabins, the summer before, when I'd come to the mountains eager to clear my head. I hadn't come with the plan of moving up, but I'd also not dreamed I'd find out that my husband David had been seeing someone else.

I knew it would not solve *all* life's problems, but the entire lifestyle here made me realize how easily I could start over. I didn't have to run away; I could simply live where no one knew me. Once I made up my mind, it hadn't taken me long to come up with the serendipitous idea to buy the cabins I stayed in and get a new perspective on life.

We had a guest coming in the afternoon, and the only vacancy we had was Number Five, now called Cedar Cove Cabin. As a rule, I always

checked the cabins out before guests arrived, just to make sure everything was in order. The moment I opened the door to Five, I took in the
recently refurbished room. I loved the scent of the newly cleaned and
oiled knotty pine walls and ceilings. I'd replaced the carpet and added
a large area rug, new furniture, and bedding. Everything was exactly as
I had designed it. None of the cabins had been restored since they were
built in the late twenties for a movie production company. Sam and his
wife had owned them for a couple of decades, and she'd passed away
years earlier. Once I had the crazy idea of buying them, Sam agreed to
sell them to me. He would stay on as "Official Innkeeper and Historian."

Cabin Number Five was by its very nature, a little freakish, and
our most legendary. We rented it out only when the other cabins were
reserved, and Sam and I'd agreed to never speak of the suicide with any
of the guests. Some things were just better left unsaid.

It was as chilly as the other cabins before the fireplace was lit, but
I always shuddered as I entered it. I recalled the quiet woman who had
insisted on seeing the cabin last winter. I'd warned her it was still clut-
tered with years of cast offs and miscellaneous junk.

Alyce Murphy had come to see the cabin where her father had hung
himself. He'd murdered his business partner and family thirty years ago;
she hadn't found out until recently he hadn't died of a heart attack as
she'd always believed. I'd asked Sam about it, and it baffled him. The
people he bought the cabins from never disclosed that minor fact when
they sold him the property.

When we made the discovery, we had two choices; if we asked any
of the 'old timers' in town if they knew anything about it, we could be
dredging up unfavorable notoriety. Or we could just tuck the knowledge
of it all away for posterity. We chose the latter: to just not talk about it.
I hated to admit I was a little superstitious, so once we'd finished the
restoration, we smudged the cabin with bundles of smoldering sage to
rid it of any taint of sadness and despair.

It made me wonder, though. What stories could these cabins tell?
I had embraced the project of buying them in all their faded glory and
kept the fragments of history Sam had saved over the years: the old

yellowed guest book, a few photos, and several boxes of assorted treasures guests had inadvertently left behind.

Our two cats, Jezebel and Socks, followed me into Cabin Number Five, just to make sure all was well, and they watched as I lit the fireplace to take the chill out of the air.

"Come on, girls," I said to them as I began to close the cabin door behind me.

I'd moved my interior design studio here to Lake Arrowhead, where opportunities to decorate lake houses and vacation homes filled me with optimism after the failure of my marriage. I'd chosen to start over, which meant I didn't have the clientele I needed to fully support myself, but finishing the cabins so we'd have rental opportunities, and my part-time job at the floor coverings store in town, helped me get started. I'd written contracts for several flooring and window coverings jobs for the store, and had already picked up one very lucrative decorating job.

One weekend while I was at the store, an elegant sixty-ish woman came in to inquire about local contractors. She had inherited her mother's lake cabin and was hoping to do some renovations once they officially settled the estate.

Her name was Carrie Davis, and her mother had lived up in Lake Arrowhead for almost fifty years, in a log home which, by her description, was filled with many years of memories.

Carrie was attractive and well dressed with trim fitting jeans and a sporty un-tucked blue and white striped shirt that hung below a dark blue pullover sweater. Her short brown hair, with just a hint of gray, accented her face perfectly. Her clear brown eyes took in everything in the store, assessing the selections and the displays of tile, hardwood flooring and window coverings. I could tell she was definitely a professional woman.

She'd lived in the home with her mother the last few years, having moved back up from Westwood, near UCLA. We compared notes on the neighborhoods down the hill, along with the clogged freeways, and I gently turned the conversation to my design services.

"I hate to admit I'm having a hard time getting started," she confessed. "Part of the charm of the house is that nothing has changed since the 30s, and I grew up with it that way. The other part is that nothing has changed since the 30s and it really needs some updating."

"That makes perfect sense. I'd love to take a look at it. It sounds like how I felt when I first saw my cabins."

"Cabins?"

"Yes." I told her about the B&B.

"You're kidding, right? I've stayed there, and they're delightful."

Her easy smile didn't hide the accompanying flush in her face.

"I have a friend. Paul," she whispered. "He actually rented one of the cabins while he was finishing remodeling his house up here."

It suddenly dawned on me.

"I remember him. But I never saw you."

"That was the intention," she laughed. "I was always home before Gram woke in the morning."

"Gram?"

"Oh, Mother."

"You're funny," I said, and thought *I just might have a new friend.*

"Will you still work with me after knowing some of my secrets?" she asked shamelessly.

"Absolutely."

"Oh, that would be perfect, Annie. Now I won't have to pay those snooty Beverly Hills decorators their out-of-this-world prices for what you can do right here!" She laughed out loud, her eyes sparkling. "I'm so glad I stopped in."

When she left, she thanked me and said, "I'll be back in soon."

I stopped for a moment and took a breath. This move to the lake was turning out to be more than I'd hoped, with new clients and locals I was beginning to love.

I met Noah for lunch at Ginny's Coffee Shop in town. Ginny and Sam were quite close, and she provided the cinnamon rolls and muffins for our guests staying in the cabins. Through the small opening into the kitchen, I caught a glimpse of Ginny's curly gray hair as she moved briskly around in the work area, helping get a large order ready to serve. She reminded me of a grandma, warm and full of the right kind of advice. She also didn't take any guff from anyone and was not shy about putting you straight if you needed it. The town loved her.

"Hey, Babe," Noah said, sliding into the booth and reaching for my hand.

"Hey there, yourself," I said, watching him settling in across from me. He took his baseball hat off and I smiled as he ran his fingers through his flattened hair. Seeing him always cheered me up. His beard had grown longer again, as had his hair, but he was still very handsome, even in his wrinkled work clothes.

"I know. Hair cut time," he said, giving me that smile that always made my heart skip.

Next to Sam, Noah was the first person I'd met when I came up here. He remodeled homes, and he took a lot of pride in his work.

When I found out David had been seeing someone, Noah was there for me, trying to help me pick up the pieces. He helped me move the last of my things from my house down the hill, although that had meant stoically standing there while David insulted him by calling him a 'cowboy.' And when I needed reinforcement, he also repeatedly reminded me that David was crazy to have hurt me like he did.

I watched Noah as he sipped his Coke. I knew he cared about me, and that made me care for him even more. He'd taken me under his wing.

"Whatcha all havin'?" Ginny asked, pad ready. She was always so perky. Twenty years ago, she lost her husband in a terrible car accident. She'd come up to the lake to get away and ended up buying the restaurant from a husband whose wife ran off with another man.

"Hey, Ginny," I said. "I'll have a club sandwich."

"I'll have a cheeseburger and fries," Noah said.

We sat in comfortable silence, and Noah looked at me.

"A penny for your thoughts."

We were going to take my new Jeep out and do some off-roading and hiking, and I asked, "We're not going to take the Jeep anywhere *too off-road* where it'll get dented, right?"

The plan was to drive off the paved roads to a beautiful outlook Noah knew and had been to many times. I was a newbie with all the mountain hazards, and my Jeep still had that new car smell, so I was careful where I drove it. I wanted at least one season before I slid and crashed into a tree or something horrible.

Out of nowhere, a sweet fragrance wafted toward us, followed by a woman who edged her way to our table.

"Excuse me. Are you Noah Chambers?" she asked, before offering her hand.

The woman was stunning. I immediately felt underdressed and insignificant in her presence. I sat there, surprised and inwardly appalled at myself.

When Noah suddenly stood up, I felt even worse.

"I'm Bunny Bryant." She gave me a quick, dismissive glance.

"I'm Annie," I said, my throat dry, my voice hardly more than a whisper.

I guessed her to be in her early forties, with wonderful blue eyes and blonde hair worn shoulder length. Her long-sleeved tan sweater was almost certainly cashmere and her tan slacks were perfectly tailored. I tried not to stare, or to check out her shoes.

"I'm so sorry to interrupt your lunch, but I was told at your job site you'd probably be here." She proceeded without giving us much thought. "I have a rather extensive project I'd like you to look at for me."

"Sure," Noah said, confidently. He pulled a chair up to the booth and offered it to Bunny, and then slid back in opposite me. "What are you thinking?"

"I just bought a home up here, and it needs a little of everything. New kitchen, bathrooms…and a list of other minor things."

I could tell she intrigued Noah, and I was sinking. He couldn't take his eyes off her. And I couldn't take my eyes off what I was sure was a

Rolex watch and an enormous diamond ring on her right hand. There was no ring on her left finger.

Noah managed a shrug. "Sounds good. What's your time frame?"

"I'd like to start as soon as possible...when would you be available to take a look at it?"

"Well," he said, taking in a deep breath, then releasing it in thought. "When are you available?"

"I can meet you any time. I'm staying at the Resort until the work is done."

I'm sure you are, I thought to myself.

Noah thought a moment more and then looked at me. I said nothing.

"I could swing by this afternoon. The guys can continue working at the job site. Would that work?"

"That would be great!" She was overjoyed.

Noah nodded towards me and said, "Annie's an interior designer, if you'd like to talk to her about what you have in mind."

Poor Noah. He had no idea what was already in the air between this woman and me. I hated to admit that if she was a cougar, I was in trouble. As for the potential opportunity for her as a client, I really didn't enjoy working with people who were high maintenance. And that's what Bunny Bryant certainly appeared to be. *Very* high maintenance.

Bunny never gave me another look. "I'll be fine. I love decorating and I already have all the artwork I brought back from Europe. In fact, I have more art and furniture than I can use."

So, I was dismissed without another glance from her.

Noah got her address and promised to meet her at three.

"I know about where the house is," he said.

Bunny stood, shook his hand again, then actually looked over at me but said to Noah, "See you later, then."

Her fragrance stayed with us throughout lunch, and then when I hugged Noah goodbye, I could still catch traces of her perfume on his shirt and hands. It smelled expensive, and I had to admit, it smelled good.

CHAPTER TWO

That night, we had rib eyes at the Cowboy Bar and I could tell Noah was excited to share about his meeting with Bunny.

Her proper name was Barbara, but she'd been called Bunny since she was a child. She came from a modest background, and met her husband, a plastic surgeon, when she went with a girlfriend who wanted to have some facial work done. They lived in Beverly Hills, in what she considered a smaller home of six thousand square feet. She and her husband were divorcing. Her husband got their second home in Palm Springs, so Bunny got to buy a home where she wanted. And she chose Lake Arrowhead.

Her new home was in Cedar Ridge Estates, a private gated community on the southeast side of the lake. Noah said it was like living in a private forest, and if he got the job, he'd take me to see it.

I already knew more than I wanted to about her, and I'd heard it was always best to keep your enemy close. I'd have to stay on guard.

"How did she find you?"

"Someone at the lumber yard recommended me when she went in there looking for a contractor. Her husband's apparently paying the price for cheating on her. She figured she didn't care how much money it would cost to do what she wanted."

I gave him a side-long glance when he said that, and I could see he hadn't realized how flippant he'd sounded.

"You're not going to take advantage of that, are you?" I asked.

"No," he said. "But I *am* going to charge what I think the job's worth and if she doesn't want to pay for it, then *oh well*. I do too many favors for people and that's fine if they can't afford to pay for it, but she can. She'll still get a fair price for the work, and she'll get a great job to boot!"

Noah drank another beer, and I had another glass of wine as we watched people getting out on the dance floor. When a slow dance came up, Noah stood and took my hand. I loved dancing with him, the way he held me close and breathed heavily in my ear. He was strong and trim and it felt good to be with someone who wanted to be with me.

That night, we planned to stay in my cabin. I had two more guests coming in the morning and I wanted to be there to greet them. Sam and I and the two camp cats made quite a welcoming committee. They'd sit at the end of the reception desk, ready to purr for any guest who scratched their chins.

Because we were in the mountains where bears and bobcats roamed foraging for food, we kept them inside during the night. I never left them out after dark. They were just as happy with that arrangement as they often sat curled up by the fireplace, or snuggled with me in bed. If they wanted a change of scenery, they'd go to Sam's, where he always had an extra cat box and their cat treats ready.

When we got to the cabin, Jezebel and Socks greeted us at the door, and once Noah started a fire and I fed them, they stretched out on the rug in front of the fireplace. I felt we were a perfect little family.

Noah reached over and did his thing that drove me crazy. First, he touched my cheek and gave me a look that left no doubt what he wanted. He kissed me with kisses that covered my mouth. He kissed my neck, then unbuttoned my blouse and kissed me between my breasts as he unfastened my bra.

I finished undressing, and he did the same. The way we fit together perfectly, melding our bodies, was so intimate and charged. I found myself again with emotion that made my eyes tear up. I'd done that a lot with Noah. He made me feel so complete and so loved. This was so different from the way David made me feel. Nine years of marriage with him had never made me feel this way. While the anger was all but gone, I still couldn't stop thinking about the years I'd lost. When Noah and I made love, the tears were for what I now had.

The next morning, we had breakfast at Ginny's. I remember when we first walked in after a night of being together, the regulars went silent and gave us a look. It was as if they'd caught us. It was obvious we were an item. But now that we were no longer a sensation, no one even looked up unless it was to greet us.

Noah had waffles, and I had eggs and toast with iced tea. I sat and watched as Noah started making out his materials list for Bunny's project. He always chewed his lip or bit on his pencil when he was thinking and I could see the wheels turning with calculations; board feet of lumber, cases of tiles, tools, labor, flex time for weather delays. All his skills and thought processes to assemble the details were impressive.

I knew he was really hoping he'd get this job, and I truly wanted him to. But I dreaded the feeling that if he did indeed work with Bunny, he would be in for a rough ride. As I continued to study Noah, Ginny reached up to the television mounted above the silverware station and turned the volume up so she could hear the news.

"Oh dear," she said.

We all listened to a news flash that a child had gone missing from their family's campsite yesterday during the day. The family of four, mother, father, the young girl and an older brother, had just finished breakfast. They were going to go to the Wildhaven Ranch wildlife sanctuary to see the animals, but when they were ready to leave, they couldn't find six-year-old Sophia Rodriguez. The Sheriff's department was starting an official search for her as the news was being broadcast.

"That little girl must be terrified," Ginny said, still clutching the remote, "not to mention her family."

A couple of customers stood by our booth to listen, and we all nodded in agreement. I remembered a missing child when we'd first bought our lake house twenty years ago, and how much it'd frightened my mother. My sister Loni and I weren't allowed to go outside until the little girl eventually found her way back to the camp.

Historically, there weren't a lot of incidents in the mountains, but Noah had told me about another missing child before I came up. The photo of the murdered little girl from last year filled the television screen, and the newscaster reminded us of that grisly conclusion with a recap of the story and more photos.

"I hope they find her and that nothing terrible has happened to her," I said glumly.

"I'm sure they will and she'll be fine," Noah said optimistically. He was trying to make me feel better.

We kept watching until another news story came on and customers filtered back to their tables. I couldn't help but think about that child all day.

Later that afternoon, Sam had a message for me when I checked in. It was from my mother.

"Your father's fallen off a ladder," she blurted when I called her back. "He dislocated his ankle and fractured the two bones in his lower leg."

"How on earth did that happen?" Images of him lying there after he'd fallen filled my mind.

"He was cleaning out the rain gutters and apparently didn't have the ladder on solid ground, so it sank into a mud patch and he went down." She was trying her best to sound positive, but I could hear the concern in her voice.

"Do you want me to come out?"

"I'd love it, but not right now," she said. "We need to get him home and set up a hospital bed in the living room."

When they retired, my parents opted to move into a retirement community in Prescott, Arizona, and their mobile home was single story and equipped with some aging in place features. My father wasn't what I would consider old, but he was in his early sixties. While he was in good shape, this was going to set him back. I had to admit that until now, I hadn't given my parent's aging much thought. They'd always been active and had had no medical issues.

"Will you have someone come out to help you?" I asked.

"Yes, the doctor is working on that now."

That was a relief.

I told my mother I'd plan to come out next week and stay a few days to relieve her. She started crying. "Annie, I hope this isn't the beginning of the end for us."

"Mother, you'll both be fine," I said, trying to reassure her as much as myself. I knew she was feeling the stress of the situation and while I wasn't really looking forward to dealing with this, I knew going to see them was the right thing to do.

Before I left, I checked on a client's orders. Grayson Underwood's project was an ongoing work in progress, and I didn't have any plans yet for delivery, so if I had to leave, this was good timing.

I stayed in the mountains for the weekend so I could spend time with Noah, and Monday morning I caught a flight out to Arizona. I planned to stay a week at the most, so I packed lightly; I could do my laundry there before I returned home.

Before they retired, my mother worked for our school district, setting up a healthy lunch program at grade schools. She also established an assistance program so students who needed help could sign up for free or reduced-price meals. However, most of the children weren't interested in eating healthier and about a hundred pounds of food a day had to be disposed of.

Exasperated at the waste, my mother set up one of the first programs to have this excess food picked up and taken to homeless shelters. When they moved to Prescott, she volunteered at the local K-6 school, and because she was still passionate about her work, she was instrumental in starting similar programs.

When I got there, I hoped I would be able to convince her that my father was going to be fine with me taking care of him if she wanted to go back to work.

My mother picked me up at the airport and, after a big hug, thanked me for making the trip. She also warned me that my father was in a lot of pain and wasn't taking his recovery well. He hated being cooped up and being fussed over.

So I was a little prepared when I saw him as I came into their house. With a slight smile, he tried to mask his misery and said, "I hope you don't mind if I don't get up. I finally just got back down."

I could see the discomfort in my father's face, and I understood my mother's concern. Although his doctor had assured my mother that he'd be okay, he looked like he'd lost ten pounds since I'd last seen him. He'd always been slender, so any weight loss, especially in his face, was especially noticeable.

Even though I could tell he was in pain, he was still very handsome. I'd seen them about four months ago, for Thanksgiving weekend, but since then I could see a few strands of gray coming in at his temples. His otherwise dark hair and strong brown eyes were still two of his best features.

"How was the trip?" he asked.

"It was good, Dad," I said, going to him and kissing him on the cheek. *"Quányù,"* I said in Mandarin. It meant get well soon. I knew he didn't speak it anymore, but I thought it was a nice thing to say. I didn't speak Mandarin at all, so on the plane, I practiced saying it.

"Are you hungry?" my mother asked. I was, so we made sandwiches. We set my father's lunch on a tray and put it on his lap. My mother and I ate on trays in front of the sofa.

I watched my father eat in silence. His eyes drooped, and he was having a hard time staying awake.

"Let me take your tray," I finally said.

He laid his head back in his chair and within moments, he dozed, his breathing slow and gentle.

I ended up staying the week, and I took over most of the day-to-day chores while my mother took advantage of getting some rest and trying to go in to work.

We talked about what they were doing prior to my father's fall, and they'd been planning a vacation to the East Coast to see the fall colors.

Obviously, it would have to wait until next year when my father could walk without discomfort.

We talked about Noah and how I was doing.

"Everything has calmed down," I told them. "I'm happy."

I talked about Grayson and how he was the perfect client and then mentioned Bunny, and we all laughed when I called her a cougar.

"I'm hoping she's not," I said, making a face.

Once I made myself relax, I actually enjoyed the time I spent with my parents. They drove me to the airport, and I insisted my father sit in the car as my mother pulled to the curb and I pulled out my luggage.

"I'll call you when I get home," I said, kissing them both.

When my plane landed, I called Noah to let him know I'd be home soon, but when there was no answer, I left a message on the office phone for Sam. The lumberyard and Sam were the best places to leave a message for him.

It always surprised me that the first part of the hilly terrain leading up the mountain was wild and almost barren, never green, always sun-baked and desert-like. There were few trees, and I'd never seen the bushes there turn green. Gradually, though, as the elevation rose and the closer I got to home, the temperature grew cooler and the green of the trees was what always welcomed me the most. I realized I was genuinely glad to be getting home, and I could hardly wait to see Noah and the cats.

They were all outside my cabin when I got there, and it couldn't have been a more perfect welcome home committee. I fed the girls and scooted them back outside. After a quick shower, Noah and I made love.

Always hungry, we had a late lunch at Ginny's, and when I saw the TV, it reminded me of the terrible story about the missing little girl.

"They found her face down in the lake," Noah said, reading my mind. She'd been molested and just tossed in there. "We're all taking it pretty hard."

CHAPTER THREE

Living in the mountains among the wildlife was still so new to me.

I was disappointed I hadn't yet seen deer crossing our property like Sam had promised. Last winter, after a fresh snowfall, I'd seen hoof marks leading across and in front of the cabins. They must have eaten berries from some bushes at the edge of the highway, for snow had been crushed down where they'd stood. It was obvious where they'd headed back into the woods behind the cabins.

Now with the warmer weather, I wouldn't see their tracks, but I did notice all the low-lying fruit from the apple and pear trees was disappearing. I had Sam help me pick the rest so we could fill a basket and leave it out. In a couple of days, it was empty.

"Do you think it was the deer, or a bear?" I asked.

"I reckon it was the deer who enjoyed our efforts since the basket hasn't been tossed. A bear wouldn't have been so polite."

I hung some bird feeders from our trees, and against the recommendation of both Sam and Noah, found something I could put peanuts in to feed the squirrels that constantly scampered about. I loved to watch them pack their mouths, then scurry away to hide their bounty.

We were averaging two bookings a week, which was a vast increase over when I first got the cabins restored, but it was nowhere near where we needed to be to make any money. I was bringing in enough to make my payment to Sam, but I needed to figure out a way to give us a kickstart.

A couple of the cabin B&Bs up here like ours also offered wedding venues, but that seemed like so much work. And even if I went that route, I didn't have anyone to manage something like that for me. The only thing I could think of doing was to increase my advertising, so I contacted the local newspaper and set up a series of ads. They offered to interview me and an article with photos came out the next week. My friend Sarah, who was a graphic designer, took the article along with photos we'd taken of the restored cabins and made a brochure for us to begin handing out.

I asked a local gift store if they'd be interested in putting something inexpensive along with a gift certificate into baskets we made with Ginny's cookies, our chocolate, a free night stay at the cabins along with a complimentary in-home interior design consultation and we gave these out when groups asked for contributions to their fundraisers.

I knew our cabins were the best dressed in town, but I had to get the word out.

Before I became an interior designer, my first real job was working in a realty office. I began making recommendations about re-arranging and staging houses that were going on the market. It had given the realtor a distinct advantage over other agents to offer this service, and I found it increased my interest in design as well.

I realized there was no reason I couldn't use my experience up here as well, so I found the most successful agent in town and made an appointment to talk to her about setting something like that up with her. She loved the idea, and I went to her next listing. We updated her brochure to include some before and after photos to show her prospective clients, and when she gave a gift after the sale, I offered her an hour of my design time, which she passed along to the client.

Being a flatlander, that spring I found out just how much I still needed to learn about living in the mountains. I already knew that during the cold months, if the temperature got too low, plumbing pipes could freeze and burst. Although the wall heaters in the cabins were older, they worked well, and we set at them at fifty-five degrees, which then meant the gas bill was always high.

My first winter had been relatively light, and Sam and Noah were always around to dig us out if too much snow collected around the cabins.

"If you leave it unchecked, it'll eventually cause damage to windows, foundations, and porches," Noah said.

"We figured that out the hard way," Sam added. "The first couple of years we were up here, we didn't do much maintenance, and we paid for it later."

The next thing I learned that spring was that we were on a septic tank. I'd noticed a foul smell outside the back of cabin number three for a couple of days. I checked the other cabins, and there didn't seem to be any issues in the bathrooms themselves.

The next time I went down to the office, I mentioned it to Sam and after scratching his head, he scrunched his mouth and said, "Sounds like we need to drain the septic tank."

"What the heck is that?" I made a face.

"Well, it's the country version of the sewer system. It's not a big deal. We just need to call the pumpin' truck to come out is all."

I didn't want to appear completely ignorant, so I tried not to panic when I asked, "And how much does that cost?" I mentally deducted another couple of hundred dollars from my tight bank balance.

"About a hundred dollars." Sam looked a number up in his book and dialed. After a few minutes, he said, "They can be here in a couple hours."

"*Great*," I said.

Within the hour, I got my first lesson in pumping.

"Ya see," the pumper said as he dug around for the lid to the tank, "First, I have to find the exact spot. Unfortunately, it's usually right in the middle of the crap. Oh, excuse me."

Not that I needed the gory details, but once he found it, he explained, "It's an underground wastewater disposal system. The poop flows from the building into a tank. It naturally separates, and the top part goes out into the drainfield, but the heavy stuff that can't be broken down by bacteria needs to be pumped. That's it in a nutshell."

That was more than a nutshell, and while he pumped, the smell was so strong I couldn't stick around; I made my way back down to the office and got out the checkbook.

"I guess, easy come, easy go," I said. "I'm just glad we don't have any guests."

Sam nodded in agreement.

Then I learned that the fireplaces had to periodically be cleaned. Sam admitted most of the guests stayed in just a few of the cabins, so their fireplaces seemed to work fine. But we had a guest in cabin number six, and she got smoked out when she lit the fire.

It was easy enough to put her in another cabin, but we ended up paying for cleaning her clothes and when we went back into the cabin the next day, the residue from the smoke clung to the new draperies and bedspread. We had to take them in to be cleaned, and then we had the carpet and area rug cleaned and deodorized.

Not only was it a time-consuming undertaking, I watched as more dollar signs flew out of my account.

In the meantime, Grayson's living room and dining room projects were ready to install, and I made arrangements to have everything delivered.

Grayson was my first client up here. The flooring store referred him to me, and he was *the* perfect customer. He'd purchased quite a large home on the lake and was interested in redecorating it.

He was in his mid-fifties and reminded me of Robert Redford with reddish hair and a trim beard. He was fit and wore his clothing like a Ralph Lauren model. On top of that, he was handsome and rich.

When I first started working with him, Noah had a feeling Grayson was interested in more than just my decorating skills. I knew how to maintain a client relationship and was not only annoyed, but offended. Every time we met to go over selections, he was a perfect gentleman and was so formal; I periodically had a hard time getting a read on him.

I assured Noah that the relationship I'd started with Grayson was totally professional.

We were on our third project, and aside from this being the largest job I'd undertaken, I had the most design freedom with him than I'd had with any other client. Grayson immediately liked almost everything I showed him, which made my job a lot easier. Sometimes wealthy customers could be challenging, but he was as perfect as he could be.

I had to admit, though, that when I met Bunny, I understood what Noah had been leery of.

CHAPTER FOUR

A few days later, I was by myself having lunch at Ginny's when I saw Carrie Davis come in. The restaurant was busy, and she was heading for the counter when I called out her name.

"Oh hey," she said.

"Join me. I was just getting ready to order."

"Great. Thanks."

Once we'd ordered, I said, "So tell me what you do up here."

"I'm a writer."

"Wow," I said. "How did you get started?"

"Well, I knew I wanted to write when I was in college, getting my teaching degree. After my son left for school, I started, and by the time my daughter Ashley, graduated my first book was at the publishers. For a while, it embarrassed me to admit I wrote romance novels, but did you know there are about a hundred new titles published every month?"

"You're kidding."

"I kid you not."

"Wow," I said again.

"Anyway, Ashley wanted to spend the summer with Gram…my mother…before she went to college, so I decided it was a good time to pack up my house and rent it out. It's what I was going to do eventually, and I figured I could write anywhere. Plus, my mother was getting older, and I wanted to spend more time with her."

"And how did you meet Paul?" I asked.

"Well, Paul has an interesting story."

She leaned in for emphasis.

"He was going through his mother's papers while he was clearing out her house, and he found some old photographs and newspaper articles. Have you ever heard of Bugsy Siegel?"

"The name sounds a little familiar."

"Look him up. He was obviously before your time. He was a mobster, and it turns out Paul is his son," she whispered conspirationally.

"How did he feel when he made that discovery?"

"Once he was over the shock of it, he started looking into Bugsy's past. At the time, he was still married, with two daughters of his own. He figured if there was nothing written about another family, it was a secret," Carrie said.

"Was he ever interested in contacting any family members?"

"Ha." Carrie chuckled. "He said, 'Not really. I didn't want to be killed.'"

"So how'd he get up here?"

"Have you ever heard of the Tudor House?"

"I have."

"Well, once he found out...he actually found his birth certificate... he came up here to see what it was all about, and ended up buying the property. He's been restoring it for a few years now. That's how I met him. They bring in music and entertainment, and I came to listen to a tribute to rock music. We got to talking and hit it off."

She wiped her mouth and put her napkin on her plate. "I'm stuffed. So, now that I've monopolized the entire conversation, tell me something about yourself."

"Well, I ran away," I said. "We had a family house up here when I was growing up, and I always remembered how the wind in the trees made me feel so tranquil. This seemed like the perfect place to gather my thoughts. And now I live here."

I told her the abbreviated version of how David cheated and my divorce and she said, "I had one of those, too."

I shared a little about Noah. I really liked Carrie, but I was also hoping I'd work with her on her house, so I tried to keep my personal issues light.

"Well, I should get back to work," I said, reaching for the check.

"No way," Carrie said, waving my hand away. "It was a treat talking with you. Let's do it again."

"Sounds great," I said, and she gave me a big hug as we walked outside.

The town library was only a few doors down from the flooring store, so with a few minutes to spare before I needed to get back, I stopped in. I hadn't been in a library for years, and I took in the woody, earthy smell… that of a building full of books. I found a pleasant-looking woman who was filling a rolling cart with books that needed to be put back on their shelves and waited.

"I'd like to get some information on Bugsy Siegel," I told her.

"I'm just a volunteer. Let me find the librarian," she said, putting the last book in its place.

To the left, in the children's section, a young mother was reading to her daughter and to the left of them a small room with a sign above the door said "Book Store."

"We have books," the librarian said as she walked up to me, "but follow me to where we have old newspaper articles." She led me to a small room in the back. "I'll show you how to use the microfiche machine and you can look to your heart's content. I think you want to be around 1945 or 46. Start there."

"Great," I said.

It took me a few minutes to get the hang of it, but I quickly found what I was looking for.

Bugsy Siegel Murdered
Rubbed out in Beverly Hills Hail of Bullets
June 20, 1947

A graphic photo of Siegel lying on a floral patterned sofa with what looked like gunshot wounds to his chest and eye caught me by surprise. The article went on to say he was shot by an unknown assailant who fired a .30 caliber M1 carbine through a window of his girlfriend Virginia Hill's home while he was reading a newspaper. She was not home at the time.

The description under the photo said he hadn't been shot in the eye as the photo suggested; instead, a bullet hit the bridge of his nose, causing the pressure that expelled his eyeball from its socket.

CHAPTER FIVE

Carrie

I still lived down in Westwood when I got the call from Mother.

"I feel so stupid," she said when she got on the phone. "I wanted to get out for some fresh air, and I should have brought that damned cane. I missed the first step off the porch and down I went. I probably scared every critter there was out there.

"My doctor said I hit my head too, and hopefully it knocked some sense into me. They want to keep me overnight to make sure I don't have a concussion. Thank god Isobel was there or...or I don't know. She's the one who called 911. I'll be fine."

"The doctor said she'll be all right," her housekeeper Isobel said when she got back on the phone. "She sprained her right ankle and wrist."

"Thank god you were there," I blurted. "Thank you so much!"

"I'll come back with my husband tomorrow and we'll bring her back home. I can stay with her until she is okay to be by herself."

"Thank you so much. I'll be up Friday afternoon, and I can stay with her over the weekend. Oh, my god. She could have been really hurt. Thank you so much, Isobel."

I ended up taking a week off so I could make sure my mother was okay.

When I called her doctor on Monday, I learned her last physical had been two years prior. I mentioned that I'd noticed she was slowing down, and I'd detected a slight tremor in her hands the last time I'd been up. She'd admitted falling out of bed and said she sometimes had difficulty sleeping. Her doctor recommended seeing a neurologist, which I thought was a good idea, so he made the appointment for her while I was still up.

She'd been diagnosed with early onset Parkinson's a few years after my divorce, and I was beginning to worry about her.

"It's not like it's going to kill me," she'd said.

"No, but it will complicate your life."

"I'm already aging in dog years. And my arthritis doesn't help."

Before I left, I hired Isobel to become Gram's companion, and I gave the school district my notice; I would officially retire and move up to the mountains once Ashley finished her school year.

A professor at UCLA ended up renting my house in L.A. There was very little in the house I needed, for everything I wanted was already up in the mountains. By midsummer, I'd sold everything else and filled a small moving truck with what I'd be bringing; clothing suited for the mountains and keepsakes from my children.

I purged my old closet and dressers and filled bags with clothing I'd donate. I brought up more than would fit in my tiny closet, so I cleared out a closet in one of the guest bedrooms, and stored my winter wear there. Christopher and Ashley's things would stay in their marked boxes stored in the garage cabinets.

It only took me a few days to re-acclimate to mountain living once I moved back up. I slept in my old room, surrounded by all my treasures; my Hardy Boys books, rocks and pinecones. Eventually, I'd probably pack everything away and be a grown-up, but for now I saw no rush.

When I was ten, Mother said I was old enough to have "big girl" furniture, so she had someone make a bed for me out of tree limbs. He also built a dresser made from wood with the bark still on it. She helped me choose a fabric, and she had a seamstress make a comforter and some coordinating pillows. She also made curtains that I could close when I didn't want the sun glaring in at me in the morning. Most of the time, I left them open, so the first thing I saw when I woke up was the trees outside my window.

I'd worn out a number of other comforters since then, but I thought about this now, after I had lunch with Annie. She was such a delight, and once I was ready, I thought she'd be able to help me keep most of the nostalgia of the house, but do the updates it needed.

I brought cookies and a soda out on to the porch and after brushing off my rocker, sat and ate them in silence. I had about a half hour before Isobel's husband Joseph was coming to go over the annual plan to trim trees and bushes for the upcoming fire season.

He'd been Mother's handyman for years, fixing frozen pipes, or relighting furnace pilots when they went out. Once Mother admitted she'd injured her back and wrist when she tripped and fell on the ice, I insisted he regularly clear the land; when there was a large snowfall, he plowed so Mother could get in and out of the driveway, and during the fall, he raked enough leaves to fill his pickup truck several times over.

Maintaining the house and property was an almost full-time task, and Joseph regularly worked the land, clearing it and fertilizing the fruit trees we had. He cleaned the walkways, sanded and stained the exterior siding and decking, cleared the gutters, and checked windows for drafts. His wife, Isobel, still did the cleaning and dusting, window washing, and clearing cobwebs from the tall ceiling in the living room. A few days a week, she'd cook for us, and I made sure there was enough food for her to take home to her husband.

While I sat there now on the porch, I thought back to when I was young and Mother would sit out here in her chair while I foraged in the forest looking for treasures I could bring back inside. I loved collecting pinecones, and in fact, they were still everywhere in the house.

When I came back up full time, even in cooler weather, Mother and I would sit bundled up in our chairs, drinking cups of hot chocolate. Last fall, we talked about what we wanted to do for Christmas. In the past, the children oversaw the decorating, but as they grew older, they didn't want to hassle with a tree.

"Remember how, after Thanksgiving, you always had a gigantic tree brought in?" I asked.

"There was nothing like the fragrance of pine filling the house, was there? And we used to make cinnamon oil to sprinkle on all your pinecones. It brought the forest right into the house, didn't it?"

"We'll have to get back into it this year," I said, looking over at her.

"Might as well do it while I still have the energy," she whispered.

"I've quit reading," she one day admitted. "It makes me crazy to try to keep my book steady."

"Why don't we have Joseph make you something to hold your book?"

"No, that's too much trouble."

I helped her sort through the books she wanted to keep, and I packaged up the rest in several cardboard boxes and donated them to the little library.

We still went for walks, but when I began to notice how difficult it was for her to sometimes get her stride, we started staying closer to home. I bought her an upright walker, which she detested.

"I'll not be caught dead with that thing," she'd admonished.

"No one will think anything about it. They'll admire you for taking care of yourself," I said, thinking logic would prevail. "Will you at least use the cane when we go out?"

She released a long breath.

"Good god, Mother, when did you get so stubborn?" I asked, frowning at her.

"It's always been there. You just never noticed."

But I'd bring the cane and hand it to her. And soon she was walking with it, even in the house.

There was an old painted mahogany drop front desk in one corner of the living room where Mother did her bookkeeping. When I came up for a visit, she'd have me organize and file her paid bills, and write any current checks that were due.

"I need a bigger lamp," she said after I came up permanently. "Unless you can see all right with this thing. I can barely read my own handwriting," she said, showing me her latest entries in her check register.

I, too, could hardly read what she'd written. I wanted to say 'you're declining so quickly,' but instead I said, "Here, now might be as good a time as any to teach me what you do. And we can go to the bank in the morning and add me to your accounts."

"You might be right," she said, nodding her head calmly. "One day, it'll all be yours anyway, so you might as well learn how to manage it now."

There were eight properties, all up in the mountains. Her bookkeeping method was simple enough, and I learned to feel comfortable with the role of her overseer and property manager. I started going with her when she collected the rents and eventually suggested we ask the tenants to drop their payments off at the house to save us a day of driving around.

I never really gave much thought to Mother's wealth. Or I should say I never dwelled on it. I wasn't interested in it, for if it was mine, it would mean she was no longer in my life. I'd have to trade one for the other, and that thought broke my heart.

A physical therapist now came to the house twice a week; Mother hated the idea, but she finally admitted she felt better after a treatment. I began helping her brush her hair and pull it into a bun in the morning, and she finally let me help her get into the shower.

"This is ridiculous," she'd say every morning. "I'm totally capable of doing this myself."

We always set Sundays aside for sleeping in and going out for brunch. After we finished getting ready, one of us would start the coffeemaker and we'd sit for a few quiet minutes, enjoying looking out at the lake.

One Sunday, I noticed Mother's bedroom door was open, and she'd pulled her covers up neatly like she always did. But the house was quiet, and as I made my way downstairs, I didn't smell the familiar aroma of coffee brewing. The kitchen was dark, as was the rest of the house; no lights had been turned on.

It felt for a moment, like Mother wasn't there, like she didn't live there with me, and I was suddenly frightened. I saw it as a forewarning of the future, when she one day would truly not be here, and I would be by myself.

I called for her, but there was no answer. I went into the laundry room to see if she was doing an early load, and then into the family room, and there was no sign of her.

Back in the living room, out of the corner of my eye, I caught movement out on the porch, and there she was, rocking in her chair.

"What are you doing out here? It's early. And chilly."

"The sunrise woke me," she said. "Look how beautiful it is, the streaks of yellow and pink in the sky. Even in the worst of weather, I've always loved this view. It always brings me peace."

"Me, too. I love looking at the water. But you frightened me. I couldn't find you."

"Oh, don't be silly," Mother said. "I'm always here."

But I knew deep in my heart she wouldn't always be.

Every week, we went to one of the same two places for brunch, and I wanted to change things up a little, so one Sunday, I suggested a new place I'd discovered.

"It's a surprise," I said. "It's chilly out, so I'll get our coats."

I got her settled into the passenger side of the car, and then turned the heater up.

"Where are we going?" she asked.

"You'll see. It's not far."

We were in a long line of traffic, which was unusual for a Sunday, and when we eventually made our way to where I could turn off, we saw the reason for the delay.

"Something must have happened," Mother said. Then she turned. "Where on earth are we going?"

It turned out Edison was working on an electrical line, which wasn't uncommon for the mountains. Trees were constantly breaking limbs and pulling down wires.

"It's called The Tudor House," I said, heading down the old road. This was one of the oldest neighborhoods at the lake, and the houses were small and built close together.

Suddenly, I turned and watched as the color drained from Mother's face. I stopped the car.

"Are you okay?"

It was almost as if she had to catch her breath before she answered, "I'm okay. I'm fine."

"You're not. You've lost all your color. What just happened?"

"It's just that I haven't thought about that place for years."

"You're familiar with it?"

"Of course." Her breathing calmed. "Everyone is if you've been here as long as I have. It just caught me by surprise. I didn't know they opened it."

"I've run into the owner a couple of times when I went there to listen to music during the week, and we'd started talking. Paul Larson is his name and he took on the restoration of the property a couple of years ago."

She agreed to go on and there was almost a look of awe in her eyes as we drove up and she absorbed it all. Once we were out of the car, she turned and said, "There was a pool over there where that concrete pad is."

And then she took in the details of the Tudor House itself.

"Needless to say, some things have changed," she said.

When we went inside, I watched her give the entire room the once over, and could only imagine what was going through her mind. Paul had told me it used to be a speakeasy.

Paul greeted us and gave me a quick hug. He took both of Gram's hands in his and told her how pleased he was to meet her. She met his smile.

"And how do you know him again?" she asked as we followed him to a table by the fireplace.

"Paul and I met when I came here to hear music a few months ago."

"I see," she said, as Paul gave us both a disarming smile. "I see," she said again.

For Mother's seventy-fifth birthday, Paul and I took her to The Saddleback Inn.

"We're overbooked tonight with reservations," our hostess said as she led us down a short hall. "We've made arrangements for you to dine in our private dining room, if you're okay with that."

"Oh, okay," Mother said. "I hope we don't feel like we're out in no-where land."

"Go ahead, Mother," I said as I held her arm.

A few moments later, we heard, "Surprise!"

Ashley and her husband were there. She'd married after graduating from my alma mater, UCLA, and they were expecting their first baby. Christopher was there with his fiancé; he was still in grad school and they'd just become engaged.

Isobel and her husband, and the owner of the restaurant, stood to one side, and then two of Mother's sisters, Nellie and Molly, stepped forward.

"Happy Birthday, Lizzie," they both said.

Mother's eyes widened in recognition and her hand instinctively went to her face.

"You're like to give me a heart attack," she said, wiping tears from her eyes. "My god, how many years has it been?"

"Too many," Nellie said, hugging her.

"I think it's twenty," Molly said.

I stayed with Paul for the week so Mother and her sisters could have the house to themselves and catch up. I took them to the grocery store so they could stock up on what they wanted for breakfast and lunch, and Paul and I took them all to dinner at night.

"Your mother was the only one fearless enough to move away," Nellie said as we cleaned the kitchen one day after lunch.

"Didn't you want to come to California too?" I asked.

"I ended up getting married to the son of the family who owned the town mercantile, and I was content with having a modern house to live in. Molly became a teacher and married a farmer's son. The boys worked our farm and built two houses so they and their wives could live there, and the youngest sister became a nurse and still works at the town hospital. If it weren't for your mother, we all would have struggled so much more."

Mother had only gone back home once that I remembered when I was in college.

"You knew she sent us money, didn't you?" Nellie then asked and suddenly appeared to have instantly regretted it. "I shouldn't have mentioned it."

"I know it was something that meant a lot to her," I said.

"Our parents were able to live more comfortably, and then they helped pay for our children's education."

"I know it's gone to good use."

Nellie hugged me.

"Thank you," she said.

"That was the most wonderful birthday," Mother told me after her sisters left. "Although it wore me out, thank you for doing that."

"You're very welcome. Are you okay?"

"Oh, yes. I'll just take a nap this afternoon."

Having company for a week seemed to drain her.

"My time is coming," Gram said as she shuffled around the house. "I can feel it in my bones."

"You'll live to be a hundred," I scoffed.

"I hope not…but it's a lovely day, isn't it? Let's go sit out on the porch."

"I'll bring your quilt."

We'd had a number of beautiful afternoons lately, not too warm; just right, and the porch was always our favorite place to be. I brought iced tea out and set our glasses on the table between us. Gram reached for her glass, and her hand shook slightly. She pulled her hand back.

"Here, I'll hand it to you," I said.

After her birthday, I started to notice more subtle changes in her. Along with her frequent unsteadiness, her speech was getting a little slower, and she'd developed a slightly repetitive movement in her fingers. She'd periodically taken naps in the past, but they were longer now and more frequent.

I knew she was noticing these changes in herself also, and outwardly, she took it all with a grain of salt. I made it a point to be with her every moment I could, and I set up a perfect space to write at the dining room table where I could be with her as she sat inside and looked out at the lake.

Sometimes I'd just sit and watch her as she picked at a thread in her blouse or hummed a tune I couldn't recognize. Then she'd sigh deeply, though not discouragingly, and close her eyes for a while.

"You'll find things about me when I'm gone," she said one night before she went to bed. "And I hope you don't think less of me."

"For heaven's sake, Mother, whatever it is, I love you and I always will."

"And don't go putting me in some old folk's home."

"Never."

She hoped to die at home, and even as I could see the time was nearing, I made sure everything was in place to make that possible.

A year later, she died in her sleep. She'd fallen again, this time breaking her hip and her back. When pneumonia set in, she never recovered. It broke my heart as she lay there in her bed and on the morning of her death, I held her cool hand until they came to get her.

She wanted to be cremated, and she'd requested no service. I wanted to have some kind of memorial, so the same people who came to her birthday celebration came to the house. Isobel cooked all day, and as we sat around the dining room table, we shared memories of Mother.

"Let's toast," I said, and we all drank. "I'll start. Gram wanted her ashes split in half," I started. "I'll scatter one half on the lake, and I'll keep one half in the house so she can stay here until I'm gone."

"That's kind of morbid," Ashley said. "What if you feel weird having them here?"

"I've ordered a nice urn I think she'd like, and I'll try to think of it as having her with me still."

"Where will you keep it?" Ashley asked.

"I'm not sure yet. Maybe on the living room mantel. So, does anyone have anything they'd like to say?"

"Let's toast," Ashley said. "Once after Christopher did something…I can't remember what…Gram told me I was her favorite and then Christopher went crying to her about something and he told me later, she said the same thing to him."

"That's because I was," Christopher joked. "Let's toast. I remember Gram having her handyman put up a hammock between the two trees

outside, and I could hardly wait to lie in it. But every time I tried to climb into it, I kept falling out of it."

"That's because you were a dork," Ashley teased.

"So were you."

"Let's toast," Ashley said again. "I remember Gram taking us to the beach at Tavern Bay Club. We brought a picnic basket, and she held our hands as she walked us into the water. We were old enough to do it by ourselves, but she wanted to make sure we knew how far we could go in. I wanted to build a sand castle, but Christopher wanted to stay in the water. Gram came back with me and got down on her hands and knees and helped me. When Christopher finally came to see what we'd been doing, he was jealous and kicked one of my buildings."

"I didn't know that," I said to Christopher. "Gram should have pinched you."

"Let's toast," Paul said. "I remember the first time I met Gram, and she looked at me and your mother for a minute, and said, 'I see.' We'd just started seeing each other, but she knew, didn't she?" he asked me.

"There wasn't much that got past her."

"Let's toast," Isobel said. "I remember the first time I broke something in the house. I thought for sure she was going to fire me. It was a ceramic bird, and I knocked it off the shelf while I was dusting. I was so afraid to tell her, but when I did, she said, 'Let's go find the glue. I'm sure we can put it back together good enough to look like new.' For all I knew, it could have been one of her prized possessions. It's still on that shelf. I think of it every time I dust."

"Let's toast," Ashley said again. "I remember Gram taking us to Santa's Village and even though we were too old for it, she wanted us to have our pictures taken with Santa. All we wanted to do was go on the car ride and the Ferris wheel. Gram loved the reindeer in the zoo. There was a shop that sold nothing but Christmas ornaments and décor all year round. Gram bought us each an ornament, and then I discovered they had drawers and drawers of miniatures."

"God, I remember that," Christopher said as a tease. "You stood there forever trying to decide what you wanted to buy. Gram told me to stop complaining and gave me fifty cents to go on another ride. When I came back, you were still there dinking around."

34

"They were all so cute, I couldn't make up my mind. I think I still have them in the ballerina jewelry box Gram gave me."

"We always got cookies from the bakery. And I thought the elves in costumes were cool. They walked around everywhere," Christopher said.

"You two used to bring friends up and have sleepovers. Bedtime was negotiable, and Gram would make you anything you wanted for breakfast. There was always plenty to eat, and one time she let you eat dessert first. It ruined your dinner, but you loved it," I said. Suddenly, my mood changed, and outwardly I tried to keep the smile on my face. "I miss her," I said, tears suddenly filling my eyes. Paul put his arm on the back of my chair and touched my shoulder, and as if no one noticed, they went on sharing their memories.

"Let's toast," Christopher said. "Remember when Mom was giving you hell about something?" he said to Ashley. "I don't remember what you did, but she went on and on about it, and finally Gram let out an enormous burp that cracked us all up."

"That was a riot!" Ashley laughed. "Gram just said, 'Oops, excuse me.' I'm sorry I'd forgotten that."

"Let's toast," Christopher said again. "I remember when I was in trouble for skipping school and Gram told me she used to do the same thing to go watch the movies in the old 'cinema' as she called it."

"Did they even have a movie theater in town?" Ashley asked.

"I don't know," Christopher shrugged. "She could have made it up to make me feel better. Who knows? It made me feel like she was a person with a different dimension. Not just some perfect grandmother."

"Gram was definitely not perfect," I then said. "Her sisters have told me stories about her growing up, and I'm sure there was a lot she'd never share. My last toast, unless I think of anything else." I giggled. "I think everyone has had enough to drink."

"Hey, the wine's going to Mom's head," Christopher chuckled. "Way to go, Mom."

"I remember Gram being there for me unconditionally. It was almost as though I could do no wrong." Then my face crumpled and tears escaped my eyes again. "She was always there."

"Joseph?" I asked, turning to him. "Certainly there must be something you remember about Mother?"

He lowered his head for a moment, then said, "Miss Elizabeth once told me she couldn't take care of the house without me and Isobel. It was near Valentine's Day. She gave me a hundred dollars, and told me not to tell Isobel, but to take her out to dinner."

He kept his head bent but looked up at his wife. Isobel began to cry.

"Hear, hear," we all toasted.

Mother asked me to live well off what she was leaving me, and then when I was ready to leave this earth to split it between Christopher and Ashley fifty-fifty. Her attorney had all the paperwork ready, and I was just waiting for everything to be transferred before I wanted to think seriously about working on the house.

"The Cabin," as she referred to it, but it was much more than that to us.

It was home.

And for now, I couldn't change it.

CHAPTER SIX

Noah got that job from Bunny, and I was apprehensive from the beginning. He hadn't even started work yet, and she'd call him at all hours, ostensibly, of course, to ask questions about the job. Noah was swept up by her flattery. I vowed to try my best to not act like a jealous girlfriend, and to be as supportive as I could be.

The truth was, the creative side of me was genuinely looking forward to seeing her home, so before any major work started, Noah took me by there. He had his own code to the gate, and once inside, he took me on the long picturesque route to the house. It was absolutely gorgeous. Cedar Ridge Estates did indeed feel like a private forest with large custom homes tucked into at least one acre parcels. I grabbed Noah's arm as I saw my first group of deer grazing comfortably as we drove by. It was incredible. I felt as though I was driving through the Beverly Hills of the mountains.

Trees lined the winding road right up to her home, where tall pine and cedar trees grew behind a continuous split-rail fence. I could totally understand why someone would want to live in this neighborhood. The driveway had an interesting curve to the left, which when we pulled in, I wondered how someone like me could successfully maneuver backing back out.

"You'd have to turn around at the garage to head back in the right direction," Noah said when I pointed it out.

A modern rectangular fountain with large bobbing copper balls welcomed us at the entry. To the right of it, small bushes in brown pots were still gently tied to keep their branches from breaking in the snow. And farther to the right, three various sized large concrete spheres sat in the center of a small cutout area.

Bunny's split level mid-century modern/rustic home was just under forty-three hundred square feet and built in the late 1940s. All the open beamed ceilings were cedar, and the twenty-five foot high ceiling in the living room was the grandest I'd ever seen. It had a sixty-foot steel beam wrapped in cedar that ran the length of the entire house. There were three en-suite bedrooms, an enormous library, a den, a wine room and a powder room. From the entrance, stairs went down to the living room/great room, then up again to the bedrooms, and up another level to the library.

I had a hard time understanding why she'd want to remodel it. It was dated with all the oak cabinets, but the library bookcases themselves were thirty feet wide by twelve feet high, and the house could have been brought into this century with the right décor.

I was inwardly opposed to making any of her intended changes to the home. But I had not been consulted; it was clearly a great job for Noah. I decided I'd need to just set my emotions aside and let Bunny do whatever she wanted. I had no say in the matter.

I suddenly felt downhearted. When we locked up the house and got back into his jeep, Noah noticed.

"I just feel like she's destroying the integrity of the home," I said when he asked. "If I could get my hands on it, it could be a fabulous period home, and it could become a European lodge instead of a modern remodel."

I felt that Noah looked at me like I was crazy and over reacting. Usually he felt the same way about changing the original character of a home, so I was a little surprised by his lack of reverence for the project.

I lifted my shoulders in response. "I don't know," I shrugged.

It really wasn't my problem, though, so I'd just have to let it go.

Noah's birthday was coming up, and we decided on the Saddleback Inn, which was a wonderful restaurant attached to charming cottages they rented out. We didn't normally dress up much in the mountains, but we both agreed this was a special occasion, so I actually put on a dress. All Noah had to do to dress up was wear a nice shirt, a fresh pair of jeans and clean cowboy boots. I made a reservation, and when we got there, we were seated at a table by a window overlooking a cabin tucked among tall pine trees.

For a minute, we just looked at each other, and he took my hand. He played with my fingers while I studied the soft hair of his trimmed beard and mustache. I loved looking at him, and I could tell by the look in his eyes, we were going to end the evening in bed. *If we made it through the meal.*

Warm bread came first, and I was starving. We had just ordered wine, when who should show up, but Bunny!

"You told me you were having dinner here tonight, and I just wanted to buy you a drink." She said, struggling with a chair.

Noah stumbled a little as he got up, then he stood and helped her pull her chair in. He gave me a wide-eyed, exaggerated look.

"I hope you don't mind."

Of course we did!

I said nothing, for fear my words would betray my annoyance, and Noah was obviously uncomfortable. He said, "Um, what a surprise."

Bunny turned to catch the attention of our server. "I'll have a dry martini," she said, then turned back to us. She gave me a forced smile, and then poured on the charm as she said to Noah, "I'm so excited about getting started on the house. Aren't you?"

Oh boy.

Her drink came, and she toasted Noah, totally ignoring me. "*Happy Birthday, Noah,*" she said in a soft whisper. For a moment, I wondered if she was going to sing to him like Marilyn Monroe did to JFK!

I was hoping she would leave as soon as she guzzled down her martini, but instead, when the server asked if we were ready to order, Noah asked if she'd join us, which, of course, she did. Then she ordered her second drink.

I don't know how I made it through that dinner. I was looking forward to a romantic evening and instead, ended up observing Bunny as she talked about what she thought was interesting in her life. How fortunate she was to have found the house, the two acres it was built on, and how she was going to have to learn how to back out of the winding driveway which could prove to be interesting if it snowed. She talked about the floor plan of the house, how she could hardly wait to decorate.

When I told her Noah had taken me through the winding roads to her house, I didn't have to force myself to say just how beautiful I thought everything was.

I wondered if I should have kept that a little secret, as I could immediately tell she wasn't pleased I'd trespassed into her domain. But then she said, "It *is* lovely there, isn't it? And once all the work is done, it'll be hard for me to not want to stay up here permanently."

Oh, dear God!

She turned to Noah and asked him about living up here.

He told her he wouldn't want to live anywhere else.

She asked about the schools here.

"Not that I'm planning on having any children."

"I made it through the local high school," he said.

She asked about his first job, and he told her how, for senior prom, he needed to earn the money to take his date to dinner and rent his tux.

He chuckled and turned red. "They hired me to dress up as a clown for the opening of the new gas station up here, and putting on the makeup wasn't as easy as I thought it was going to be. I had to wipe it off and start over a couple of times."

Bunny giggled. "I can just see you walking around, tripping on your big floppy shoes."

He'd never told me that story, and I grudgingly admitted I was resentful.

"What's worse is this kid came up to me and asked me to do a trick. I was hot and tired, and I told him I didn't do tricks. When he persisted, I told him clowns could be mean and to scram."

"You didn't," she squealed.

40

"I did, and I felt bad about it later, but the kid had no idea who I was, so I was in the clear. Later, though, kids from school started driving by and throwing water balloons at me. The place was a mess by the end of my shift."

"Did you do it again?" I asked, mostly to be part of the conversation.

"They wanted me to, and I could have used the money, but there was no way I was goin' back there. My mom ended up giving me the rest of the money I needed. I think she felt sorry for me. I sure did."

"Tell me another story," she cooed.

"Yes, do," I added. Throughout it all, I sat with a pasted-on smile and by the time dinner came, my jaws were getting tired.

"Well, when I was a junior, I took a job at the grocery store, before the big supermarket opened, and I mostly stocked shelves. Then the meat manager asked me to clean the case. So I had to actually climb into the meat case with a bucket of warm water. The minute I got in there, I could see someone I knew come around the corner and it was a girl I had a crush on. There was no way I could climb out of the case quickly enough to avoid her seeing me. So when she saw it was me, she cracked up. All I could do was wave at her and feel stupid."

"You have the most interesting memories, Noah," Bunny laughed. "I can't think of anything like that ever happening to me."

It wasn't so much that Bunny was heaping it on, but that Noah was such a fool. She was toying with him, and he was falling for her shameless flirtation.

"Excuse me," I said as I got up to use the restroom.

"Oh," I heard her say as I walked away. "I almost forgot to give you this."

When I returned to our table, Noah was standing there with his new leather work belt on and I'm not sure how I managed it, but I said, "Wow, it's wonderful."

When dinner was finally over, we walked Bunny to her car. She gave Noah a hug and a kiss on the cheek. When we got back into his car, of course, I could smell her fragrance and all thoughts of spending

41

a romantic evening making love in front of the fireplace immediately left my mind.

I'm the type of person who needs a clear mind during sex. If I'm thinking about a million other things, then I don't connect. Not that I've had that problem with Noah, but I just knew that I wouldn't be able to focus on *us* if he stayed with me that night.

"I know we'd planned on being together tonight," I said as we pulled into the cabin's parking area, "but I have to admit, Bunny really ruined my evening," I said.

"I know she sort of barged in, but are you sure?"

I could tell I hurt Noah, and at that moment, I really didn't care.

"Yes. I also had too much wine, and I'm sleepy." That part was true. I'd had two large glasses of wine and that much wine made me groggy. I reached over and gave Noah a kiss and inhaled Bunny. "You don't need to walk me in. I'm fine. The kitties will protect me." Then I got out.

I fed the cats and then started a fire. I sat on the sofa facing the fireplace and watched the flames dance to their own beat.

It startled me when, about a half hour later, I heard a soft knock at my door. I pulled my curtain aside so I could see outside, and Noah gave me a silly grin. When I opened the door, he had a bouquet of flowers in his hand and offered them to me.

"Pretty please?" he asked with a mock pout.

How could I refuse him?

"Okay," I said, "but you definitely need to shower first."

After Noah fell asleep, I did my best to do the same, but I couldn't stop my mind from wandering. I thought about everything from Bunny's house to Bunny herself. I recalled her saying she might want to live up here permanently and wondered what had become of their home in Beverly Hills. I wasn't worried about Noah, but I definitely didn't want to run into her in town. And then random thoughts about David and thoughts of anger jolted me more. I wondered if he was with the woman he'd been seeing when we were married. I wanted to throw my happiness in his face. But then I had to push those thoughts aside and try to think

42

about my new life up in the mountains, and how meeting Noah had changed my life. I was now content.

I finally got up and put another log on the fire. I sat back on the sofa and immediately Jezebel found my lap. I didn't mean to, but I laid my head down on the arm of the sofa and fell asleep. In the morning, I woke to a terrible kink in my neck and a strained back muscle.

Mid May, on a clear warm day, Noah and I took a boat ride from the Village to the Art and Wine Festival hosted by the Rotary Club at the Tavern Bay Beach Club. There was beer, wine tasting, entertainment and exhibits by local artists. I hadn't attended before, but I saw an opportunity to advertise the cabins, so I'd donated a gift basket for the silent auction. I was glad I thought to bring extra brochures for the cabins so I could set them out on the table next to my sign. It looked like there were none on the table.

It was always interesting going somewhere with Noah. I watched the locals greet each other with a smile and a hug or a pat on the back. He knew just about everyone, and he'd bring me up to date on the local scuttlebutt. Most of the time, it was telling me about doing a job for someone, but every now and then, he'd offer up a tidbit of dirt.

He pointed across the way to a large man wearing a cowboy hat.

"John's son just got married," he said, raising his eyebrows in mock surprise. "They're due to have a baby."

"Hey you two," he then said to a middle-aged couple. "How's Jeff?"

"He just re-enlisted. He was in Germany, but now he's at Fort Meade."

To me, he said, "Jeff and I played football together in high school. That is, until my mom found out."

"How could she not know?" I asked.

"Well, when I was a kid, I'd had rheumatic fever, and was in bed for months. The doctor told her I'd not be able to play any kind of sports, so when I wanted to try out for the team, I forged her signature on the parent's approval form."

"How'd she find out?"

"Would you believe the newspaper ran my photo in a game and, well, that was it?"

Noah gave Jeff's mom a hug and then we walked on. I stopped and touched his arm.

"Are you okay now?"

"I am. I get a clean bill of health, every checkup. The service didn't want me then either."

"Well, that's a relief!"

"Hey, Annie," a voice behind me called out.

I turned, and it was Carrie walking towards us with a handsome man.

"Great to see you. This is Paul," she said, taking his arm.

"Hey there," I said, shaking his hand. "This is Noah."

"I saw you have a basket in the auction? I told Paul I'd met you."

"Yes, I thought it was a great way to get the word out about the cabins."

I wasn't sure what to divulge about his past, so I said nothing more.

"Have you eaten anything yet?" Carrie asked. "We're starving."

We made our way to the food tables and bought tickets for appetizers. Carrie found an open table, and we all sat.

Noah went to get us some wine.

"So, Carrie tells me you're going to help her with the house," Paul said.

"I'm still working up to it," Carrie said quickly. "I keep thinking about my mother, and I know I'm being a baby."

"You're not," I said. I didn't want her to feel the least bit uncomfortable about us working together. "You'll know when the time is right, then we can tackle a little bit at a time. This has to be overwhelming."

"More so than I thought it would be. But soon," she said, taking a sip of her wine.

"I hear you're a transplant too," I said to Paul.

"Yeah. I was born and raised on a small ranch in Rancho Santa Fe. I learned to ride a pony I named Cinnamon because she was so red. The deal with Mame, my mother, was that if I wanted to keep her, I had to clean all the stalls and feed and water the horses. Carrie told me she shared about my father. Obviously, he wasn't around, but there was a hired hand named Jim who taught me how to groom them. I learned how to fix the arena fencing, and how to level out and lay new gravel down in our circular driveway when it needed it. I think that's how I got interested in working on properties. Speaking of which, have you been to the Tudor House yet?"

"I'm ashamed to admit, I haven't. But I'd like to,"

"We'll have to have brunch one Sunday," Carrie suggested.

"I understand it had quite a history," I said.

"It used to be a speakeasy," Paul said.

"And *I* understand you own the cabins Carrie and I have stayed in. We should exchange brochures if you have some."

"That'd be great," I said.

"Let me know when you want to meet," Carrie said, as we all got ready to leave. "I'm there almost every Sunday."

Memorial Weekend was the official start of summer in the mountains. Boats that were stored during the winter in a big warehouse down the hill were brought back up and put back on the water, and for several weeks before the big weekend, there were always personal trucks towing boats up Highway 18.

It was also the biggest garage sale weekend of the year. I'd been to garage sales before, but had never seen anything like what happened up here on the three-day weekend. Everyone who had something they no longer wanted posted a Garage Sale sign on almost every tree leading to their home.

I had to convince Noah to drive me around, since he was more familiar with the streets than I was. He'd never been interested in garage sales in the past, but once he saw the things we could get at bargain prices, it piqued his interest. We found some old prints for his cabin and a rustic cabinet he could set his television on. I found this wonderful old writing desk made from logs and asked Noah if I could store it at his house.

"It'll fit perfectly in the sunroom," I added.

Bookings increased with the pleasant weather and just when I had a few extra dollars in my savings account, our washer quit working. Sam couldn't recall whether he and his wife had ever replaced it, so it was probably over twenty years old. We needed a new one quickly, and no one could deliver to the mountains for almost two weeks. Thankfully, Noah said he'd take me down to the Sears in San Bernardino to pick up a new one. I decided if I could put it on my charge account, I might as well get a new dryer too, hopefully averting another emergency if *it* suddenly quit.

CHAPTER SEVEN

In mid-June, I met Grayson so he could check out the progress of his living room and dining room. I'd brought in an oversized red Persian rug, and two matching brown leather sofas which faced each other, separated by a plank cocktail table. Because there was track lighting, we didn't need end tables with lamps, so instead I had four custom tree trunk tables made to sit at the arms of the sofas. They could be used for drinks or just kept as accents.

Two contemporary tan leather chairs and ottomans flanked the windows, opening out to trees and the lake. Next to each, floor lamps would provide enough light for reading. In the dining room, I did slightly winged tan leather Parsons chairs with a rustic planked table. Over the buffet were three rectangle mirrors hung from sets of deer antlers.

I could tell Grayson was happy, which, of course, reinforced that I'd done some of my best work here. While I took into consideration each of my client's personal tastes and preference when I worked with them, I ultimately wanted the finished look to be something I could live with myself. And I'd accomplished it here.

"Sit with me in this beautiful living room," Grayson said. "Every time I come up here, I feel you've outdone yourself. And I couldn't be happier." He'd brought out a bottle of wine and two glasses.

I could not stop the trademark color from rising in my face. I hated that trait!

"And I have to admit, the way you 'color' " he said, doing quotes with his fingers, "is quite refreshing."

Of course, this made my face even hotter.

"It's obviously a trait I'd love to lose. It sometimes doesn't allow me to show a poker face when I need one," I said. "I'm still hoping to grow out of it." I managed to laugh.

"I hope you don't. Will you have wine with me this afternoon?"

I decided to have a glass, so he poured us each one. We sat in relaxed silence and admired the room. The house was wonderful to work with and the room was very welcoming.

"Annie, I have a proposition for you. And I'd like you to think about it."

I tried to read him, and guess just what that would be.

"I have a small ranch in Montana that could definitely use you…" he leaned forward on the sofa. "Now before you say no, it's not that far away and I have a friend with a plane who can take us there." Grayson drank from his glass.

I was at a loss for words. I looked at him for a moment and he was appraising me. I tried to gather my thoughts, and then asked, "What are you thinking you need? Furniture and accessories? Remodeling?" My imagination ran wild.

"No remodeling. The house was finished when I purchased it several years ago, and it came with the previous owner's furnishings. I just never changed anything. But now that I've seen what you can do, I'd like to decorate it to my taste."

"That sounds reasonable. What type of home is it? Mountainy or contemporary?"

"Definitely mountainy. It's a log house, more of a remote retreat on acreage, which was the point when I purchased it."

I'd never been to Montana before, so my mind conjured up images of expanses of land and it definitely sounded exciting and challenging.

"When would you want to start? You've given me several projects already…which is fine…I just wondered about a time frame."

"I'd like to get started on it while we're on a roll. If you look at it and we figure out what you'd need to order, then hopefully we could finish it before the weather turns."

I tilted my head in thought. It *could* be done, but we'd have to get started now. I'd pictured a small plane, but had never flown in one; but people did it every day. I'd also have to figure out how to charge him for my time. I definitely had the resources, but I'd also have to figure out where I'd ship everything.

"Do you know any businesses in town that could take delivery of furniture and boxes? Manufacturers won't deliver to a residence. Or we'd have to ship it all to one place and truck it in."

"I know people in town who could accept delivery. Sound interesting?"

"It does." Then he read my mind.

What a fabulous opportunity.

"You'd figure your time, say for a weekend, and then charge what you normally charge."

"When could we go?"

"We can work around your schedule."

"Ok, just let me think about it. Can I call you this afternoon or tomorrow?"

"That'd be great. I'm hoping you accept the job." Grayson gave me an intriguing smile, which I should have recognized as a sign my life was going to get complicated.

Oh dear, Noah wouldn't be at all pleased.

And he wasn't.

I told him that evening after we'd had dinner. We were at my cabin, and I'd tried to figure out a way to gently break it to him that I was definitely interested in the project. I could use the additional income to make an extra payment on the cabins, which would put me ahead with Sam.

I needed more clients up here, so between the cabin restoration, Grayson's lake home and now the Montana home, I'd have three new projects to add to my portfolio and to show prospective clients.

49

"We'd need to go soon so we can get everything ordered and placed before the weather changes. I'd love to tell him yes," I said, giving Noah a weak smile and silently asking for his blessing.

He stiffened. I searched his face. First there was surprise, then comprehension, then a slight collapse in his posture.

"I don't like it, Annie," he said, running his hands through his hair. "I really don't feel comfortable with you going off with him like that." His face was set, his jaws clamped, and he fixed his eyes on me.

We'd had a few conversations related to this in the past. Noah didn't trust Grayson, and I could see why, now that I'd met Bunny. But I didn't agree. Sure, Grayson could be the perfect man for *someone*, but while I was attracted to him, I couldn't picture myself *with* him. I couldn't seem to make Noah see that.

"Come on, Noah. He's just a client. And a really good one at that. I don't know why you're so worried about him. And *me*, for that matter." I tried to hide my annoyance with him.

"Annie, I don't trust him," Noah almost pleaded with me.

I sighed loudly. I knew I'd get opposition from Noah, just as I knew he was suspicious of Grayson's intentions, but Grayson had crossed no lines with me. Was Noah showing a possessive side to him?

"I'm trying to respect your opinions here, Noah, but I also know that this is exactly what I've been hoping for. I feel better about everything since I've moved up here, and this is just a stepping stone to getting established again. I understand how you feel, but I just don't see it. I'm not interested in Grayson's lifestyle. I need normal. And this is a great opportunity for me."

Noah turned to me and took me by my arms. "Annie, if you take this project, then you're disregarding how I feel."

I immediately felt backed into a corner, and I didn't like it.

"Then you're pushing me into making a decision I already wanted to make. I'm trying to work with you on this, but you're ultimately making me want to take the project even more."

His logic was understandable, but when did I get to start doing what I thought was best for me?

I'd sensed this would not end well. And it didn't.

"Then you've made your decision, and I'm not part of it." Noah collected his jacket and left.

I stood there fighting tears of anger. I drew in a deep breath and called Grayson.

"I hope I'm not calling too late. I'll take the job," I said when I had him on the phone.

"Wonderful. I'll make the arrangements. Any days better for you?"

"I'm available anytime."

I was convinced I'd made the best decision, but also miserable that I'd been forced to give Noah an ultimatum. This was a perfect time for me to grow not only my design business, but to learn to stand on my own. And I was determined that no man was going to hold me back.

Part Two

At a Crossroad

CHAPTER EIGHT

Two weeks later, I met Grayson at Cable Airport in Upland and his friend flew us to Thompson Falls Airport in Montana, where we were met by a car. It surprised me to see patches of snow scattering the ground.

The "small" ranch sat on twenty tree-covered acres with a clearing for the house, stables, and a pond that looked like a small lake. The setting was majestic, right out of a magazine. The only thing missing was the name of the ranch on the head gate.

The entire house was built from logs, including the covered exterior walkway leading to the front door. It was probably twenty feet in length, with slate and tree trunk columns, and a huge antler chandelier was centered in front of the hand-hewn front door. It had a large open floor plan, with five bedrooms, four bathrooms, a home theater, a family room with a pool table and bar, and a kitchen to die for.

There was a separate guest house with two bedrooms and two bathrooms, and a three-car garage. The property was spectacular!

"Grayson, this is absolutely wonderful! It's heaven."

"I rather like it myself," he said, bemused.

"I'm sorry. It just took me by surprise that there could be something that could take my breath away." I looked at him. "You chose a slice of heaven!" I paused and cleared my throat. "Ahem" I laughed, "back to professional mode!"

"Happiness becomes you."

"I can't help it."

And I couldn't. If I was going to run away, this was where I'd want to go.

"I'll show you to your room, and then we can have a quick bite. I had my housekeeper bring in lunch."

Grayson led the way up hand-hewn half log stairs, then down a hallway lined in logs.

My bedroom was also log walls, with knotty pine vaulted ceilings, and a large en- suite bathroom with a tumbled marble and stone shower. The furniture was a combination of old and new, and the window treatments and bedding were dated. The carpeting was older, too. I'd have to do an inventory when I got the grand tour.

I unpacked the few things I'd brought; toiletries and my own wash cloths, which I'd use to remove my make-up. Even in a hotel, I didn't like to leave dirty linens behind. Then I went downstairs to where Grayson was setting lunch out on the kitchen island. The kitchen was incredible; the stainless stove and oven was at least sixty inches wide, the island top was maple butcher block, the cabinets were darker hickory, and the countertops were granite. I didn't enjoy cooking, but I could love this kitchen!

From where we stood, we looked out into a dining area and large living room with a rock fireplace.

"How can you possibly have enough time to spend quality time in your homes?" I asked, amazed.

"It's difficult—once you've finished the decorating, I think I'm going to have to spend a couple of weeks at a time in each to really get the full enjoyment out of them. I think you like this home even more than the lake house."

"If I had to choose, I'd have to say yes. This is incredible. I'm sure you've figured that out!"

"This could be perfect for you. I picture you here. When we've finished lunch, we can take a tour and I'll show you what I'd like to do. Unless you're tired and want to relax a little."

"No, I'm fine. I'd love to see the rest of the house," I said, trying to take it all in.

We ate grilled chicken sandwiches with avocado and chocolate chip cookies for dessert. I hoped we weren't going to have a large dinner!

Grayson started the tour in the living room and dining room and asked, "What are your thoughts?"

"I think you could use a larger dining room table, but I like the setup." I said, making some notes.

"I agree. What about the living room? The furniture's a little worn. I do have the guest house that we could move all this into. What do you think?"

"I think that would be great. You could also introduce a deep, rich south-western look in here, with a Navajo rug."

In the family room, I suggested new light fixtures over the pool table and bar area, and thought some old paintings would look great on the log walls.

Then we moved upstairs into the bedrooms and bathrooms.

"I'm thinking the log furniture is okay, but all the bedding and window treatments need to go," Grayson said. "And I really don't care for the carpet in any of these rooms, but it gets cold here so carpet is better than hardwood."

"Well, since I think we'd have a hard time matching the hardwood in the rest of the house, why don't we replace the carpet with something more updated?" I suggested. "I'm sure I can find something up here and we can make arrangements to have everything installed when we're ready."

"Good idea."

Grayson was beyond an ideal client. Tomorrow, before we left, I would find a floor coverings store and take Grayson with me to make some selections. I'd then get a sample of what we decided on so I could come up with some bedding and fabric options.

I didn't need to do floor plans for the bedrooms since we were keeping the existing furniture, but I did make some notes on how I could rearrange things. I measured the windows for new draperies and measured the beds for bedding. I took some photos of each room so I could remember what was in each one to make accessory selection easier.

When we were done, Grayson suggested we both retire to our rooms to take a break. He told me he'd made dinner reservations at one of his favorite restaurants. I wasn't ready to think about food yet, but I knew I would be later.

"We can try to squeeze in a quick tour of the property before we go," he said.

Once in my room, I brought out my drawing paper and started drawing the rooms. I'd brought the phone book up, and found a flooring store that seemed to have everything I'd need. I called to tell them I'd like to bring a client in in the morning and we set a time.

I needed to take a quick nap.

About an hour later, I woke up and for a minute couldn't remember where I was. The Montana house! I stretched, yawned, and then went into the bathroom to see what damage my nap had done to my hair and make-up. I quickly touched up my hair and went down into the living room.

Grayson was reading in one of the overstuffed chairs and looked up as I entered the room. For a moment, I felt like I was in my own home and my husband (or lover) was waiting for me. I'm not sure why that image entered my mind.

"Did you nap?" I asked, sitting in a chair opposite him.

"I did. I can only sleep for about twenty minutes, or I feel groggy for the rest of the day," he said, putting his book down.

"I usually feel that way too, but I must have needed the sleep. I'll be awake in a few minutes."

I got up again and stood by the windows overlooking the trees. "You said you had stables too," I said, "but I don't see them."

"They're to the left of the house. If you're up for a quick tour, we can head over there. It might be cool so get your coat." Grayson went into his room and came back out with his heavy jacket on.

There were several outbuildings; the two largest were a stable for 12 horses with a tack room and an indoor riding arena. Another was a barn, and the last one was a bunkhouse.

"Are these horses yours?" I asked, looking inside.

"No, I don't ride, but I love having them here. I lease out the stables to a young couple who board and train. It works out well as they are always on the property, so my caretaker has help if needed."

"I haven't been on a horse since I was around ten. There were stables in our neighborhood, but I was always a little afraid of them. I knew they sensed it, too. I think I rode maybe twice and then decided that horses and riding weren't my passion. These are beautiful though," I said, walking into the barn. "I can definitely appreciate their beauty."

Next, we went out to the pond, with a water feature in the center that sprayed water in a mesmerizing pattern.

"Does it freeze in winter?" I asked.

"Yes."

"You don't stock it?"

"*Good heavens, no. They'd be gone in a heartbeat,*" he said. His tone shifted.

I was sure he hadn't meant to be unkind, but he made it obvious I'd blundered.

"Oh," was all I could think to say as I stepped back.

Grayson immediately understood what he'd done, and quickly said, "Animals in the wild will eat whatever fish we'd hope to keep. Bear, fox, and it wouldn't be a pretty sight if they left remains all over the grounds."

To change the subject, I sighed and closed my eyes.

"It's so green and beautiful here," I said.

"It'll start turning brown in a few months."

Suddenly, thoughts of Noah rushed into my mind, and I missed him. I thought he would also think this was beautiful. "I can just imagine it when it snows. It has to be absolutely gorgeous."

"I'd love for you to see it. Depending on how long it takes to redecorate, we may have snow by the time we finish." Grayson took my arm and guided me back to the house. "The ground isn't always level, so just watch your step," he added.

I was grateful for his support as I tried to watch where I was walking, trying to take in everything around me.

"It's getting cool, so we should get back into the house where it's warm," Grayson suggested.

"I agree. It really got cold quickly."

Once inside, I stood by the fire to warm up. Grayson hung his coat on a coat rack made from a tree trunk, but I wanted to keep mine on for a while longer.

"We have a while before our dinner, and if you'd like to read, I have a library in my study. You're welcome to select something."

"That'd be great. I always enjoy a good book and forgot to bring something."

I came back in a few minutes with two books I hadn't read.

"Are you that quick of a reader?" Grayson asked, raising his eyebrows.

I laughed. "No, I just couldn't decide which one I wanted to read."

I alternated between reading and making notes of what I thought we could do to update everything. We sat, deep in our own thoughts, for almost an hour while the afternoon turned into early evening.

"Well," Grayson said, breaking our comfortable silence. "We'd better start getting ready for dinner. It'll take us about a half hour to get there, so we should have plenty of time." Grayson stopped to look at me. "See you in about fifteen minutes?"

"Sounds good," I said, putting my book down and heading towards my bedroom. I decided to wear my hair up and quickly clipped it into a twist. As I dressed, it surprised me I was getting hungry after that big lunch!

"You look wonderful with your hair up," Grayson said when I came back into the living room. I could see his eyes taking me in, and I felt my face color. 'Looking wonderful' wasn't my intention, but I couldn't escape the feeling of confidence and pride.

The emotion in his expression surprised me.

"I've warmed the car for us, so we'll be comfortable," he said, motioning me to head outside.

Indeed, the car was warm, and it felt great as it had gotten even colder outside now.

As he'd said, it took about a half hour to get to the restaurant, and I caught myself looking at Grayson's profile as he was driving. He was very pleasant to look at, and it was unfair that men seemed to improve with time, where women tried desperately to keep from showing their age.

When we arrived, Grayson gave his name to the hostess, and wanted to be sure we got the booth he'd requested. When she told him it would be a few minutes, his impatience showed.

"That's okay," I said. "It'll give me a chance to look around."

I could see why this restaurant was a favorite place for Grayson. Like his house, it was built out of logs, with tall wood ceilings, and large rustic western oil paintings filled the walls. The dining tables and chairs were made of smaller logs, but upholstered for comfort. The floors were stained concrete and filled with discarded peanut shells from previous diners.

It was a perfect blend of rustic and elegant. We were seated in our booth, and Grayson ordered wine.

"What do you recommend?" I asked when the server gave me a menu.

"I can order for us if you'd like. Their Chateaubriand is excellent."

"Sounds delicious. Please go ahead."

Our waiter brought our wine, and once our glasses were full, Grayson toasted.

"To an exciting new adventure."

Grayson ordered the steak, with au gratin potatoes, asparagus and blue cheese salad wedges. I knew I'd never be able to eat it all, but was going to give it my best try. I'd worked up an appetite after all.

"So, what do you think of nature paintings like these for your family room?" I asked, pointing to several with deer and bear.

"Always working…I think they'd be perfect."

"Good. I'll look for some."

"So, how is everything going with your cabin remodeling?" Grayson asked.

"Very well. It's a subject I love talking about. I'm actually finished. It was mostly cleaning and decorating."

"And you've started marketing it?"

"We've got brochures and I've started advertising in the local paper. Everyone reads it when they come up."

"I can see the pride in your face. It lights up when you're talking about it."

"Sam, the previous owner, is going to stay and help me run it, which is perfect. I will definitely need help, especially as my design business grows."

"So you're happy there? With how things are going?"

"Very," I said, taking a sip of my wine.

The salad came, and we ate in silence for a few minutes.

Then, as if it was the next natural thing to talk about, Grayson asked, "And how about your friend?"

His question caught me a little by surprise. He was obviously talking about Noah. On one hand, I thought, there was nothing wrong with him asking, but then on the other, it was crossing the line a little. I considered how to answer that question…then thought the truth was always best.

"We're having a minute," I finally said.

Grayson looked at me like he wasn't quite sure what I meant, and then comprehension made him nod his head in understanding.

"Tell me what you're looking for in life, Annie."

This question also surprised me, so I didn't answer him right away.

"Let me tell you something about me first," he said, "to make you feel more comfortable." Grayson sat back against the booth. "I married at a young age, while still in college. We had two children, both grown now, of course, and as much as I hate to admit my age, I have two grandchildren.

"My wife," he said, then corrected himself. "My former wife and I are still close, but we ended up not having a lot in common, which happens in a lot of marriages. She still points out that she did all the work raising the girls, and I worked and made a lot of money. Eventually, we decided we should try to begin again on our own before we were too old."

Grayson chuckled, but I could tell he was unaccustomed to sharing this much about himself. "We were both forty-five then. And it's been ten years."

That made him fifty-five!

Dinner came, and it gave me a chance to think about what to tell him about me.

"Well, your marriage sounds a lot like mine," I began. "I'm not really sure when it started, but we also grew apart. The problem was that instead of talking about it, we both pretended we didn't have a problem until I found out my husband was seeing other women." I still felt humiliated, but I wasn't going to let it show. "I had already come up to the mountains to try to figure out what I wanted to do with my life, and when he wasn't honest with me, the decision to divorce was already made for me."

Grayson put his hand on mine and said, "I'm really sorry, Annie. You're obviously not the only one that's experienced this. And usually the better of the two ends up in pain. But it sounds like you made the best decision. You'll see that one day."

I took my hand away in the guise of wanting more wine. I hadn't intended to have Grayson's sympathy.

"And what about your friend?" Grayson asked again.

I'm not a very good liar, so I've learned to try to tell the truth as often as I can. I didn't want to open any doors, and I felt the conversation was possibly heading in a direction I wasn't sure I wanted it to.

"We care a lot about each other," I said. "But I don't want to do anything on the rebound. I have to be honest with you," I started, "he was not the least bit happy I decided to take this project."

I couldn't believe I'd said that! I instantly felt I'd betrayed Noah's private feelings.

"I could tell that he wouldn't be," Grayson said, taking another sip of his wine. "I recall when he came up to us in the coffee shop. He tried to act nonchalant, but it was obvious he was more than a friend."

My thoughts went back to the time the two had first met. I had a meeting with Grayson at Ginny's to show him some things for his Arrowhead home, and Noah came in. He'd said he'd seen my car. Grayson had been his normal polite self, and Noah had stiffened at the sight of us.

"Kind of like Noah's new client, the cougar," I said, laughing lightly.
"Oh?"

Now I'd done it, so I continued. "His new client is stunning, and she treats me like I'm not there when she talks to Noah. So I can relate a little to how he's feeling."

"That's interesting." Grayson was silent. He then said, "I can't imagine anyone making you feel less charming and beautiful than you are."

I know I looked surprised, for I certainly felt that way.

"I'm serious."

I took another sip of wine, then Grayson refreshed my glass. While I was holding it, his hand went to my bracelet, and he fingered one of the charms.

"Does this have significance?"

I said, "My mother and father gave it to me one year for my birthday. I don't wear it often as it gets caught on things and I don't want to lose any of the charms."

"Well," he said, finishing his wine, "I've eaten way more than I should have. Would you like dessert?"

"Oh, my gosh, no. I don't think I'll ever eat again."

I could tell he was studying my face, and it made my pulse quicken. Was he interested in me, after all?

Grayson raised his hand to get our waiter's attention, but when he was not immediately acknowledged, he grimly set his mouth, and then, as if knowing he'd done that, relaxed his jaw. When the head waiter came by, Grayson said, "I tried to get the attention of our waiter. We're ready for our bill," and within moments he was presented with our check and he tucked his credit card inside the folder.

Grayson asked for our car.

"I don't want you to get a chill, so wait a few minutes before you come out," he said.

It was freezing cold now, and I got a chill, anyway.

As we drove away, I said, "Dinner was indeed delicious, Grayson." I folded my arms into each other to help warm up. "Thank you very much."

"My pleasure." He looked over at me. "Are you toasty yet?"

"Yes, almost there. And the wine has made me sleepy," I said, yawning.

I'd been wanting to ask him about his name, and so I took this moment to do so.

"It's very English sounding, isn't it?" He answered with a question. "They named me after my great-great-grandfather, whose family at one time had privileges and land bestowed upon them by the King. However, over the years, because it has become so expensive to run a household like that, my family has since made the home available to the public. It works out well for them."

"Do you ever go back?"

"Not really," he answered somewhat indifferently. "I've never been close to my European side of the family."

"I have no claim to that kind of heritage that I know of. Born and raised in Southern California."

"And your family?"

"My father is Taiwanese and my mother is German and Norwegian. He came here to go to college and met my mother. They fell in love, but when he told his family about his impending marriage, he was told he was not welcome to return. They believed that 'race married race' and 'religion married religion'. My father told them he would never return then."

"Times have changed since then. Did he ever go back home?"

"Yes, when his father died, my mother convinced him to go back. We all went, my sister and me too."

"And how did his family react?"

"His brother and mother embraced him." I paused. "Isn't that a shame he lost that time?"

"Yes, well, parents don't always make the soundest of decisions."

"Possibly."

"I don't know a lot about my grandparents, and times were a lot different then."

"Where are your parents now?" he asked.

"In Arizona." Almost as an afterthought, I added, "I have a sister that I don't regularly see."

"That happens too."

Back at the house, Grayson stood behind me to help me out of my coat, but turned me so that I was facing him. I could feel the nearness of our bodies. He held my arms first, then leaned in to whisper in my ear. He smelled of musk and his fine leather coat.

"I'm a very patient man, Annie, but I'm persistent. I know what I want, and I usually get it." His voice was deep and sensual.

When he released me, I could see the sexual magnetism that gave him such confidence; it showed in his eyes, and I was too startled to voice any objection. I found his nearness both appealing and arousing, and my unexpected response to his touch confused me. I'd found him attractive, but I hadn't seriously thought of having him as a lover.

He touched my face, then my lips, and it was disturbing…the way I felt, not the way his touch made me feel.

He studied my lips, then my eyes, and said, "We can have breakfast in town tomorrow before we go to select flooring. Then we can leave for home. See you in the morning." And he turned towards his bedroom.

Stunned by his declaration, I stood motionless while I gathered my thoughts. What on earth had just happened? I waited until I was in my bedroom to take my coat off as I still had goose bumps, not only from the temperature outside but by what Grayson had just said.

Did he mean he intended to *have me?* Deep in thought, my hand went to my face, my fingers played with my chin.

Could I indeed live with someone like him? I could see why an older man could be interested in a younger woman: after all, David had once been interested in me.

Had he been thinking about me that way since the beginning? He'd always been very charming, yet polite. Very casual, though, and not overbearing. I'd never picked up on those vibes from him, but thinking back, tonight he did touch my arm, and then my bracelet. Had he touched me before and I just thought he was being a gentleman?

Once in bed, I couldn't help but think of Noah, and how I'd felt about him when we first met. It wasn't like I was instantly *'in love'*, but I found him attractive. His legs, his arms…and of course I was still married…

I closed my eyes and thought of how Noah made me feel. The ways he touched me, to show me there could be more to sex. Then I tried to think about Grayson in the same way. What kind of lover would he be? Stiff and more interested in his own gratification? Or gentle, having had experience with women over the years, and knowing what they wanted… what they needed.

Sleep eluded me as I couldn't help but think how my life could take a dramatic turn. One thing I knew for certain was I missed Noah and was hoping to see him when we returned. I needed to see him in a new light.

The next morning, I felt drained. Grayson must have noticed as he asked, "Did you sleep at all last night?"

I was honest with him. "No, I really didn't."

The same car that had picked us up at the airport now came to take us back. There was a small café in town where we ordered breakfast, and it was obvious Grayson watched me as I picked at my food. Out of the corner of my eye, I watched him too. However, I tried to avoid actual eye contact.

"What size shoe do you wear?" he asked out of the blue.

"What?"

"What size shoe do you wear?"

I told him. "Why?"

"Just curious."

Once at the floor covering store, I was more relaxed and preoccupied, looking at different options for the bedroom flooring. I showed Grayson a couple of choices, and he said he'd be happy with either, so I made the final decision. As with the last time we shopped together, I sensed the salesperson looking at us both, wondering what the relationship was, but not being bold enough to ask.

Grayson gave them the address and the contact information to get in.

"It'll take about six to eight weeks for everything to come, so we have time to get flooring done before we come back, then I can finish the rooms in two days," I said. "Are you okay with that?"

"Absolutely."

When we finished, the car took us to the airport. On the way, Grayson took my hand but looked straight ahead. I looked down at our hands, then up at him. He truly was handsome, with fine lines in his forehead, and furrows between his eyebrows. Lines under his eyes and at each corner just enhanced how attractive he was. His beard was very short, with a darker red on his mustache and under his bottom lip, and grayer along his jawline. His eyes met mine and the tenderness in his expression surprised me. I didn't pull my hand away, but instead, struggled with the uncertainty that played in my mind.

CHAPTER NINE

The temperature was 102 in San Bernardino and it lowered significantly as I headed back up the hill. In my mind, I'd been replaying my meeting with Grayson and how he'd made me feel. It wasn't easy for me to put my finger on it. In more than one way, he reminded me of David; in social settings, his feeling of self importance was so transparent it was borderline offensive. He expected others to follow his lead, and he had obvious expectations from those around him. He didn't hesitate letting you know it, either.

These were all traits of someone so successful, and I admired him for that. Despite all that, I realized just how easy it would be for me to get involved with him. It wasn't what I thought I'd wanted, but I couldn't stop my mind from wondering about a life with someone like him.

Was it better pretending these feelings didn't exist? Or to act on them, possibly regretting that choice for years to come?

As I pulled in to our parking area, my stomach dropped. Why had I expected to see Noah standing there waiting for me…helping me stay on track?

He was everything I'd hoped for; he was kind, thoughtful and loving. And most important, I admitted, was his devotion to me. I didn't have to compete with anyone or anything to keep him interested in me. I think down deep, it disappointed me he didn't have big dreams and his tendency to walk away from me when we had a difference of opinion was maddening. It was also childish.

I checked the outside thermometer as I set my bags outside the office; it was eighty-five! I wanted to check in with Sam. As usual, he was napping in one of the chairs and sat up when he heard the door open.

"Sorry, Sam," I whispered.

"Ah, just resting my eyes," he said, getting up. He had that sleepy look about him, trying to pretend he was awake.

"I'll come to you," I said as I sat in the chair next to him. "It's hot in here. Do we have a fan?"

"I'm good. Have a good trip?" he asked.

"Oh my gosh, it's so beautiful there. I couldn't believe it." I said. "And it's really a good job, so I'm excited about that; perfect timing to be able to replace our roofs. I know you've said we could make it for another winter, but after all the work we've done, I don't want to take any chances." I sighed. "Did Noah finish repairing the window in cabin two?"

"Yes…he did. And he asked me to tell you he's gone back to Colorado to get a little more work done there. Unfortunately, it seems like it's an open-ended project," Sam mumbled. The look in his eyes betrayed his casualness.

I turned and stared at him, wordless. I'd done it. I'd sent him away. I could suddenly feel my body sag in resignation. For appearances, I tried to maintain my composure, but it was almost impossible.

How could he have left without saying anything? Without even leaving me a note. This was definitely not a good sign. Either he had a legitimate reason to leave, or he was sending me a message that he would not be here for me when I returned. And little did he know this was when I needed him the most. I'd made my decision to accept the new job from Grayson, and it wasn't what he wanted.

I knew Sam was watching me and I didn't care. Tears welled up in my eyes, and I stood to leave.

"I'm so sorry, Annie," was all he could say. "He'll be back. He's just working off some steam."

I cried all the way to my cabin. Jezebel and Socks came running as I opened the door. I let my bags drop and went to the bathroom where I could wash my face. The harsh reality of it all reared its ugly head when I looked at myself in the mirror. I'd created all this myself.

I fell on my bed and covered my face with my pillow, trying unsuccessfully to control my sobbing. I hadn't really cried in so long; it surprised me how long it took me to relax my breathing.

More than anything, I desperately needed Noah. I needed him to hold me and to tell me everything was going to work out. That he'd be back, and that he understood my decision to take Grayson's job. But that meant I would have to admit that Grayson had had me on his mind after all! Noah had been right.

My despair then turned to resentment and anger. Swallowing a sob, I took a deep breath, then forced myself to remain calm. The sun was just beginning to set, and I was hungry. I opened a box of crackers and found a jar of peanut butter. The combination was not my favorite, but by eating it, I felt this was how I could punish myself.

That night I woke from a terrible dream. In it, I'd set aside my relationship with Noah to remarry David. We were inside a store and David was getting impatient, as was his custom. Once outside, we sat, and I tried to figure out why I would possibly go back to him. This wasn't the first time I'd done it.

I thought of Noah and how I'd begun a wonderful new life with him, and he'd stepped aside so I could go back to my old life. Would he take me back again? How was I going to get rid of David?

When I finally got up, I felt drained, and the dream stayed with me most of the day. I'd never once given a thought to going back with David. Maybe I was transferring Grayson for him. Who knew?

I hadn't slept well in days, and my mood was foul. But I was determined to work through this, however it ended. I had no way of knowing what would happen when Noah returned, so I decided I was just going to have to live with whatever happened. And the only way I knew how to pick myself up was to immerse myself in my work.

I got out my notes from the Montana house and found all the samples of fabrics and bedding from my own cabins. I didn't want to duplicate what I'd done for myself, but there were some options that I hadn't gone with and those would work for Grayson. I found a few smaller pieces of furniture that would fill in empty spaces, and I started looking through my accessory resources.

I ordered everything and made arrangements to ship it all to the person Grayson knew in town; I then called them to let them know approximately how many packages and boxes to expect. I asked if they would let me know when everything had arrived so I could schedule the return trip to get everything set up.

I left a message for Grayson, letting him know I'd call him when we could expect to go back.

CHAPTER TEN

While I spent the next weeks awaiting delivery of Grayson's accessories for the Montana house, I was hoping I'd hear from Noah so I could decide what I wanted to do.

If he came back, and if he apologized, I'd know we had a chance to try to work things out. And then I would have a clearer direction of which path I was going to go down. While we'd never said it, I thought I loved Noah, and I was pretty sure he loved me, too. We still had a long way to go in our relationship, especially if every time we came to a major obstacle, he ran for the hills.

Grayson had made it very clear to me he was going to continue on his quest. Part of me felt terribly guilty for even considering having an affair, if that's what one would call it. Now that Noah and I were together, thoughts of having sex with someone other than him had never crossed my mind. However, that hadn't been the way when I was married to David. Even though our relationship was waning, what kept me from being unfaithful then, was I felt we were both still committed to our marriage.

But Noah and I weren't married. We shared a special feeling for each other, but there was no spoken commitment or a formal arrangement between us. We were just us. And I thought for sure he was the one for me.

It surprised me when, about a week later, I received a package; there is no door-to-door mail delivery in the mountains, so everyone has a post office box. I had to wait at the counter to see what it was, and it dashed an unrealistic hope that it might be something from Noah as I saw it came from Saks Fifth Avenue. I waited until I got back in to my car and then opened the box to find a fabulous pair of chestnut color fleece-lined boots. The note inside said, *'For when we get snow.'*

I was dying of boredom and anticipation, so I drove out to visit to see my parents. My dad was doing really well, and I was glad I'd made the effort. Mostly, we sat outside and read, and one day we packed sandwiches and went to the lake to have lunch. My father wasn't up to walking far, so we took a quick trip along the banks. It was even more peaceful and relaxing here than in Lake Arrowhead, because there were no power boats in the water. I'd needed cheering up, so I'd purchased a new fleece lined suede jacket in the Village before I left, and I was glad I'd brought it for even in summer the evening cooled off. It and my new boots kept me warm.

My father suggested dinner at the Saloon where we'd eaten with Noah, but I suggested we try somewhere they liked. I had mentioned nothing about Noah and me, assuming they'd think our problem was all my fault and I didn't want to be thinking about him while we ate.

However, that's *all* I could think about.

The six-hour drive home seemed to take less time than the one out, and I used this time to sing out loud to music on the radio and to let my mind wander. Desert terrain and succulents were not my favorite scenery, so it was easy.

Just like I'd never seen it snow until I lived in the mountains, I'd never seen cactus growing, or maybe I never paid attention to it before my parents moved. What was interesting to me was the most well-known cactus was the one with the least personality. It was the saguaro; the tree-like cactus with arms, and the Arizona state flower.

I much preferred the evergreens in the mountains.

I finally got the call that all the packages for Grayson's house had been delivered, so I called him and we set up the trip back. It somewhat surprised me I hadn't heard from him in the meantime, except for getting the boots. He was an interesting man; if he wanted what he wanted, he certainly was patient. I had to admit, I was getting a little nervous.

I met Grayson at the Ontario airport again, and as his gaze took in my entire body, I could tell I flushed. The same pilot who flew us before gathered my luggage, while Grayson held his hand out to me. I took it and he brought me close to him, and said, "I want to capture the sight of you in this moment, and freeze it forever."

The first thing I thought was, *what a turn on that was;* the second was, *I have to focus on getting the house redecorated,* and the third was, *I knew I was definitely beet red!* He gave me a gentle kiss on my cheek and walked me toward the plane.

I had to admit that I basked in his open admiration of me. That was the most romantic thing anyone had ever said to me. For the entire flight, I felt on and off surges of electricity go through me, like butterflies and adrenaline combined.

The inevitable outcome of this weekend was that we would sleep together, and my life would change forever.

We landed, and once we were in the car, I asked if we could stop and pick up some of the things I'd ordered.

"I've already had them delivered," Grayson said. "There was too much to fit into the car and I wanted it to all be at the house when we got there."

"Great. I'd like to get started right away."

"My housekeeper Irma will be there with lunch and to help you unpack everything."

"Is there an iron and ironing board?"

"I'm sure there is."

The minute we opened the front door, I smelled lunch, but was more interested in looking out at the trees. I walked to the floor to ceiling windows and smiled.

"The grounds will start turning brown from the summer, but the trees are still so beautiful," I said.

"It's quite a sight in fall," Grayson said, coming to stand next to me.

I turned to see they had stacked all the boxes to one side in the entry, and it looked a little overwhelming; but I would figure it all out. Lunch was also laid out in the kitchen, and it looked wonderful. Fresh fruit, Caesar salad with chicken, sparkling water and, again, chocolate chip cookies.

"After lunch?" Grayson motioned from the boxes to the counter.

As before, lunch was delicious.

I knew this was going to be a pivotal time for me and Grayson. I was here not only to complete the project, but I was here to see where our relationship, whatever that was, was going to end up. I tried not to watch him as he ate, but I wanted to see how I felt about him, if I had any strong feelings one way or another.

Until our first trip here, there hadn't been a strong magnetic draw to him—like there had been with Noah almost from the start. Grayson must have sensed me watching him, for he turned to look at me and I could tell he had his mind on other things.

Irma appeared as if called. "You like me to clean up first, Mr. Underwood?"

"Yes, thanks, Irma," Grayson said.

Obviously, he was accustomed to having someone like Irma around. I wasn't used to having anyone "clean up" after me. I'd had a housekeeper for years but was insistent upon cleaning parts of the house before she came. I didn't feel someone else should have to pick up my laundry and clean my sinks.

Grayson went promptly to his chair in the living room and started reading one of his newspapers. It didn't look like he was going to help, and unconsciously my brows furrowed, but I shrugged it off and went to work opening the boxes. As I unpacked everything, I set it aside per bedroom; I would work in the master bedroom first.

When Irma was finished in the kitchen, she joined me there where the ironing board and iron were already set up.

"I do that for you," she said to me.

"Let me just finish this bed skirt, then you can help me lift the mattress off," I said, removing the skirt I'd just ironed. I tried to keep it from touching the floor.

We got the bed skirt set, then the sheets and the duvet cover. Next came pillow shams and accent pillows, and I stood back and looked at it. It looked great. Next Irma ironed while I started hanging the new curtain rods. Once those were up, the drapery panels were added and again I stood back and admired the finished project. I looked at my watch and couldn't believe it was mid afternoon already. At this rate, I'd never get finished with the other bedrooms.

While Irma dusted, I set out the accessories I'd planned for the room, and took away any leftover packaging materials. Then I could hardly wait to ask Grayson to come see the room.

When I got into the living room, he was on the phone and whispered he'd be right with me.

I didn't want to interrupt him, so with the little energy I had left, Irma and I took the rest of the bedding and accessories to their respective bedrooms upstairs. Might as well get a head start in the morning, I thought.

"Will you be able to come back tomorrow?" I asked Irma.

"Yes. I come in the morning and make a nice breakfast for you, and then we can go to work. But I can stay for a while longer now to get more done."

"Are you sure?"

"Of course."

"Sounds wonderful, Irma, but it's a lot of work for you."

"Is okay. Mr. Underwood is a good man," she said, then went into the next bedroom.

We got everything ironed and ready for tomorrow.

Irma left, promising to be back in the morning.

I was tired and needed a sit down break. I sat in the chair I'd used the first time I was there, and rested my head, my hand under my chin, then closed my eyes.

"Tired?" Grayson said, setting his paper down.

"Yes. It's not very professional, but I need a few minutes."

"You don't have to always be professional around me. I will not pick on you for being tired. After all, you've been working while I've been reading the paper and on the phone. You and Irma have done all the work."

"Still…"

"I was thinking of dinner at the local coffee shop if you're good with that? Tomorrow we can have a nice dinner."

"Sounds good to me. Do I need to change my clothes?"

"No. You're fine the way you are. Rest a little, then we can go." Grayson went back to his paper.

About an hour later, we were sitting opposite each other at the Round Up Café looking at menus. We shared a club sandwich and French fries. I was planning on getting a hot fudge sundae after.

"I haven't been up to the lake in a while, or I would have asked you to dinner," he said.

"Oh, I meant to tell you again. I love the boots. I brought them, although I'm not sure why I thought it was going to be cold enough to wear them. These fries are nice and crispy," I continued, putting several at a time in my mouth.

"I usually stay away from fries, but these *are* good."

We were making small talk, and it felt very stilted!

"Tell me something about your work," I suggested.

"Well…my staff does most of the work now. I'm very lucky to have talented people who work for me. I've found I enjoy pursuing my real estate projects a little more lately. It's the hunt to find the properties that make financial sense with a quick payoff once I've invested in improvements."

"Are you into commercial properties, or residential?"

"Mostly commercial, but I'm open to just about anything."

As soon as our waitress came back, Grayson asked, "Dessert?"

"Actually, I'd love a hot fudge sundae with no nuts or whipped cream," I said.

"That sounds good; I'll have one as well."

We sat quietly waiting for our sundaes and I played with my straw cover, giving me something to do with my hands while we waited.

"Yum," I said, when the sundae came. Then I added, "I don't know where I'm going to put this, but it's perfect."

Grayson watched me for a moment before he ate.

On the way back to his house, Grayson took my left palm and brought it to his lips, kissing it softly. The feel of his beard on my skin was very sensual. I knew this was a preamble for what to expect when we got home.

Even for the beginning of August it had cooled down quite a bit, and when we got inside, I didn't want to immediately take my coat off. Instead, Grayson lit the fire, and I stood by it for a few minutes.

I wanted to relax in a hot tub, but there wasn't one in my bathroom, so I opted for a hot shower. I stepped out of my clothes, leaving them in a pile, then turned the shower water on and let it get warm while I grabbed a towel. I'd ordered new fluffy ones, and I could hardly wait to have them wrapped around me when I got out.

I pinned my hair up, as I didn't want to wash it at night, then stood in the floor-length mirror to give myself a critical look before I stepped inside the shower. The warm water felt wonderful on my skin, and I considered making it hotter, but knew that I'd come out bright red if I did. I let the water run down my back as I tilted my head side to side, and then I heard the shower door open and Grayson came to stand behind me.

He rubbed my shoulders and kissed my neck, and it sent shivers down my spine. He then turned me to face him and, with the water still running against my back, he kissed my lips, and then found my breasts. He also found the place that made me catch my breath, and I wasn't sure I'd be able to stand.

He turned the water off and wrapped the towel around me and led me to my bed. The fireplace was burning, so the room was warm. He lay down beside me and touched me again, but this time it was his turn to drive himself into me until he satisfied himself and then me again.

Dear God, I thought, what just happened? I'd never experienced such quick hands, and I was absolutely drained, but I felt a distance between us, even while we lay there afterwards. For one thing, Grayson didn't feel warm and fuzzy; he felt rigid, like there was no emotional attachment. It was almost impossible to describe—no soft motions, but ones that were more perfunctory or automatic. It was strange, and I had a hard time putting a finger on it.

First time sex, at least for me, was always nervous and self-conscious, so I tried to set those thoughts aside. I also was somewhat surprised at my silent but curious response to seeing a man with reddish brown body hair. It only made sense when I thought about it, that if a man had brown hair on his head, he'd have brown hair everywhere else, but I'd never thought about red. And I wasn't certain I wanted to run my fingers through it.

Lying on his side with one arm over me, Grayson fell asleep, but I felt fidgety. He snored a little, and I had a hard time getting to sleep, so I finally eased his arm off me and slipped out of bed. I also wanted to visit the bathroom.

Instead of getting back into bed, I sat in one of the upholstered chairs by the windows and watched him. I eventually leaned my head back and fell asleep. When I woke in the morning, Grayson had left the room, so I got up and took a quick shower. The warm water felt good on my skin, and I washed my hair. It would have all day to dry, since I forgot my hair dryer.

When I finally made it downstairs, Grayson was dressed and having coffee. It was only eight, but Irma was already there, ironing in one of the other bedrooms.

"Good morning, my dear," Grayson said. It made me feel like something he'd say to his wife.

"Good morning, sir," I replied, responding to the formalness.

He looked up at me for a quick second, and then went back to his paper. "We have a light breakfast set out, and then I know you want to get back to work."

We finished the second and third bedrooms before breaking for lunch. Having Irma there was a tremendous help. I brought in the accessories for the living room and dining room so I could place them right after we ate. While the main furniture hadn't been delivered yet, I wanted to get an idea of what the room would look like when it was finished.

After lunch, I wanted to get my bedroom done, so I brought everything we needed into the room. Grayson followed me in and closed the door. He stood behind me and put his arms around me, cupping my breasts, and then whispered into my ear, "I have quite an evening planned for tonight." I had to admit it sent goose bumps down my spine, but then I wanted to break away before Irma came up.

I must have turned ten shades of red when Grayson opened the door, and Irma was standing there. We had exhibited no sign of a relationship, unless Grayson had told her, and I thought I was going to die. She just looked down and came into the room.

She ironed while I placed the accessories and hung artwork, so by the time she was ready, we could get the room done relatively quickly.

The house really turned out super, and I was a little disappointed that Grayson hadn't been more demonstrative about how he felt about everything. I gathered all the trash and, with an armful, asked him, "Where would you like me to put all this?"

"Oh, Irma can take it to the garage. It'll be picked up this week."

I looked at her, and then guiltily transferred everything over to her, but not before I found trash bags for everything.

When we finished, I joined him in the living room and sat for a minute enjoying the view of the trees out the expansive windows. I couldn't tell how warm it was, so I grabbed my coat and I went outside to get some fresh air. It was warm out, but invigorating. It was so quiet my footsteps audibly crushed against the gravel and pine needles, and then the sounds of the horses caught my attention. I continued walking and turned in that direction, but wasn't paying attention to the uneven ground and lost my balance. I didn't hurt myself when I went down, but immediately hoped no one saw me fall. I knew I'd die of embarrassment if anyone did.

I picked myself up, brushed my pants off, and decided I'd had enough of an adventure for the afternoon. When I went back in and hung my jacket up, Grayson asked, "Where'd you get the dirt on your jeans?"

"Oh," I said, "I tripped."

"Are you okay?"

"Yes, just feeling like an idiot."

"Well, *that,* you're not," he said, giving me another look, and then going back to his reading.

Okay, I thought to myself as I shrugged. I wondered just how many papers he read in a day.

"I'm going to go up and take a quick shower. When is our reservation?"

Grayson looked at his watch. "We need to leave in a little over an hour."

"Great. Meet you back down here?"

"Maybe," he said. It was obvious the look he was giving me had a double meaning, and of course, I blushed. "You're quite charming when you do that," he said.

I took a quick shower and then soaked in the tub to ease my tired muscles. I also locked my bedroom door so I could relax and have some time to myself. After savoring every minute of the warm tub, I put my hair up, touched up my makeup, then put on a comfortable but warm outfit of black pants, a black and white polka dot shirt with a fold down collar and cuffs and a short black leather jacket. I don't change my purse often, but I'd brought along a new leather one I'd just purchased and tucked in my gray and black plaid scarf for later. If Grayson was going to dress like Ralph Lauren, then I was going to co-ordinate with him.

And sure enough, when I went downstairs, Grayson was standing there waiting for me in his leather boots, black jeans, white sweater and a camel overcoat. He looked very handsome. I could tell he appreciated the way I looked too, by the way his somewhat stern look softened as I came down the stairs.

"You locked your door," he said, annoyed.

"I just wanted to soak in the tub." I was a little taken aback that he would admit he'd tried my door.

"Well, we should get going," he said, grabbing our coats off the hall tree.

Once we got in the car, I wanted to let him know it disappointed me he hadn't commented more on the house, but I wasn't quite sure how to bring it up without sounding defensive. I thought about it and eventually came up with, "You've said little about the house…do you like it?" There it was.

"Oh, I'm sorry. I thought you'd be able to tell I was very happy. I should have said something. And not just because you brought it up, *I am* really pleased with everything."

He looked at me, and part of me felt a little childish for mentioning it.

"I'm sincere, Annie. You've done a wonderful job bringing the house up to date. I'm eager to see the new furniture when it comes in."

"I'm glad you're happy. I want to get some photos before we leave tomorrow."

"Definitely."

I studied Grayson as he drove and wondered what a life with someone so complex would be like. Then I couldn't help but wonder what he had planned for this evening. I knew for certain it would not be boring.

We pulled up for parking service, and as the valet came to my side of the Range Rover, Grayson said, "I'll get that for her."

He guided me towards the restaurant door. Suddenly I could feel the heat of his hand on my back, and I recalled his touch on my bare skin.

Once inside, we waited for the hostess to acknowledge us, and I could tell Grayson wanted to make a point when he said, "I requested a booth, so I hope there's no problem. *The last time we were here, we had to wait.*"

The hostess was obviously accustomed to dealing with the demands of the public, for she was extremely polite as she showed us to our booth. I, on the other hand, wanted to fade into the background. I looked at Grayson and he didn't seem fazed. I tried to push images of my ex-husband behaving similarly from my mind, and a small alarm went off as I involuntarily tensed my neck.

"I think we should have prime rib this evening," he said.

I agreed, and when our waiter came back to the table with our wine, Grayson ordered for us.

"We'll each have the prime rib on the rare side, with au jus on the side, and the creamed corn and spinach in their own plates. And the Yorkshire pudding on separate plates. What have I forgotten?" he asked to no one in particular.

"Nothing I can think of, sir," the waiter answered.

"Ah, butter."

Then we toasted. "To a wonderful evening with a beautiful woman," he said with confidence.

I rubbed the goose bumps on my arms, suddenly feeling chilled.

"Yes, to a wonderful evening," I responded, and sincerely hoped I wasn't heading down a dark path. I rolled my head from side to side to stretch my neck muscles.

"Are you okay, my dear?"

"Yes, just tired muscles from working on the house. I'll be fine once I have some wine." And to that, I drank.

When we got home, the surprise was the hot tub warmed and ready for us, with rose petals along the edges, and chilled champagne in a bucket. I don't know what I expected, but sitting in the tub sounded luxurious. Grayson undressed first, then stepped down into the tub and stood there waiting for me. I was struck again by his body hair and I was hoping I could learn to accept it without constantly being aware of it. I suddenly felt very self-conscious. He'd seen me without clothing, but I felt totally exposed while I undressed and he watched me. He then reached for my hand as he helped me down into the tub. I was grateful for the concealment and the heat of the water.

He poured us each a glass of champagne and then toasted me again. "You've done a wonderful job with the house, Annie, and I apologize for not acknowledging it sooner. Sometimes I treat people like they are my employees, and that's not always good either!" he admitted with a quick laugh.

He set his glass down, then took mine and set it down as well. He kissed me then and his lips were soft. While he touched me under the water, he kissed my neck, which seemed like his favorite spot. I'd seen movies where couples made love in a pool, and wondered what it would feel like, and I had to admit that it didn't feel like I'd expected. I had a difficult time focusing on myself, so I just encouraged him to please himself. He didn't seem to have a problem with that.

We sat in the hot tub for a while, and the blend of chilly night air with hot water was a perfect combination. Grayson eventually climbed up out of the tub and helped me out, putting a thick towel around me first. We then went through the French doors into the master bedroom, and candles that had been burning filled the room with a soft fragrance.

I was content with calling it a night, but Grayson seemed to want more.

"I must make sure you also feel the satisfaction of our lovemaking. Let me make you happy too," he said, laying me down on his bed.

He definitely knew what to do to make a woman reach orgasm, but as with the night before, it felt like he had it all figured out, like it was a routine. The evening ended in a mutually satisfactory conclusion, but I didn't feel warmth. Or love.

CHAPTER ELEVEN

As much as I wanted to go back to my own bedroom, I stayed for a while with Grayson in his bed that night. He seemed to feel comfortable as he had no issues quickly falling asleep and yet even though I was right next to him, I again felt a distance from him that was hard to describe. I didn't bask in the lingering fleshy scent of our lovemaking.

I'd made a terrible mistake in letting it go this far. There was no way I could fit into his world; not that I wasn't good enough, but I didn't want the lifestyle he offered. And I wasn't even sure what that was, to be honest. I didn't want three houses, and I didn't want to go from place to place. I also didn't want a lover who would live in one place and visit me where I preferred to live.

I didn't feel like I belonged here, and I knew this wasn't the person I wanted to spend the rest of my life with. Suddenly I turned cold, and I shuddered with dread.

I was back to where I started. Even though Grayson was lying right next to me, I was alone. I didn't have Noah, and what I'd just done was the worst mistake I'd ever made.

I sat up for a minute to make sure I didn't wake Grayson, and then I went to my bedroom. I wanted to take a hot shower and at least try to get some sleep. I also wanted time to think on my own about how I was going to tell Grayson this was not going to work out.

If I would have thought this through, I would have told him after we got home. But for some reason, I decided that I would tell him before we left the house in the morning. Looking back, I don't know why I was so surprised at his reaction.

Grayson hadn't come to my room in the morning, but instead had gotten ready and was at the kitchen counter having coffee when I came down.

"You left my bed again," he said bluntly.

"I woke up then couldn't go back to sleep, and I didn't want to disturb you."

I decided to sit and talk with him.

"I see," he said, coolly, and he hadn't taken his eyes off me.

"Grayson," I started, "we need to talk about us." I felt the best way to get it out was to just start.

"Indeed?"

I couldn't tell by the look on his face what he was expecting, but I could tell that his body had stiffened.

"You've done everything right…and you've been the most gracious host…but I never should have allowed our relationship to get this far." There, I'd said it.

All he did was look at me, but I could see the change in his demeanor. He straightened his back and his face had suddenly turned a blotchy red, as if I'd slapped him.

The room had gone so silent, I could hear actually hear the silence in my ears.

"And here I thought I'd made you happy," he finally said, obviously offended.

"You did…" I started, but he didn't let me continue.

He stood and came to where I was sitting.

"Look at me, Annie," he demanded, the beginning of rage filling his voice.

His sudden action surprised me, and I couldn't help but sit back in my chair. I was unnerved, and I knew I could not disguise my unease. His eyes had turned icy gray instead of the beautiful blue they really were.

I looked down, not wanting to meet his eyes.

What had I done?

"I told you I was a patient man, and that I know what I want. And you knew that when you came here." His voice was now laden with full on rage. "I think you know how I feel about you...I've been trying to step back and let you have your freedom, but I want you to be part of my life."

He then grabbed my upper arms and brought me to my feet. He tried to kiss me. The force with which he held me was hurting my arms, and thoughts of him being near me right now were repulsive. I turned my head away from him.

At that moment, sheer panic filled me, and I wasn't sure if he would just let me be, or physically assault me. I wanted to maintain my composure, but also wanted there to be no doubt I would fight him.

"Let me go, Grayson, you're hurting me!"

A sudden chill filled the air, and for a split second, I saw such rage in his eyes, I knew he could do just about anything. My temper rose, almost matching his, and I repeated in a low voice, *"Let me go or I'll fucking kill you."*

I don't know if I was more frightened by the thought that I could actually do that, or that he would try to beat the hell out of me. So I just pulled myself away from him and watched him withdraw.

"Annie," he said in a much calmer voice, but I was halfway out of the kitchen and up the stairs to my room.

I locked my door and stood against it, not so much to keep him out, but to give me something to lean on while I caught my breath and waited for my heart to quit pounding in my chest.

When he knocked on my door, I involuntarily started shaking, and of course I didn't answer him. That terrible feeling of anxiety rushed through me and I somehow willed myself to breathe deeply, and eventually I started calming down.

I sat in the chair by the window and used the images of the trees to help me focus. I eventually closed my eyes so I could concentrate on my breathing.

I had to leave, and there was no way I could fly back with Grayson. I'd forgotten my room had a phone, and I quickly dialed the operator.

"I need a cab now," I urgently whispered.

I quickly packed what I'd brought and then picked up an umbrella I'd seen in the closet in case I needed to defend myself.

When I looked out my door, thankfully Grayson wasn't there, so with my heart still pounding fiercely in my chest, I made my way downstairs, grabbed my coat, and left the house.

There was no place to really hide outside, but I stood out of view until the cab pulled up. I think I literally jumped in and closed the door as quickly as I could. It was like I had to be sure the boogie man hadn't followed me in.

When we got to the airport, there was an open flight to Ontario, so I booked it. I knew Grayson would not come after me, but while I waited, I made sure I sat with my back against the wall so I'd be able to see if anyone was following me.

Thankfully, I'd met Grayson at the airport, so the minute I got off the plane, I ran to my car. I sat in the warm silence and cried. I knew there was no one there, but I was afraid he'd followed me and would at any minute knock on my car window.

I should have found somewhere to calm down before I drove up the mountain, but I wanted to get home and lock the door to my cabin. I was still a bundle of nerves as I drove the winding road, but somehow, as I did, I found myself relaxing with the turns, and by the time I reached the cabins, I knew I was going to be okay.

Everything was as it had been before I left—and why wouldn't it be? No one had changed anything. But no one had done what I'd done.

That was when I started crying again. Noah had been right about everything. I never should have taken this job.

I whispered, "Please come home."

CHAPTER TWELVE

Carrie

After running into Annie at the Art Festival, I knew I'd need to begin sorting through Mother's things or she'd think I'd lost interest in working with her. But every time I opened the door to her bedroom, Mother's fragrance and the thought of her not being there overwhelmed me. I'd open her drawers or closet doors and promptly turn around, closing the door behind me as I left the room.

I'd collected several empty boxes, but they remained at the foot of the stairs, waiting for me to find inspiration to get started. It finally came when I had the brilliant idea of starting downstairs where there were fewer personal memories. I had a few days before I was leaving to go on a short book tour with a group of other romance writers, so I grabbed a few of the boxes and brought them into the living room.

My goal was to find things I wasn't interested in keeping when we started updating. I started with the bookcases, where I pulled down books and magazines that were more clutter than ones of interest. I loved Mother's collection of gourds and Santa carvings, so without spending a lot of time, I rearranged some books and found room to show them off. I put everything I didn't want into the boxes, and I would let Isobel sort through it all before I donated it.

I found that by just getting started, it motivated me to do more, and in no time, I filled all the boxes I'd brought home. I hated to lose my momentum, so I continued to pull things I could live without and I moved my writing aside and found room on the dining room table and kitchen bar area to store them.

Tomorrow I'd go to breakfast and stop at the grocery store and buy large trash bags and see if I could collect more boxes.

I ended up filling the back end of my car with broken down boxes, so I had to stop at the postal store next door and buy packing tape and a dispenser so I could reuse them. I was on a roll.

I'd purposely left the door to Mother's room open before I went out, daring myself to work in there when I returned. I brought some of the boxes and the trash bags up and stood in the doorway for what seemed like an eternity. Everything smelled of Mother.

I thought the closet would be the easiest, so that's where I started. I began at one end and made two piles on the bed; one was for items I thought could be washed and donated, and another for Isobel to go through to see if she could use or give away. Anything that smelled musty and couldn't be washed and freshened went straight to the floor. I'd put it in trash bags when I was finished.

I took a break and had lunch outside on the porch where I'd be able to relax and listen to the quiet. I watched as a bird ate from our feeder, and in the distance I could hear a woodpecker doing its business.

Mother's throw was still tossed across the back of her chair, and more than once, I expected to hear her voice break the silence.

"I miss you," I said.

I poured another glass of iced tea and went back upstairs. I began going through the smaller dresser and sorted underwear and stockings; things that wouldn't be of use to anyone. I did fold heavy socks and mittens that were in good shape and put them on the bed near the clothing; someone would be able to use them. I folded several piles of scarves; Mother had so many, some I'd never seen her wear. Pullover sweaters and pajamas filled two drawers, and half of them looked new.

The top drawer of the taller dresser had some trays of jewelry, most of it costume. Mother always wore her real jewelry; a necklace with a locket that had a picture of my grandfather and her in each frame and her wedding *rings. She'd often tell me that's all she really cared about. I added everything still of use to a small box and set it next to the clothing on the bed.*

The second drawer was filled with what must have been my grandfather's things; ties, a masculine jewelry box full of tie tacks, cufflinks, a pocket watch and fob, an 1898 silver dollar money clip, and several rings with various stones in them. I discovered a pearl-handled revolver, covered in a soft cloth, and as I unwrapped it, I could immediately smell the metal of the intricately carved barrel. I didn't check to see if it was loaded; instead, I quickly recovered it and set it back in the drawer. I'd already decided to keep everything that was his, and I'd find a nice box to put everything in. Maybe a wooden one, something I could keep in a closed cabinet.

The rest of the drawers were filled with old photos, albums, funeral service acknowledgements, birth and christening announcements, my high school and college graduation diplomas, and some embroidered cloth handkerchiefs.

I discarded announcements about people I didn't know, along with old photos with no names written on the back. I loved seeing the photos of Mother and my father, though. They looked so in love and they made such a handsome couple. In these photos, they both seemed so happy. I swore I could see a twinkle in their eyes when they looked at the camera.

There were photos of my mother when she was a child, and some with her family on the old farm. And of course, photos of me and my children.

On top of some old newspapers were black and white images of women dressed in slinky gowns, standing with men in tuxedos. Some of the women were quite glamorous and smoked from long cigarette holders. I was certain several of them were of my father, standing with just his legs spread akimbo, or sometimes with his elbows also bent, holding his long coat open. If I didn't know differently, I would have sworn he was wearing a shoulder holster. If he was the only subject in the photo, his look was serious, as most old photographs were.

There were several that looked like Mother so many years ago, with other young girls who were casually dressed, and it looked like they were standing in front of a three story English Tudor building, similar to the building across the street from the Tudor House now. I glanced through a series of photos of what looked like the interior of a lounge of some type. Expensive looking sofas and chairs were set around large Oriental rugs, and mostly men sat and appeared to talk, some with cigarettes dangling from their lips. In several photos, there were gaming tables and some of the well-dressed ladies stood behind men playing cards.

Old newspapers were from up in the mountains, and when I saw an exterior image of what was now the Tudor House, it felt like I had the wind taken from me. These were photos similar to, if not the same as, what I'd seen of Paul's.

I skimmed several of the articles from the late 20s to the mid-30s. There were photos of Bugsy Siegel helping a woman out of a car, others of well-known actors coming up to the mountains, including Jack Benny and Jimmy Durante.

And then between the newspapers was a death certificate.

Deceased: Thomas Meyer
Residence: Illinois

It was my father's.

Date: November 3, 1934
Place of Death: Los Angeles, Ca
Married
Husband of: Maryann Goldmann Meyer
Cause of Death: Gunshot injury, catastrophic injury to the head,
   damage to the brain

Mother always said he'd been killed in an automobile accident...

CHAPTER THIRTEEN

Carrie

The only person I could talk to was Paul.

"Bring all your photos," I said.

I hadn't seen all the photographs he'd told me about, but I was eager to see them now and to show him what I'd found. He was down in Rancho Santa Fe, checking the property, and wouldn't be back up for another day.

It was impossible for me to concentrate on anything but my discovery. I cleared all the knickknacks off the dining room table and put them on the coffee table. I was going stir crazy. I had enlarged copies made of the photos I'd found, I went to the grocery store and mostly just roamed the aisles, stopped at the post office, and did my rental property banking, but I couldn't stop thinking about what it all meant.

The moment Paul came to the door, I literally dragged him to the dining table where I now had everything laid out. I decided to set the scene a little by showing him the revolver and the newspapers first.

I then went to the photos.

"These look similar to mine," he said, taking a few of them from me.

"Look," I said, "Here's the inside of a gaming room, and then look at this." I handed him the photo of the Tudor House. "It's your place."

"Holy shit, it is," he said.

"*Let me see your photos.*"

"*Here they are.*"

He handed me what he'd brought, then said, "I think we may have some that are very similar. Look, these look like some of the same women, and yours are definitely the speakeasy. This is crazy."

"*Let me see your mother, Ida Mae.*"

"*Here they are with some women I don't recognize.*"

"*Well, guess what? This one is a photo of your mother with mine,*" I said, shocked.

"*I need a drink,*" Paul said. He'd been pacing the floor and finally fell into one of the chairs in the living room.

"*It gets even crazier,*" I said, bringing us both a glass of wine. "*I've also found my father's death certificate. And it says he died of gunshot wounds.*"

Suddenly, my eyes filled with tears.

"*His name was Thomas Meyer, not Davis, and he was married to Maryann Goldmann Meyer, who lived in Chicago. Mother always said he died in a car accident, but that's not true. And I don't think they were married.*"

CHAPTER FOURTEEN

My life had turned black and overwhelming. Melancholy came upon me in waves, and I found myself with no energy to get up and get out of my own tracks. Thankfully, I had enough munchies for me and food for the cats, as I never even ventured outside my cabin for two days. Silence and sleep were what I seemed to crave. The cats loved it.

When I began feeling claustrophobic, I wanted to walk the grounds. I tried to keep the cats inside before I closed the door to my cabin, but they rushed out. I managed to walk the border of the ravine behind the cabins, and the girls followed me as I made my way along the edge, thinking I could easily miss my step and fall. The image of me lying there with broken bones and calling for help at first didn't bother me. I was already falling—the only difference was, when someone came to rescue me, I'd feel like the fool I was.

Thinking it would be Sam, and how he'd be unable to drag me back up, made me realize punishing myself was actually being selfish.

I felt worse than when I left David, I think, because I'd brought this down upon myself. I'd done what I wanted, even though I knew down deep I might be headed for trouble.

When I willed myself to clear my thoughts, I did. I'd focus on knots in the pine ceiling or stare into the unlit fireplace. When I allowed myself to think, I tried to put my thoughts into categories; one Noah, one Grayson, and lastly, David seemed to worm his way in.

With Noah, I missed his embrace, the feelings of his legs wrapped around mine, the gentle way he kissed me on the neck. He was a good man, and I'd betrayed him. I hadn't intended for my relationship with Grayson to go so far. I missed Noah's friendship and encouragement. But he'd walked away from me, and now I wasn't sure he would come back and be a part of my life. How could I face seeing him in town?

Grayson was hard to pinpoint; he had the look, and the way he carried himself...well, that certainly let everyone know he felt he was in charge. Those attributes were definitely admirable, but he'd set up a huge barrier around himself. He needed to be strong to be successful in what he did, but the aloofness was a definite turnoff. In fact, the personality traits he had that were like David's should have sent up red flags in the very beginning, but I had missed them. He had a constant need to always be in control, and with that, he wasn't able to see that others needed something more.

He had obviously been with a lot of women, for he knew what to do to bring pleasure, but his lovemaking was mechanical and lacked intimacy. That's the word I'd been looking for, what I had been trying to figure out. I'd never be able to share a life with someone like that.

And then there was David. He'd built some walls around himself too, distancing himself from that same intimacy. I ended up following in his path, accepting what I had always thought was normal, until I met Noah. I'd blamed myself for his straying, but enough time had passed that I now realized it was David's way to constantly feel superior. He'd thrown away our marriage. The way our lives were was what ultimately pushed me away. Certainly, I was also at fault; no marriage fails because of just one partner. Somehow, there is something they both are, or aren't doing, to keep the relationship alive.

My three men. Where did I fit into all these relationships? What had I done, or not done? No one can give one hundred percent every day, all the time. But where had I gone wrong with David? Part of it was ignorance of youth, but on the flip side, he gave me the opportunity to grow and develop. That part of our marriage was positive.

Where I went wrong was not trying to keep our relationship alive. By the time I found out about the other woman, it was too late. If I was totally honest, it had been too late even before then. I don't know if I could have ultimately changed the direction of our marriage, but I could have recognized the signs.

How do you do that, though, when you have no life experience, or you have the idea that once you get married, you live happily ever after?

With Noah, I could sense he was interested in me when we met, but I had made no decisions about what to do with David yet. So starting a relationship wasn't on my mind…we grew into learning about each other and caring.

And Grayson, he had never been an option, but I let him in. Sure, he was attractive and stylish, and that was appealing, but I was never instantly interested in him. I had too many things going on to think about further complicating my new life up here.

I should have never taken the Montana job, but I was trying to establish myself, and I needed as much income as I could generate. I'd made the huge mistake of combining my personal life with my professional one.

Then another realization struck me. I needed to bill Grayson for everything I did in Montana. What if he decided to not pay me? *Shit. Think.* Relief flooded my mind as I remembered he'd already paid me for all the furniture and accessories; it was just going to be my time that was lost. Thank God! I would eliminate any further communication with him by not billing him for my time. That would solve that problem!

I should have left the boots there. That would have made it clear I didn't want to see him again. Dammit. I got up, found them, and set them outside my door.

What if he showed up here?

If I thought about that logically, he wouldn't want to take any further chances of injuring his pride. I was certain he'd disappear from my life. *But would he?* Yes. Knowing him, he would.

Part Three

Picking Up The Pieces

CHAPTER FIFTEEN

In some ways, I craved the solitude, even if all I thought about was life itself; my life and where I would go from here. But by day three, my hibernation was making me restless, and I longed to get some fresh air. I changed my sheets and brought all my laundry down to the office.

I could tell Sam was pleasantly surprised to see me as he said, "Well, it's good to see you're still alive and doin' okay."

"I'm good. Just needed some downtime," I said, as I came around the counter to look at the guest log.

I'd only been gone over the weekend, (plus the three days of hiding in my cabin), so I knew there really wasn't much new. But I needed to do something with my hands.

"So you finished with that project?" he asked. I thought I noted a slight raise in his left eyebrow. It was his way of asking if I was home for good.

I could feel my face heat up, but said, "Yes. And honestly, I'm glad it's done. Doing a job so far away is really draining. When the furniture comes in, I don't need to go back. A delivery service can bring everything into the house."

He nodded.

"Thank goodness Grayson's housekeeper was there to help, or I never would have finished it."

"Oh, does she stay there?"

I gave him a look. "No, she cooks for him, and came in to help me."

"Just askin'."

I could tell I'd spoken sharply. "Sorry, I didn't mean to snap."

"Well, we're all glad you're back. The girls did fine, but they missed you," he said, referring to Jezebel and Socks.

"I missed them too," I said, then smiled. It's funny how when people refer to your children, or your pets, you smile. The girls were my babies, and I loved them dearly.

"Well," Sam said, pointing back to the booking calendar, "We have a new reservation; a couple up for the weekend, so that's a good sign. Someone else called and asked about availability for a few dates, so that's positive too. I think all your hard work is paying off."

"I don't know what I'd do without you, Sam," I said, going over to him and giving him a big hug.

"I just want you to be happy," he said, hugging me back. He then held me at arm's length, and asked, "Speaking of which, have you heard from Noah yet?"

I didn't mean to, but I let out an enormous sigh. "No, I haven't heard from him. I hate that he's still gone."

Sam wrinkled his face then said, "I didn't get a chance to tell you when you first got back. He came back while you were gone. Said it was to check in to see how the boys was doin' workin' at that Bunny's place."

Shit. He'd come here, and of course Sam must have told him I was in Montana. If he still cared about me, that news had to have been pure torture to hear. And what was worse was that everything he was imagining, was indeed happening. I could feel myself heat up again. Damn it!

"Did he say when he was coming back?" I tried not to appear too anxious, but I knew Sam could read me.

"He did." Sam gave me another hug. "You know, I'm not so old that I don't see what you're going through. And what I *do* know about life is that things have a way of working themselves out. He just needs some time."

I didn't want to be so dramatic as to run out of the office, so I pretended to take my time, but by the time I made it outside, I'd started crying again. I'd really made a mess of things.

That night I tried to drink myself to sleep. I was exhausted, but no matter how I tossed and turned, I couldn't get comfortable. I didn't want to admit how frightened I'd been, but I'd set myself up for what had happened. I'd brought it on myself and now I might lose Noah.

I needed to talk with someone, but calling my parents was out of the question. I could never tell them what I'd done. I thought about calling my old friend Sarah, but I hadn't spoken to her about private matters in years, and it would also embarrass me to tell her how I'd ruined everything. I couldn't just call her out of the blue and cry on her shoulder.

So I decided to call Laura. I hadn't seen her since our grand opening, although we'd talked on the phone a couple of times. Aside from Noah, she was the first person I met up here, and we'd become fast friends.

She'd finally found 'Mr. Right' when he came up to the mountains for a weekend with his buddies. They'd met at the Cowboy Bar, our old stomping grounds, and hit it off. I was thrilled for her, but I missed her terribly. Plus, she did my hair, and I had found no one up here to replace her.

I told her I needed to see her, and we set up lunch for the next day. We'd meet halfway between the mountains and where she was now living in Newport Beach.

Suddenly, just the thought of seeing her lifted some of the heaviness I felt. It was the first positive moment I'd had lately. I truly looked forward to seeing her; we had a lot of catching up to do.

CHAPTER SIXTEEN

We met at the Mission Inn in Riverside. It's a beautiful old hotel with great restaurants and the downtown area is closed off to traffic, so people can walk around the area and shop in wonderful stores.

I soon realized I'd dressed too warmly in a pullover sweater and new boots. I'd forgotten the temperature down there could be between ten to twenty degrees warmer than it was up in the mountains, and I immediately felt the rush of heat as I got out of my car. I waited under one of the large trees at the entrance until Laura found me. Opposite my gloominess, she looked radiant. She'd cut her hair and wore jeans with a paisley print top.

I was glad I'd made a reservation because they were busy as usual and it took us a few minutes to check in. Thankfully, we were seated in a shady area out on the patio where it was cooler. We ordered iced tea, then we gave the menu a quick look before we both decided to have Cobb salads.

"Looks like you need a hairdresser," Laura said, looking at my hair.

"No one can replace you," I said, giving my shoulders a shrug.

"Why not try Raymond in the old salon? He has a great following."

"I've been planning to, but have had a lot going on lately."

"Well…tell me."

"I will, but first tell me how you're doing. Are you happy?"

She leaned forward in her chair. "I am. In fact, I'm wondering when the other shoe is going to drop. Things are that good. I hate to sound like such a romantic, but our relationship is strong, I truly like the kids and I'm surprised they haven't been a burden. My appointments at the new salon are picking up, and I love living in Newport Beach."

"Wow," I said. I hadn't realized I too was leaning forward to listen to her, and I sat back and took a quick sip of my tea. I slowly nodded my head, embracing her news. I managed a smile, hoping it came across as being sincere.

We both took bites of our salads.

"So tell me," Laura said again.

I knew I wasn't able to conceal the defeat in my voice and face as I spoke.

"I think I've done it this time," I started.

Laura's brows rose slightly. "Pray tell."

"I think I've done some irreparable damage to my relationship with Noah."

"Well, don't stop. Spit it out," she whispered anxiously.

"Everything was going so well with us. Our bookings are up at the cabins. I actually have some cash in the bank…"

"And?"

"You know, I'd started working with this client, Grayson Underwood. And Noah has hated the idea all along. He always felt Grayson wanted more than a designer/client relationship, and I kept assuring him I didn't see it that way…"

Then I told her everything, and I watched as her face took on looks of surprise and concern. She didn't interrupt me, and she didn't admonish me, for which I was grateful. If the situation were reversed, I'd never want to do that to her.

"Well?" I finally asked.

"*Well*, is right." She sipped her tea. "Let me get my thoughts together."

Laura took a deep breath and closed her eyes. I watched as I envisioned a hundred different thoughts going on in her mind.

"First, I don't think you made a mistake. I think you acted on what you thought you wanted to do. Did you start out intending to have a relationship with Grayson?"

"No. I thought he was handsome, but I was interested in Noah."

"Well, Noah left. And he did it, in my opinion, when faced with potential competition for you."

I sighed. "But he did have a job opportunity in Colorado."

"Annie, he didn't even tell you he was leaving. That's running away. Noah's a great guy, and I think he really cares about you. But he can't run away when things get rough. And even though you ended up having an affair, *one*, Noah had already left you, and *two*, you're still trying to figure out what you want to do with your life after David. All of that is natural. Ask any shrink," and now she smiled.

She leaned back in her chair. "Would you have done that if Noah was still in town?"

"No," I said quickly.

"I think you did nothing wrong, and if you hadn't opened the book to see what being with a different person could be like, you wouldn't have been fair to yourself."

I knew what Laura was saying was logical and made sense, but while those thoughts had run over and over in my mind, I still felt like I'd betrayed Noah.

I couldn't believe I still had an appetite, so I went back to my salad and changed the subject.

"So, how's Jason's doing?" I asked.

"Jason's business is good; I've told you it's working out with the kids, and I actually like having a family. I've met his parents, and the mom's family, and we all seem to get along. Sometimes it scares me."

She pushed her plate away and let out a sigh. "I'm stuffed. I feel like this time just might be the right time for me. And Annie, you'll find the right thing too. I can't imagine Noah staying away forever."

Then I told her he'd come back while I was in Montana, and her expression changed.

"Oh, oh," she said.

"I need to figure out whether to call him."

"Will you tell him?"

I'd already thought about that. "No," I said. "I don't want to hurt him more."

Laura nodded in thought.

I looked at my watch, then said, "Well, we should probably get going, so we miss some traffic going home. I've loved getting together and we need to do it again. And not so long in between."

"I agree," she said as we hugged.

I mulled our conversation over in my mind as I made my way back up the hill. We were both right, but sometimes when you've done something you hadn't intended to do, like sleeping with Grayson, it was hard to justify your actions. I had done nothing wrong. Noah was not back in my life. And for all I knew, he could have been with someone else, too. We both had the freedom to do what we wanted.

I had no way of contacting him. Assuming he still cared about me, I knew it must have devastated him when I wasn't there. If it were me, all kinds of thoughts would have been running through my mind; bodies entwined and another man seeing me the same way Noah saw me when we made love. And if it could get any worse, imagining that I would choose to be with someone else. My heart broke for him.

When I got to the office, Sam gave me a message from Carrie Davis; she was ready for us to get together and get started on the restoration of her cabin.

Hoping I'd catch her at home, I gave Carrie a call. She was back from her book tour, so we decided to meet the next morning. I had breakfast at Ginny's first and felt awkward, wondering if I wore guilt on my face, thinking everyone knew what'd done, but no one seemed to give me a second thought.

CHAPTER SEVENTEEN

When I found Carrie's "cabin", it wasn't a cabin at all. It was huge, and right on the lake with a lawn in front that led down to the water. It was built in the late twenties out of logs and it was wonderful. She greeted me at the front door and stood aside while I made my way inside.

Even though it hadn't been updated in years, the home was incredible, and I was dying to get my hands on it. I could smell the years of people living there…not unpleasant, but more of old furniture, old clothing in the closets and old wool rugs.

"Carrie, this is spectacular," I said, gravitating toward the large windows that faced the lawn and lake. "This area reminds me of my parent's lake house."

"That's right. You'd told me they'd had a place up here. I love the tranquility, don't you? Always have."

"I have to agree. I've always loved it here. I have a lot of wonderful memories."

"I'm sure you thought I'd never get around to working on the house. I've started doing some sorting. It's a lot harder than I thought it would be," Carrie said, looking around the living room.

"Well, I'll do my best to preserve what you want to keep and accentuate what you want to update. I just want to light a fire and curl up in here." I let out a deep breath. "Where should we start?" I asked.

I set my bag down and pulled out my notebook and pencil.

"Whoever designed the house, had an eye," I said.

"Let's start here," Carrie said. The kitchen, pantry and laundry room were on the west side of the house. "I'd eventually like to replace this old tile bar and countertop, but I still like the cabinets. And there's nothing to do but reorganize the pantry. In the laundry room, I'll replace the washer and dryer and I'd like to replace the counter in there too. I think these are the same appliances Mother bought years ago. In the old days, we had to hang our laundry outside to dry and when it was especially cold out, it sometimes felt like everything was still wet when we brought it back in.

"We could always tell when the deer came through the hanging clothes, for even though we made sure to securely clip them to the line, we'd find a few pieces on the ground, often trodden with hoof marks. Mother would get cross, but she'd pick everything up and refill the hamper. 'Those darned deer,' she'd say, then give me a wink."

We stood at the window looking out at the lake for a few minutes, and I could tell Carrie was lost in thought.

"I've started taking down and clearing out things that I can live without. I thought if you saw it with everything Mother collected over the years, you wouldn't know where to start. I have boxes of things you can look at if you want to."

The living room and dining rooms were only separated by what I was certain were authentic antique Persian rugs.

"I'll have the floors waxed, and the rugs taken out and cleaned. What do you think I should do with the walls?"

"I have them in my cabins, and I had them waxed, and they turned out very nicely."

"You may not care for the taxidermy, but it fits so well up here," Carrie said, pointing to a large, mounted deer head on the fireplace. "There's more in the family room."

"I wouldn't want to shoot anything myself, but I love the look."

"When I was very young, I asked Mother about them, and there was the oddest rabbit I'd ever seen. It's right here still."

It clearly surprised me when I saw it.

"It's a taxidermy creation from the 1930s, mounting small deer horns to jack rabbits. Isn't it funny?" she giggled. "It's called a Jackalope. For years, I had a hard time understanding it wasn't real."

"I think I've seen something like it in one of the antique stores I went in to with Noah, but was too embarrassed to ask what it was. The next time I see one, I can sound 'all knowing'," I said.

I followed her upstairs, and she said, "The bedrooms need new bedding and window treatments, and they'll be cleaned and ready. I'll lay out what I'd like to keep on the beds."

She led me to her mother's room and stood at the open door and I hadn't realized she'd held her breath until she slowly let it out.

"I've had the hardest time with this room," she said. "Thankfully, Gram…Mother, didn't die up here, or I don't think I'd be able to sleep here, but I'll most likely wait until all the work is done before I move in here. We can do this room and leave mine for last. That's where I've been staying."

"I don't see a problem with that," I said, going ahead of her and looking closely at the room.

"And last, is the library," she said, going back down the long hallway. "It's actually one of my favorite rooms in the house."

We walked up three steps to another level, and the amount of books filling four walls of built-in bookcases momentarily overwhelmed me. Pheasant mounts flanked the tops of the bookcases, and two oak library ladders leaned against opposite walls.

"Gram taught me at a young age about caring for books. I wasn't aware at first that some of these were limited and first edition printings. She'd remind me, 'Rule number one is to keep the books away from sunlight and dampness. Then, don't dog-ear the pages, or leave the book open and face down.' I've done that with my own books if I didn't have a bookmark handy," Carrie said conspirationally. " 'Opening the book widely can damage the spine', which I also often did, and last, 'don't wrinkle or damage the dust jacket'. When I was young, I kept a notebook about what I did and didn't like about a particular book I'd read. Sometimes I'd get so caught up in the story, I'd forget to write anything down, and that's when I'd realized how much I'd actually enjoyed the book."

"Where did she collect all these?" I asked in awe.

"I'm not really sure. She went to a lot of garage sales. Every time I went with her to one, we always lugged boxes of old books back to the house."

We made our way back down into the living room, and Carrie said, "If you have a few more minutes, I've made some iced tea and we can sit on the porch. It's also one of my favorite places."

"Sure," I said, setting down all of my notes.

"Take the chair with the throw on it. It was Mother's, and she'd love to have company," Carrie said mischievously. "When I came back up here after my divorce, I found such peace just sitting out here."

"I felt the same way. I told myself I wasn't alone, and that plenty of other women had left unhappy marriages. We have something in common. In between bursts of anger and feeling sorry for myself, I finally realized I'd be all right."

"Me too. Oh, I have something to show you."

I sat and closed my eyes as I rocked in Gram's chair. I just about jumped out of my skin when a black and white cat jumped onto my lap.

"Well, hello there," I said, quickly recovering.

"*Sadie*," Carrie scolded. "You frightened our guest."

"I didn't know you had a cat," I said, petting her.

"She mostly hides under the bed. She was Mother's, and she misses her terribly."

"I have two cats. Socks and Jezebel."

Once Carrie set the tray with our drinks down, she went back inside and brought out some old photos.

"I wanted you to see these. I found them when I was going through Mother's things, and I showed them to Paul."

There were two young women, standing next to old cars parked in front of a Tudor style building.

"This was the Tudor House," Carrie said. "The woman on the left is my mother, and the one on the right is Paul's."

If I'd come across these photos in the cabins, I'd never have been able to figure out who they were, and I thought it was interesting she wanted me to see them.

"I found some other things too, and something disturbing. I've come to understand my parents were never married...just before I left for my book signing, I went through all Mother's belongings, and I found things that honestly threw me for a loop."

Telling me about her discovery surprised me. I didn't know if I'd be that forthcoming with someone I hardly knew.

"I shared this with the ladies in my writing group while we were away, and while we all agreed this was an enormous shock, we also decided this could be my next book. It'd be a romance set up here in the mountains. Mother told me before she died I'd find out some things about her, and boy did I."

Carrie put her tea down.

"But this is what I wanted to show you," she said, handing me another photograph. "How far back do your guest books go?"

I looked at the photo of the same two women, and there they were, standing in front of one of my cabins.

CHAPTER EIGHTEEN

"Give me a few days to come up with some ideas," I said as I packed up my bag. "And I agree with everything you're thinking of doing. I'll have some great things to show you, and I'm dying to get back to the office and look at the guest books. I'll let you know if I find anything."

When I got back to the cabins, I went directly to the office.

"Sam, you'll never believe this," I said, setting my bag down. "I need our guest book for 1929. I've met someone whose parents stayed here then."

Since we weren't sure when it was exactly, we started in January. We found plenty of one night stays, but it wasn't until the end of March that we came across 'Mr. & Mrs. Thomas Meyer'. Cabin Three was checked off until the end of April.

I called Carrie right away.

"I found them. They were here!"

My mojo was back. The next morning, I made a trip down to the design center where I could pull fabrics and furniture for Carrie's house. When I got back, I went through all my samples from my trip last year to the furniture market when I was restoring my cabins. There were plenty of options to present, and I hoped I wouldn't overwhelm her.

When we met again, I started my presentation in the master bedroom.

"I thought this room could use a rustic but slightly feminine look, so while keeping the vintage rugs, I thought we could do drapery panels on the windows, a red plaid reading chair by the fireplace, and two leather chairs in the corner."

"I love it," Carrie said.

Three of my favorite words.

"I've always slept on the right side of the bed, so I'd like to be sure to have a good reading lamp on the nightstand."

"I sleep on that side too. I did when I was married, and I've never changed."

"How funny our habits are."

I continued. "For the bath, I'd love to see double vanities along one wall, and new rustic tile for the shower."

"We can do the same in the guest bathrooms," Carrie suggested.

Then we worked our way downstairs.

"I'd love to see stationery drapery panels on either side of the two sets of windows, and I have a couple of ideas for chairs and new sofas." Then I pushed it a little by asking her how she felt about a huge antler chandelier hanging in the living room and was pleasantly surprised she liked the idea. Lighting over the dining table would be different, and I showed her my idea for that, too.

"Am I overwhelming you?" I asked, hoping my eagerness for the project wasn't too much for her.

"No, it's perfect," she said, pleased.

"I love the library as it is, but I think we can break up placement of all the books with some curiosities, as I call them, like this armillary and these pipe stands. I also think hanging some of these unframed paintings on the bookcase itself adds a lot of intrigue."

"I'd never thought of that, although thinking back, I believe I've seen photographs of library shelves filled with all kinds of wonderful things, including paintings. I like it."

"I saved the kitchen for last, since I really wanted to preserve it. Colored appliances are all the rage right now, but I think we should use stainless. It's a newer look, and I think it's classic, meaning it'll never go out of style. We can put in a new sink, but I'd like to keep the cabinets and do what's called 'live edge' wood on the counters and bar tops." I'd brought an example of that also so she could see what that looked like.

Carrie nodded and said, "I think you've hit the nail on the head with all this. I love your ideas and really wouldn't change anything you've shown me."

I was delighted…beyond exhilarated!

"We don't have to do it all right now," I said. I wanted her to feel comfortable with the plan.

Carrie stood at the windows facing the lake and took a moment. "Let's start downstairs. I'll find someone to take the rugs out and vacuum them thoroughly, and then I'll find a hardwood specialist to add life to these floors and walls. If you go ahead and order everything for down here, we can do the kitchen too. Then we can start upstairs. Sound okay?"

"Sounds really exciting," I said. "I can hardly wait to get started." I took a few more measurements of the kitchen area, and then I wrote down what we were doing in each room so I wouldn't get myself confused once I put all the samples away. Carrie sat and took in my process.

"It's very interesting to watch you," she said. "As a writer, I create differently. I loved observing your presentation. You exude passion and I had no problem visualizing the end results. I can tell you love what you do."

"I do, and sometimes I have to be careful if I'm really excited about a project. Like this one, that blends the old, or what you already have, with the new, adding only what will keep that look timeless."

I started gathering all my paperwork and putting it into my bag.

"At least you don't have to carry samples with you," I said, then smiled. As with the first time I'd met Carrie, I liked her.

"No, but I *do* need to carry notebooks around. I'm afraid if I don't have them, I'm lost if I want to write something down. I've done that for years."

On the way back to my cabin, I couldn't help thinking how much I enjoyed working with what a client already had, and it made me think of ways I could add that to services I already offered.

Since I'd missed lunch, I decided to stop and grab a bite to eat. I'd sit and make some notes. I couldn't decide between the grilled chicken sandwich at the Grill or a club at Ginny's. It turned out it would be neither, for as I slowed down to find a parking spot between the two, I saw Noah's jeep covered in mud. He was standing with an attractive young woman and talking to Bunny Bryant.

As if I needed a double punch to the stomach, notice of his arrival was there in the stack of messages Sam had taken for me while I was down the hill.

"He's back in town," the note said.

CHAPTER NINETEEN

The temperature had fallen into the fifties and yet I was feeling stifled by the heat in my Jeep. As soon as I unloaded my car, I brushed the leaves off my Adirondack chair and sat for a few minutes. Soon Jezebel and Socks were at my feet, rubbing my legs, and I petted them both. I felt their unconditional love, and it lifted my spirit a little.

For once, the quiet of the mountains wasn't enough to bring me the comfort I sought, so I went inside and grabbed my jacket and headed for the Village. I'd forgotten how all the stores set out decorated scarecrows for fall, and while most of the displays were already up, a few of the stores were out working on theirs. I'd wanted to do that at the cabins too, but at that moment, it was the farthest thing from my mind.

I bought some duck food from a Girl Scout who'd set up a small table and tossed handfuls of it out onto the lake. It was almost as though an announcement went out amongst them, for in no time, a raft of ducks, some with their ducklings, were heading towards me from all over, joining the feeding frenzy.

I smiled.

How simple their lives were.

Once the food was gone, I sat on the bench in front of the art gallery and just breathed in the cold air. Everyone who passed me was bundled up in jackets, scarves and mittens, and I wished I had brought something to keep my hands warm. I'd have to remember to keep my winter gear in the Jeep.

A brisk wind whipped the water, and I felt like that was what my life was like. The sky was turning gray and another bitter gust of wind chilled me. Visitors were hurrying past me to leave and I decided to go home myself and sit in front of my fireplace.

I stopped in to check in on Sam first, and I'd forgotten I'd left the cats outside before I left. They were both sitting on the counter grooming each other and they looked up at me as I came in, as if saying, "Where were you?"

"I'm so sorry, Sam. I totally forgot they were outside," I said, going to pet them.

"They're fine. They just came down to visit, is all. It's getting cold out there."

"I know."

"I'm assuming you got my note. About Noah bein' back?"

"Yes," I said, "And I saw him. With Bunny and another attractive woman."

"Ah. Well then," he said, raising an eyebrow. "That'd be Charlotte. His old girlfriend."

"*Great*," I said miserably.

"I can't tell you much about her, but I can tell you about his time in Colorado if you're wanting to hear it."

"Yes," I said. "It's been on my mind."

"Well, I know I'm tellin' secrets and all, but he was pretty miserable. There was plenty of work to help keep him occupied during the day, but there was also plenty of drinkin' afterwards. The way he told it, drinkin' too much was his way of dealing with it all."

A knot formed in my stomach.

"He told me there were times he'd wake up drunk and still go to work. Now that's not too smart if I tell you truthfully, but then again, like I'd told you before, me and my wife never had any problems that made me want to go off the deep end."

I felt my jaw began to quiver, and it was all I could do to control my tears.

"Now I'm not tellin' you this to make you feel worse. I'm tellin' you this so you'll know you can fix it. He knew you were home, and that's why he came back. But I think you're goin' to have to be the one to make the first call."

"But what about this...Charlotte? How does she fit into the picture?" I asked, with little hope.

"Well, that's just a monkey wrench, if you ask me. Noah didn't know she was comin' up, and it's caught him by surprise. I think if you've got your mind made up, you can plead your case."

That night I cried myself to sleep, thinking of how I'd wanted to change my life, and how I'd now made a mess of it all. I promised myself that when morning came, I'd call Noah.

I wasn't sure where he'd be. I didn't know if Charlotte was going to be an obstacle and if she was staying with him. And I didn't know how he felt about her. Either way, I would be the first to break the ice and see what happened. If he had moved on without me, then I'd have to live with that. But if he still cared about me, then we needed to try to work something out.

I was too nervous that next morning to eat breakfast, which was a first for me. But I wanted to get the call out of the way.

I dialed his number once, and then quickly hung up hoping his phone hadn't rung. What if she was there?

"Just do it!" I said to myself.

So I did. I dialed his number again, and my heart pounded fiercely as I waited for him to pick up. He seemed to take forever to answer and for a moment I thought it was going to go to the answering machine, but finally he answered.

"Hey," I said.

"Hey," he finally said.

I tried to make light of everything and said, "So I'm back and the project is finished. Thank goodness." But he was silent. I went on, "I figured if I waited for you to call me, it'd never happen, so here I am." Now that was the dumbest thing I'd ever said. Shit. "I didn't mean it that way."

He still said nothing, and I wanted to know where I stood, so I said, "I've missed you, and I'd like to see you." By now, the tears were streaming down my face, and I sniffed.

"I've missed you too. I've been busy, and so have you…"

Then I heard a woman's voice in the background and, half in anticipation and half in dread, I asked if he could talk.

"Yeah, sure," he said. "That's Bunny. She just stopped by."

Double shit! In my heart, which was sick with dread, I'd been afraid he had found someone else. Here he was, back and working on Bunny's job again.

I couldn't let it go.

"Can you come by tonight?"

He didn't answer immediately, and I dreaded the worst.

"Yeah, sure," he said.

I could tell he didn't want to talk in front of her, so I told him to come by after work, and he said he would.

I hung up, but a stab of guilt took me by surprise, and I felt utterly miserable.

The day seemed endless, and no amount of sitting outside and trying to relax worked. I was tied up in a knot. And it was my own fault. I couldn't eat. If only I could sleep away the time it would pass faster, but I couldn't sleep either. I tried walking around the property, which usually always made me calm down, but I was still filled with uneasiness.

What if he just didn't care anymore? Should I tell him the truth? No! Stop it! I had a hard time controlling my thoughts. "Please brain, just turn off!" I said aloud.

At around four, I took a hot shower. I had visions of him coming into the cabin and of finding me and holding me while we both stood under the hot water. But of course, that never happened. And I figured if I stayed in the shower much longer, I'd look like a prune when I got out.

So I dried my hair and wore it down like Noah liked it. I wore nothing but my robe, like I'd done the first time he'd come back from

120

Colorado. If it worked once, it would certainly work again. There'd be no doubt in his mind what I wanted. And I wanted *him*.

I poured myself a glass of wine and gulped it down. On an empty stomach, it immediately went to my head. But it relaxed me slightly. I'd just poured another glass when I finally heard his Jeep pull up in the parking area and my heart raced again. After taking another gulp, I refilled my glass.

I waited for his knock on the door before I opened it and then had this horrific thought that he wouldn't be alone and I'd be standing there literally and figuratively exposed. And humiliated beyond belief.

I knew the minute I looked at him that he was mine, but that something had closed in him, like a door. I knew I'd broken him. He tried not to show it, but I'd already seen it. It felt like I'd pulled a plug, or pulled the stopper, and water was swirling down a drain.

"Thank you for not making this harder than it is," I said softly, fighting an overwhelming desire to pull him to me. My heart pounded against my ribs.

"I don't think you realize just how hard this is..."

And then I knew for sure he knew what I'd done.

His eyes probed my face, his fingers caressed my cheeks. There was a long, empty pause, and the silence was heavy. I suddenly felt the full weight of it all, and I'd done it to myself. I wished for comfort, for someone to tell me everything would work out, but there was no one there but Noah.

I waited until he'd seen what he'd wanted of me, and then I dropped my robe and thought he was going to break the door down to get inside.

We stood for a moment just looking at each other, and he smelled so good and clean, I couldn't get enough of him. He finally came to me, but he was limping.

"*What happened?*"

Instead of answering me, he brought my body to his. He covered my mouth with his, and then when he caressed the spot he sought out, his touch made me tremble.

"Why did you stay away?" I asked, crying.

"Shh," he said, touching my lips with his fingers. We moved to my bed where I welcomed him into my body.

And of course, afterwards I cried.

"What did you do?" I asked later, referring to his bandaged knee.

"Well," he made a face. "I was still in Colorado," he said sheepishly, "and I wasn't paying attention. I'd been drinking too much and was getting behind in my work." His voice trailed off.

"Although some days I could hardly get out of bed in the mornings, I insisted on going to the job. Unfortunately, my skilsaw clipped me just above my knee as I was cutting a board. It looked worse than it was with all the blood, but I tied a shirt around it and got myself to the emergency room, and I only needed about six stitches."

Of course, I knew why he'd been drinking. I didn't know whether to cry again, or be angry with him for being such an idiot.

He then asked how everything went in Montana, and I did my best to answer honestly.

"It went well enough. When I was finished, everything looked great, of course," and I smiled, "but I wouldn't take that kind of job again. I made good money, but at what cost?"

"And what was that?"

That's when he looked at me and, for a slight moment, I wondered if he was baiting me. A long moment passed as he waited for me to speak. I hoped my internal conflict didn't show on my face.

But I answered with confidence and a sigh, "Travel back and forth, making arrangements to be out of town. Plus, having a huge deadline to get the project finished in a two-day period. It was all more than I anticipated, and I know it caused a problem between us, and I'm really sorry."

He nodded as though weighing in my answer and deciding if it was going to be acceptable. He seemed to be satisfied.

"Well, I'm glad it's over," he finally said.

"I am too."

"Are you?"

"Yes."

I finally asked, "Who was it you were with yesterday? I saw you with her and Bunny yesterday."

Noah tilted his head, as though reliving a memory.

"She's one of the gals I told you about. She didn't want to live up here, and I didn't want to live down the hill. She's the one who ended up getting married."

"And?" I prodded.

"I had her grandmother's old china cabinet in my storage shed. I'd promised her I'd fix a broken leg on it, but then never heard back from her. She came up to take it back down."

"How did you feel seeing her again?"

"Oh, mixed, I guess. I knew a long time ago we would never work out, but it's odd to see someone you once loved."

"Did she say how she was doing? Was she happy?"

"I didn't ask. Truthfully? I didn't care. She seemed happy enough," and he shrugged.

I'd decided to never tell Noah about what happened with Grayson. What could I say anyway that didn't sound regrettable on all counts? I felt for the sake of our relationship, we'd be better off leaving it alone.

And on the other hand, we never spoke about how he avoided confrontation by leaving when he questioned his relationship with me...and when I needed him most.

For now, I was happy we'd come this far.

CHAPTER TWENTY

I was eager to see the progress Noah had made on Bunny's project, but I didn't want to go by unannounced. I also didn't have the combination to the gate, so I suggested we could meet at the job then go have lunch. I could tell he was looking forward to showing me how far they'd come.

I didn't see Noah's truck when I pulled up, but I could tell men were working, so I went ahead in.

"Hey there," a voice called out to me. It was one of Noah's friends.

"Hey Billy," I called back.

He came from the back and said, "Noah will be right back. Make yourself at home."

Only a contractor or another interior designer could look at a home under construction and see the beauty in it. It looked great. There was still a lot to do, but I could definitely see it taking shape.

"It looks great, Billy. How's it going?"

"Good," he said, wiping his brow on his shirtsleeve.

I was dying to ask him what it was like working with someone like Bunny, so I did.

"Well, even for her age, she's pretty hot. You'd better watch it," he said with a wide grin. "She's still trying her best to get her hooks into Noah."

I shot him daggers.

"Not that he's been interested," he stammered. "He's managed to get away with murder, though. Gettin' her to do extra work."

"I'll bet," I said, shaking my head. "Mind if I check it out?" I asked, but I'd already started looking around.

"Be my guest. I need to get back to work," he said, putting his work gloves back on and heading towards the kitchen.

I knew I'd never be involved with this project, but I could picture it in a lake house décor, off whites and blues. I'd keep the oak ceiling and open beams, and…and then I heard Noah's voice.

"Hellooo." He called.

"Yoo-hoo," came a woman's voice right behind him.

I found my way back to the front of the house and there stood Noah with a sheepish grin on his face, behind Bunny, who was making her way over the rubble on the floor. He shrugged his shoulders.

"Hi, you two." I said, as cheerfully as I could.

"Look who I found outside," Bunny said, almost cooing

"I see." I said. "Be careful in those heels."

"I was out shopping and I wasn't planning on stopping by, but I couldn't help it. I had to see what was new. It's looking wonderful, isn't it?"

"I think so. It's a beautiful home, Bunny. And when you're finished with it, it'll be fabulous." Boy, did I lay it on, and I could tell she was delighted.

"I told Noah I'd take him to lunch, but he said you two were already planning on going…so why don't we make it a threesome?"

If I'd had a drink, I would have choked on it. But instead, I quickly weighed getting stuck with the cougar, or not having lunch with Noah.

"Let me just look around, then I'm ready to go," she said. "*Billy…* can you give me a strong arm to hold on to?"

Noah and I exchanged glances, and he just rolled his eyes and shrugged.

He showed me into the family room where they'd added pine paneling, a new fireplace mantle and a stone hearth. They'd completely torn out the kitchen and replaced the oak cabinets with maple and black granite tops. Top of the line Sub Zero appliances sat in the middle of the floor awaiting installation.

All the bathrooms had new cabinets, tile countertops and showers, and I cringed when I saw what she'd chosen for colors. Instead of going with either a stone or neutral look, each bathroom had its own combination of oranges and golds.

"She picked it," Noah said when he saw the look on my face.

"Obviously, money doesn't guarantee taste," I whispered.

I felt like a snob, and I'd seen enough. I was ready to leave.

Just down a short hill and a quick turn to the right was the small town of Cedar Glen where we decided to eat. We each drove our own cars and met at the Cedar Glen Inn, a well-known family-run restaurant, similar to Ginny's. Noah and I had eaten there before when we'd taken the Jeep out. Autographed photos hung on knotty pine-paneled walls, and old-fashioned curtains and valances hung on the front windows. They always served more food than what we could eat, so most of the time we tried to split a meal.

Next door was the Cedar Glen Trading Post, where local contractors and homeowners alike, could buy hardware, paint, fishing gear, guns and ammo. The son-in-law had just taken over the business after his father-in-law retired, and every time we'd gone in there, the old plywood flooring reminded me just how long the store had been there.

Parking, especially during lunch hour, could be a challenge, but we managed to find three places. I ended up parking in front of my favorite store, Timberline, which was next to the Trading Post. It was always filled with wonderful antique and vintage furniture, paintings, florals, pillows and mountain accessories. I never went in there that I didn't buy something. The rest of Cedar Glen consisted of the hair salon where Laura used to work, a yarn shop, barber shop, thrift store, the post office and the Malt Shop.

In the eighteen hundreds, Cedar Glen was a lumber town. Its horse-drawn wagons transported lumber to be made into boxes and crates for the citrus industry down the hill. Hook Creek flows through there and was named after John Hook, who built his cabin there. Hook Creek was where we did most of our off-roading, so while I wasn't an expert in geography, I was a little familiar with the area. Cedar Ridge Estates, where Bunny's home was, was just up the hill above Cedar Glen.

"Lunch is on me, so order what you want," Bunny said in a bubbly voice as she opened the menu.

We ordered and then sat for a few minutes in what *I* thought was an uneasy silence. But in no time, Bunny got us back up and running by talking.

"I just love what we're doing to the house, don't you, Noah?"

"Yes, I do," he said. "It's really coming along."

When there was finally a pause, I said to Noah, "I have some ideas for Carrie's kitchen and bathroom, if you'd like to stop by." I put my hand on his, and it didn't go unnoticed.

I'd meant to show him the counter top ideas I had and kept forgetting.

"I can hardly wait to start decorating," Bunny said, drawing attention back to herself and pulling out some magazine pages. "I've been collecting room ideas like crazy." She showed me a few, and I had to admit I liked a lot of them.

Of course I couldn't just sit there, so I started commenting on some of them, and it surprised me she agreed with me on some thoughts. I knew she'd never hire me as her designer, and I was okay with sharing some of my opinions. I gave her some ideas I'd had when I was walking around the house earlier, and she actually listened to me.

We ended up having a pleasant lunch, and I thought I'd escaped her scrutiny until she brought up my project with Grayson.

"So," she said, "I understand you just finished a big job in Montana?"

She looked directly into my eyes, and I was certain it was to ferret out any juicy details.

Although heat rushed up my neck, I took the cue and replied, "*I did.* And if I may say so myself, it turned out great. It was an exceptional experience, but I don't think I'll take another job so far away. Too many working parts."

"I see. I heard your client was very wealthy."

I couldn't help but look at Noah and he met my gaze. Why would he tell her something like that?

"Money helps…doesn't it?" I said coolly.

"It certainly does, my dear. And I also understand he's quite handsome."

What a bitch!

Noah had been sitting tipped back in his chair, which he often did in a casual setting, and I thought he was going to tip himself over when I said. "Actually, he might make a good person for you to meet. He's single."

She tilted her head, seemingly deep in thought, and said, "Hmmm. That might be interesting." But she was looking at Noah.

I made sure she saw me kiss Noah goodbye as we left.

CHAPTER TWENTY ONE

Since I didn't have anywhere to receive boxes for Carrie's project, I'd asked Liz at the flooring store if I could use the store as my shipping address. I was still working part time, and I knew I'd be taking up precious floor space, so as soon as something would come in, I'd load it up and take it to Carrie's where we could use the garage for staging.

Carrie had made quite a bit of progress on her own, getting everything cleaned and ready for me. She'd been in a couple of times and brought me up to date on all the progress she'd made getting the log walls and wood flooring cleaned and oiled. She'd put off having the rugs brought back until we were ready. I could tell she was excited, and I remembered how I felt when I started the restoration of my own cabins. Even though I was in the business, I still wanted everything done overnight and I never wanted to lose sight of how my clients felt once we made the decision to start a project.

While we hadn't become social friends, I'd come to know a young woman who also worked in the store. She was in her early thirties and still lived at home so she could help care for her mother, who was showing signs of dementia. There were three sisters, so each shared in caring for her, but Lilly was not married or in a relationship, so more responsibilities naturally fell on her.

Even in the short time I'd worked in the store, I couldn't help but observe Lilly's calmness when she received calls from either her sisters or her mother. I knew that the money she earned from working went towards keeping the household going, and my heart went out to her. I hadn't been around many people who were going through something like this, thank god, and I couldn't believe how strong a person she was. Of course, there were days when I could tell she'd been run through the wringer; dark shadows deepened her eyes, and I could sometimes recognize the heaviness in her step. But she never complained, even when I asked how she was doing. Many times, I wished I had that strength and character.

I asked Lilly if she'd be interested in making a little money by helping me work on the house, once everything came in for Carrie. Her face lit up, and I could tell she'd welcome the opportunity.

A few days before an unexpected deluge, I stood outside the cabins and marveled at the dark gray skies, and how they made such a beautiful backdrop for all the mountain's trees. We needed the rain, but in the next few weeks, we had back-to-back rainstorms resulting in flooded streets and rockslides along the highway. County trucks worked around the clock to keep the roads clear, and in some places, water rushed so furiously, the fire department provided sandbags to keep the local businesses from being inundated with overflow from the sidewalks.

The town was virtually empty and several stores put Closed signs up in their windows. We ultimately had no customers, but I volunteered to keep the store open, mostly, I think, to sit and watch the rain. It had an almost calming effect on me. We became the local drop off point for UPS and any special deliveries. Even the grocery store across the street had few customers.

In the early afternoons, Noah would make his way to the store and we'd huddle under an umbrella and walk a few doors down to Ginny's, our only source for nourishment.

Thankfully, our roofs survived the downpour, and our porches elevated the cabins and office, which allowed rainwater to either gather in any low spots we had or to naturally make its way into the ravine behind the property. Jezebel and Boots only ventured outside once, and when they got drenched, they ran back in to my cabin into towels I used to dry them off. They spent the rest of the storm curled up in front of the fireplace.

Noah and I were in a good place; after the first urgency of our lovemaking, I'd sensed some hesitancy on his part to return to the assumption we were back together again. I'd felt it too.

Even though the weather had turned unusually cold, we'd gone to the Village and sat on the bench we'd sat on the first time we'd taken the boat out. We could see our warm breath in the air. We still hadn't spoken directly about what had happened in Montana, and sometimes Noah's silence made me uncomfortable.

I'd tried to think of what I'd say if he ever came out and asked me what had happened. I'd never wanted to crush him by telling him the truth.

He put his arm around me and pulled me close. His eyes were still firmly planted on the lake.

"What do you really want, Annie?" he asked.

Before I could answer, my mind raced with thoughts of Grayson. I'd been fairly successful in pushing them away, however, every time I saw a black Range Rover, my stomach churned, and I couldn't help but remember the way he'd looked at me the last time I'd seen him.

I knew this would always haunt me.

I laid my head on Noah's shoulder and answered, "I want to be happy."

The minute we had a break in the weather, and when one of Lilly's sisters could be home with their mother, I met her at the store and Noah helped us pack up his Jeep with the rest of the boxes we had for Carrie. Once it was all inside her garage, we set up staging tables and we unpacked and sorted everything. From here on out, regardless of weather, we'd still be able to work.

I brought an ironing board and iron, and Lilly started opening and ironing the draperies and pillows shams.

"Let's start in Mother's room," Carrie suggested. "I'm ready to see what you have in mind." So, we started in the master bedroom and hung the drapery panels, then set up the bedding. The red chairs hadn't come in yet, but I set a copper pot filled with red flowers and white baby's breath next to the fireplace to add some color. We rearranged the artwork, and I brought in some old books from the library to set around the room.

"I'd like to hang these of my mother and father," Carrie said, showing me some newly framed photographs. "Or, since they have a back on them, we could use them on the dresser. Whatever you think."

There were three of them, and I set them on the tall dresser around a container I'd filled with artificial pine branches with small pinecones.

"We can set these here for now, and when the room is finished, you can decide if you want to move them. I bought some pine fragrance, and I figured you could spray these periodically if you want the true scent of the trees."

"Great idea," Carrie said.

"Are you feeling better about your discovery?" I asked.

"I am. I've run it by Paul, and I'm definitely going to write their stories, or at least what I think might have happened. I'll have to do a lot of research about the period, but I think it'll be interesting. We can use the cabins too, if you wouldn't mind."

"I'd love it. What a great idea." I thought for a moment, and then said, "I can put the books in the cabins for our guests. Of course you'll have to autograph them."

For one room, we'd decided on a large-scale brown and tan plaid comforter with a mix of that same plaid and faux animal skin pillows.

The other guest room's comforter was a mountain green and tan plaid with brown trim, faux leather shams, and bear appliquéd pillows. I didn't always like to do matching curtains, so we hung some brown fabric with large accent buttons on the windows.

Carrie wanted to leave her bedroom for last, so we moved downstairs to the last bedroom. It was a little more mountain glam with a new brown and teal wide striped rug, with just tan blankets and teal and brown embroidered pillows on top of the bed. I brought along a couple of white faux fur pillows to mix in, and a fur throw for the bottom of the bed.

"You've pushed the envelope, Annie, and I love it."

"I was hoping you would," I said, pleased.

We'd finish the kitchen and bathroom updates when Noah could pull away from Bunny's house, and even though we were waiting for some living room furniture, we were able to get a jump start on accessorizing. It was fun and challenging to use a lot of the artwork and memorabilia Carrie wanted to incorporate, but that also made for a totally custom look.

Lilly was a natural at sorting and organizing and with her help, we finished the first phase of the job in two days. As soon as Carrie paid me, I wrote Lilly her check, and I could tell she was proud of herself and grateful for the opportunity to earn a little extra money.

Carrie was ecstatic as well. While we were there, she'd go from room to room and just sit there "treasuring the memories and basking in the charm of it all." Her creative words, not mine.

Unfortunately, I hadn't finished taking many pictures at Grayson's, so I wanted to make sure I got plenty of them here. Carrie thought it was a great idea and even offered to pose in a few of them so I could use her name. I asked if she minded if I contacted the newspaper and she thought it would be a super plug for both of us. "Author moves back to Lake Arrowhead," or "Local Designer and Author Re-Write History." She was full of clever things to say.

We finally had our first big snowstorm, and while it wasn't my first time seeing snow, it still mesmerized me as I watched the snow, which seemed almost weightless, land on the tree branches and fall to the ground. I wished I could sit outside and listen to the snow absorb all the sounds of the rest of the world.

That's how the mountains usually made me feel.

CHAPTER TWENTY TWO

We hadn't been to the Cowboy bar for weeks, so Noah and I made plans to meet there for a steak, and then listen to music. He called me about a half hour before I left my cabin to let me know that a good friend that he'd grown up with had shown up unexpectedly and he wanted us to meet.

Noah and Josh were sitting at one of the tables we usually sat at, and I watched for a moment while they rough-housed a little, nudging each other and laughing. It looked like they were on their second beer, so they were feeling relaxed.

Noah saw me as I joined them and said, "Josh, this is Annie."

Josh's blond hair was also long, but where Noah wore his in a ponytail, Josh let his hang almost to his shoulders. He was very handsome and I could see how women would be attracted to him. He stood also and shook my hand.

"Glad to meet you, Annie. I hear you're the one who's getting old Noah to finally settle down." And he laughed.

Noah's face reddened.

"I don't know that I'm the one who needs to settle down," Noah said playfully, as Josh sat back down. "Wine?" he asked me.

"Yes, thanks."

While Noah went up to the bar to get my drink, Josh raised an eyebrow and jokingly looked me up and down, nodding his approval.

"Glad you approve," I said as I hung my purse on the back of my chair. "So, you're originally from up here?"

"Yes, I am. Grew up with Noah. He had the life I wanted. That is, until he lost his parents," Josh said without shame.

"Here you go," Noah said, handing me my wine glass. I took a sip before I set it down. "Getting to know this guy?"

"Yes, I am."

"I'm kind of the drifter...right, man?" Josh said, taking a drink of his beer and grinning at Noah.

"You could call it that," Noah answered. "I can't tell you how many times he tried to get me in trouble."

"Me? You were a little crazy, too. Remember that time we raced our motor bikes around the school and someone called the cops?"

"Unfortunately."

"Whose idea was that?" Josh asked.

Noah shrugged.

"Or when we lit old man Wilson's trashcan on fire? Whose idea was that?"

"Ditching school wasn't my idea," Noah said. "I knew we'd get caught, but you finally convinced me to do it. I never could sign my mom's name. Or that time we took two girls to the movies and one of the fathers came in looking for them?" Noah looked at me then. "Apparently, they weren't supposed to leave the house that night. That was embarrassing."

"Ol' Noah seemed to figure out what he wanted to do when he grew up, and I followed as much as I could. We worked for the same contractor, so I'm thankful to them both for teaching me a trade. Have hammer, will travel," Josh laughed.

"Josh is a carpenter too, and when he's up here, I always try to get him to work with me."

"Where have you been?" I asked.

"When I left here a couple of years ago, I had a housing tract down the hill to work on, and that kept me busy until recently."

"Didn't you meet a gal?" Noah asked easily.

"There's always a gal. This one seemed like a good one, but things just didn't work out between us."

"I'm sorry," I said.

"Well, it gave me an opportunity to get back up here and check in on my buddy." He tilted his bottle to Noah's as a toast.

"I just might have some work for you if you're interested."

"Sounds good."

"I also have an extra bedroom, if you want."

"Sounds like you've got everything I need."

"I'm starving," I said, ready to order.

"Then let's order," Noah said, squeezing my hand.

"So I hear you bought some cabins?" Josh asked.

"I did. And I love it up here," I said, filling him in on all the details.

When I finished, Noah asked him about his parents.

"Dad remarried last year, and they moved to Northern California. I talk to him a couple times a month and he seems happy. She seems pretty nice, and if she makes him happy, then I'm good with that."

"What about your mom?"

"Well, she's still reeling from him getting married again. She wasn't happy *with* him, and she's not happy *without* him, I guess. She's still down in Moreno Valley. I stayed with her about a week before I came back up here. I feel bad because she's miserable, but there's nothing I can do about it."

"It's harder for women to find men than it is for men," I offered. "Especially as you get older."

"She'd probably have more of a chance to find someone decent if she quit partying so much."

"I'm sorry to hear that," I said.

"That's life," Josh said and sighed. "So, what's this job you have?"

"Well, it's a pretty big project for a lady, and I'd like to get it wrapped up. There's definitely enough work. I could use the help. I'll take you by the place tomorrow and you can get started if you want."

"Sounds good," Josh said, getting up. "Another brewskie?" he asked Noah.

"Sure."

"I feel kind of bad for the guy," Noah said while Josh was up at the bar. "He seems a lot mellower now, but he needs to find his home."

While we ate, Noah and Josh talked about growing up, and I saw a more mischievous side to Noah than I previously had.

"Hey, remember when you dressed up as that clown?" Josh laughed.

"Or when you got that job working at the restaurant and forgot to put the lid on the trash?" Noah asked. "And a bear tossed everything? Did you lose that job, or just come close?"

"Just came close. It wasn't like they had ten people lined up to take my place."

They looked at each other, almost trying to outdo the other.

"Or when we took your jeep out to Deep Creek, and we got a flat? You had to call your old man to come get us."

"And I wasn't supposed to take it out. I didn't have my driver's license yet."

"Boy, did you catch hell."

"Well, as usual, I'm stuffed," I said once I'd finished eating. "As soon as I can waddle out of here, I'll leave you two to continue reminiscing."

"*Hey, Josh,*" a gal said coming up to the table. "*Wanna dance?*"

"Sure," he answered, and then got up.

"Sounds like you two were pretty close," I said.

"We were. Still are. Along with Sam, he was there for me when I lost my parents. He's really a good guy, just needs to find the right woman."

"Sounds like you," I joked.

Noah leaned in and kissed me. The music ended and Josh took his chair back at the table.

"Well, I'll let you two get caught up. Try not to drink too much." I kissed Noah. "And introduce him to Bunny," I said.

"I said the *right* woman."

"Who's Bunny?"

"Oh, you'll find out soon enough," I said as I grabbed my purse.

Sure enough, Josh met Bunny. In fact, she joined us for lunch that next day and she was practically hanging all over him. He was loving every moment of it.

"So I see you two have hit it off," I said. Noah shot me a look that could have killed.

"What a surprise," Bunny said. "Just what I needed."

Images of them together almost made me want to laugh. Was I mistaken, or did I see Josh actually move her hand slightly so he could open the menu?

"Well, let's eat and get back to work," Noah said, trying to get things moving along. I could tell he felt a little uncomfortable with Bunny's show of affection towards Josh.

I reminded him that Sam's surprise seventy-fifth birthday was the next day, and to try to keep it a secret if he saw him before then. It was going to be at Ginny's, and she had everything planned.

"I can't believe Sam's that old," Josh commented.

"Join us," I said.

"I will."

I'd asked Lilly from the store if she'd help me decorate the back of the restaurant, so the next afternoon, we laid out a dessert station opposite where the buffet was going to be. I'd come up with a few games that didn't take group participation. I set up a jar of cotton balls, one of jelly beans, one of marbles and one of macaroni, along with a paper for guests to write down their guesses. I'd brought gift certificates for the winners.

In a small town, it was difficult to keep any secrets, but Sam was genuinely surprised when he got there and we'd filled the restaurant with his friends. Although the invitation had said no gifts, there were plenty of birthday cards with everything from gift certificates to movie tickets and confetti in them.

Although Bunny hadn't been personally invited, she came as Josh's guest, and I saw several people roll their eyes when she passed them. Oh well, as long as she now had her hooks in Josh instead of trying to interest Noah, I was fine. It gave them both someone to be with.

Ginny outdid herself and served pot roast, mashed potatoes, mixed vegetables, and salad.

"To a great guy," Noah toasted.

"To Sam," everyone chimed, drinking from their glasses.

"To Sam," I added. "I couldn't have done it without you."

Everyone chipped in cleaning up and in no time, we wrapped everything up and put any leftovers away. We didn't have guests at the cabin, so Sam stayed with Ginny; I went to Noah's, and Josh stayed with Bunny at the resort.

The next Monday, Ginny had surgery on her right foot. She'd fallen and broken a metatarsal bone many years ago and had developed some type of bone spur, and it was driving her crazy. She'd put off having something done about it until temporary over-the-counter protective pads no longer provided her much comfort.

"I'm like most people," she said. "I wait until the pain is almost unbearable before I opt for surgery. But I can't afford to be off my feet."

With surgery on a Monday, she'd have three normally slower days to keep her foot elevated, and then she'd be able to stand with a boot. Sam stayed with her to make sure she did what she was supposed to do, which was to only get up to go to the bathroom. It was good they had each other.

CHAPTER TWENTY THREE

The fog, which didn't normally make its way inland enough to reach the cabins, had filled in around the trees, turning the mild day into a chilly one. While I hated driving in it, I loved the almost melancholy image it made. I pulled into the Cabin parking area and grabbed my two bags of groceries. I hadn't worn a warm enough sweater, thinking the day was going to stay comfortable, and I was chilled; I wanted to hurry in and start a fire in my fireplace.

It wasn't until I got about twenty feet from my cabin that I noticed a man stepping out into my path. It was Grayson. I stumbled on one of the rocks lining the walkway, and dropped one of my bags, the corner tearing as I let it fall to the ground.

What was he doing here? I was more annoyed than I was afraid, but when he called my name, suddenly my body had an even greater chill that felt like it went down into my bones.

"Annie," he said again calmly.

What I wanted to say was *"Leave!"* but what I ended up saying was, "Why are you here?" I didn't move. My warm breath dissipated in the cold air.

"We need to talk." He'd come a little closer now, and I could see the determination in his face. And then I saw a flash of tired sadness, but it quickly disappeared. His shoulders sagged, and it suddenly reminded me of how David had looked once when he realized he'd been broken.

"I'm sorry, Grayson," I said, trying to remain calm. I could see anger building in him, and I didn't like it. His mood had changed swiftly.

"I told you, Annie, that I knew what I wanted. I told you more than once. And I thought you were of that understanding when you came back to Montana."

"Grayson, I never should have gone with you. I knew I needed to finish your project, and I wasn't even sure *what* I wanted."

"And what is it exactly that you *do* want?"

His words bit at me. It was the same question Noah had asked. I knew the answer, but I it sounded false with him.

"I want happiness. And love," I said, almost feeling like a child.

He said nothing, but just looked at me, frowning slightly, like those words were foreign to him. Then he stepped closer and said, "Let me help you with your groceries," he said, less menacing.

He bent down, but I said sharply, *"I'm fine. I don't need help."*

My words seemed to cut through him. When he stood, he was so sickly looking and pale.

"Please, Annie." He came closer again and gently reached for me. "I need to see this work out. I thought I could make you happy."

My heart almost broke for him. Ever since I'd known him, he'd been so sure of himself, and so strong. I just stood there now, for I didn't know what else to say. He came closer again, this time close enough to grab both my arms and pull me towards him.

"You need to go, Grayson. You're hurting me. I should have never let our relationship go that far. I need you to go, and you need to leave me alone." I could hear the harshness in my voice, and I meant it. "It's cold out here and I want to get inside."

Grayson's entire demeanor changed again. For the first time since he'd come here, I wondered how far he'd take this and I was feeling uneasy.

With his left hand, his fingers dug into my arm.

"Ow." I winced and tried to pull my arm away.

His right hand went swiftly for my shoulder and he pulled me down, my knees landing hard on the gravel.

I wasn't sure what he was planning on doing; surely he wasn't thinking of killing me. But I was finally afraid. I knew from that angle I couldn't effectively reach out to him. I would have knocked him down if I could have.

Then we both heard the cock of the shotgun and froze.

"I'd let her go if I was you," Clearly and firmly, Sam's voice filled the air around us.

At first, Grayson didn't move or release his hold. I was sure he had anticipated no one stopping him from doing what he was planning on doing. Whatever that was.

"Let her go or I won't have any problem shooting you," Sam said coldly.

Grayson released me, and I fell the rest of the way to the ground.

Time stood still for the three of us, and no one moved. Then I heard the crunching of tires on the parking area gravel, and Noah slammed his truck door closed and he ran down to where we were.

He was seething, and Grayson turned from bright red to gray.

Continuing to hold the shotgun in one hand, Sam put his arm out to stop Noah from reaching for Grayson. Once Noah calmed down a notch, he reached for me and helped me back to my feet. My balance was off, and he led me to one of the Adirondack chairs, but quickly turned to face Grayson, who by this time had stiffened and regained some composure. I could see his fists were clenched so tightly, his knuckles were white. Did he think he could take on Sam *and* Noah?

"If you ever come near her again, I swear I'll kill you," Noah finally said.

By this time, the fog had completely engulfed us and it seemed an appropriate ending as Sam pushed Grayson away from us, but not before he turned towards me and smiled coolly. They all but disappeared in the distance.

I watched as Noah clenched, then unclenched his fists again before he came to me. There was no way he couldn't have figured out that I hadn't been totally truthful with him about the time I spent in

Montana. He looked raw, and it broke my heart. It nauseated me as I let him see me.

"Let's get inside," he finally said, pulling me out of the chair. He opened my cabin door, and the cats rushed out. As I turned on a light, he picked up my groceries and brought them in. The cats ran right back in so I could feed them. I was on autopilot as I opened a can of food and put some on two plates. I then lit the fireplace, but I wasn't able to even look at Noah as he stood with the bags, standing by them on the counter.

"Why don't you take a hot shower," he said then, his voice slightly shaking.

I'd broken his heart!

I did take a shower, and as I let the hot water envelop me, I couldn't control the tears. I felt so ugly when I cried, but I didn't care. Part of me hoped he wouldn't be there when I got out, knowing how I'd look, and then the other part wanted to have him hold me.

I wasn't sure that he would even want to see me again. I'd hurt him more than anyone deserved, and I wouldn't have blamed him if he walked away from me for good.

Somehow, my tears seemed to stop, but I had those awful breathing spasms that come after an unusually hard cry. When I came out of the bathroom, Noah was there, sitting on the sofa, staring into the fireplace.

He got up and held me in his arms, and I started crying again.

"You're fine," he said, trying to soothe me. "You're fine," though his voice was strained.

He brought me back to the sofa where it was warm and we sat there with his arm around me. I leaned my head against his chest. I wasn't sure what he would ask me, or how much I'd tell him. And at that moment, I wasn't sure that I deserved someone like him.

This was the second time he and Sam had come to my rescue, and I hated it. Two different men had tried to control me, and both times, my loves, Noah and Sam, had stood up for me. It humiliated me.

We sat in silence, looking into the flames of the fire for what seemed like hours, and periodically I glanced at Noah and watched the light from the flames flicker on his face. When it grew dark, we went to bed. When I woke in the middle of the night, we were still lying next to each other, with cats as our companions, and I fell back asleep.

When I finally woke, I felt dreadful.

CHAPTER TWENTY FOUR

Noah was gone. I was hoping I could just erase what had happened, and never have to face Sam or Noah again, but I knew that wouldn't be possible.

Noah left me a note letting me know he'd gone to Bunny's, so at least I knew where he was. I decided to go into the office and see if Sam was around so I could thank him for coming to my rescue. Again.

He was sitting behind the counter when I came in and he gave me a wicked smile.

"Now that was the most exciting thing that's happened since last year." I could tell he'd forgiven all.

I shook my head and gave him an exaggerated smile in return.

"How did you know he was here?" I asked.

"I saw that bastard walking through the parking area, but there was no car. So I assumed there was a possibility he wasn't really an invited guest."

"No, he wasn't."

"I checked on him a couple of times before you got back, and he was just waiting there, so I held tight to see what he was up to. And then I thought I should call Noah since he'd had that phone hooked up at Bunny's. I wasn't sure when you'd be back, and it might have been a false alarm, but I didn't want to take any chances."

"Oh, Sam," I said, exasperated. "I've made such a mess of things, haven't I?"

"Well, now, I don't think so. I *do* know that if that fellow wouldn't have released you, I'd a had to shoot him. And I would have done it, too."

"I think you *would* have you crazy, wonderful, man." I went around the counter and gave him an enormous hug. "And I love you."

"Well, now, don't get all weepy on me."

I was still hanging on to him when I said, "I don't know what to tell him."

Sam put me at arm's length and said, "That's entirely up to you. But Noah knows he shouldn't have just left you to fend for yourself. That's something he'll have to live with. And you know that life is full of surprises and opportunities, and sometimes you just have to do some explorin' before you know what it is you really want."

I started crying again, and I knew I looked like hell, but I didn't care. I was really hoping to get all this crying out of the way so I could get back to normal, whatever normal was.

"My advice is to just give it some more time. You two will work it out. I'm certain of that."

"I hope so," I said, as I left the office. I was still blinking a few tears away as I made my way back to my cabin. The forest had become quiet, which I loved, and the only sounds were the crunch of gravel as I walked down the path. I picked up a few large pine cones to add to two of the cabins that were reserved for the weekend; I'd rinse them, and add pine scent before I set them out.

I needed to splash my face with cold water and then feed the cats. Thankfully, I didn't have to see anyone important today, but I was also getting hungry so I'd have to go get something to eat and everyone would see my blotched face!

I stressed all day about what to say when I saw Noah, but I could tell by his stride as he walked up to my cabin door that he was okay.

"Hey," was all I said to him.

"Hey," he said back. "Bunny and Josh want to go to dinner tonight."

Part Four

Pinecones and Garland

CHAPTER TWENTY FIVE

It was almost Thanksgiving again, and I needed to talk to Noah about what he wanted to do. I'd never cooked a turkey, but I could do that if we went to *his* cabin, or we could eat at Ginny's like we did last year. I wondered about going to see my parents, but we had three cabins rented and I knew I'd feel better if I were here for our guests.

By mid afternoon, I felt an annoying scratch in my throat and my nose started running. Neither was unusual because I'd always had allergies, but this felt different. By the time Noah came by, I used the cross sign to ward him off. I knew I was coming down with a cold, and while I'd probably already passed it on to him, I didn't want to take any chances. I did ask him if he'd go to the drugstore to get me cough drops, syrup and Vitamin C for both of us.

I took a hot shower and put on heavy pajamas and socks, rekindled the fireplace, and then lay down on the sofa.

"Are we okay?" I asked when he dropped everything off.

His eyes were dark and serious, but then he sighed, almost as if in resignation, and said, "Yes."

"I'm so sorry, Noah. For everything, and now what I think is going to be a doozy of a cold. Thanks for picking everything up for me." I rubbed my eyes and then felt the warmth in my face. I was hoping it was just from the fire and not the beginning of a fever.

"You'd better get home and bundle up. Don't kiss any strangers," I said lightly. "I'm going to try to go to bed, but I usually can't sleep when I feel this way." Then, as an afterthought, I said, "Can you tell Sam I'm going to stay inside for a few days? He can always call me if he needs me."

Cold air was rushing in as he opened the door to leave.

"Oh, and can you bring some firewood and leave it on the porch?"

I waited until I could hear his truck door slam and when I could no longer hear the crunch of gravel under his tires, I took two Vitamin C, and opened the bag of lozenges. My throat was killing me.

My colds had a pattern.

Day one: Sore throat.

Day two: Stuffed nose and crackling in my ears.

Day three: Stuffy nose, runny nose, crackling in my ears, and the beginnings of a cough that sounded like I was dying. Plus, I couldn't lie down, so I had to sleep upright in a chair.

Days four and five: incessant coughing and crackling in my ears.

I'd called my parents to let them know I wouldn't be coming out and, and coughed for effect. It relieved me to hear my sister Loni was going to go see them. There was no mention of her husband making the trip, which, of course, made me wonder if they were having problems, but it was none of my business. I didn't bring it up, and I was sure I'd hear about it after she left.

By Thanksgiving weekend, I didn't sound like I was walking around with the plague, so I was able to greet our guests. We had a light dusting of snow on that Wednesday, and a storm that dropped about six inches on Thursday, so I had to use the Jeep to get our visitors in Black Bear Cabin (number Two) to their dinner destination at the Resort. The couple in Woodhaven (number One), came up with their chains, so once Noah cleared the berm in the driveway, everyone was good to go.

Josh and Bunny joined us for our dinner at Ginny's. I personally couldn't see it as a long-term relationship, but Bunny was glowing and

Josh was smitten with her. It seemed she couldn't keep her hands off him. They gave romance a new meaning.

While we held hands, Noah and I had never been publicly demonstrative about our relationship. He would always do little things, like wiping something from my face, or tucking a loose strand of hair back behind my ear. I knew it wasn't fair, but comparing us now to Josh and Bunny, I felt like we were an old married couple.

I sometimes felt the axis of our world had changed, which would have made sense. I'd catch him looking at me for periods of time and then, when my eyes caught his, I tried to read him. Afterwards, he always had this flicker of emotion in his eyes, and I wondered what he was thinking. I'd give him the most genuine (and seductive) smile I could, and he'd smile back.

After the incident with Grayson, Noah was more urgent and greedy for me, as I was with him. We'd settled back in to our comfortable and untroubled lovemaking again, for which I was grateful. Noah was the most attentive lover I'd ever had, and his touch was soft and caressing.

CHAPTER TWENTY SIX

Carrie

Before Thanksgiving, two new places opened in the village, just in time for the Annual Fall Festival. There was a line outside one of them, the Coffee & Company gourmet coffee shop and bean supplier for diehard java connoisseurs, like me. The moment I walked into the store, I inhaled the all-encompassing aromas and I thought I'd died and gone to coffee heaven. I felt rushed with so many customers in the store, so I only bought two bags of coffee for myself and would come back before Christmas to pick up some gifts.

The other one, Up In Smoke, was the new BBQ restaurant, and they had set up tasting tables with samples outside. People waited two and three deep, and I thought about avoiding the crowd when I saw Annie waiting.

"Hey," I said as I came to her in line.

"Carrie! Wait for me, and I'll bring you a sample."

A few minutes later, she handed me a small plate with a taste of pulled pork and meat from a beef rib.

"This is delicious," I said. "I'm so glad they've opened up."

"Me too. I've been meaning to give you a call to see how you're doing. The rest of the furniture should be in soon," I said.

"And I've been meaning to call you too. I wanted to wait, but I've actually stayed in Mother's room, and I think I'll be okay."

"Of course you will."

"I'm ready to work on my old room whenever you have time. The kids are all coming up for Christmas and I'd love to have the room finished so they can see the house."

"Sounds great. I have time next week. Just let me check with Lilly to see when she's available, and I can give you a call."

A large wagon filled with hay and people pulled up in the parking lot next to us.

"Super. Are you going on the hayride?"

"I hadn't thought about it."

"Well, why don't you ask Noah, and maybe the four of us can go and then have BBQ afterwards. I'll look up the dates."

"I'm sure we'll be available any time that works for you," Annie said. "In fact, here's Noah now. This BBQ is delicious," she told him, giving him her last bite. "How does a hayride and dinner here sound?"

"Good with me. For as many years as it's been going on, I've never gone on it."

"There you have it," Annie said.

"I think they're having a holiday show here, too. Maybe I could check that out? Would you go?"

"It sounds like fun. We'll have to bring blankets! I remember coming here for the summer concerts. And particularly one summer when I was ten, I had a crush on a young man who worked at Ginny's. I was so silly then, and when I waved at him, I thought for sure he was going to come up to me; but then I saw he was with a beautiful blonde girl and I thought I was going to die of embarrassment."

"That's such an awkward age, isn't it?" Carrie said with a slight smile. "I remember coming here every summer when Gram was alive. We'd pack a picnic and sit and listen to the different bands. We quit coming once it got too hard for her to walk around, and I haven't been back."

"Maybe we can go with you this summer," I suggested.

"That sounds great. I'd like that." She sighed. "Well, I'm going to stop by some of the hand-crafted booths, then head for home. I've started some research for the book."

"Are you going to write it?"

"Paul gave me his blessings, so that's all I needed."

"I think it sounds exciting. People up here will definitely want to read it. I'm sure the newspaper will write about it. In fact, they might even know people who lived up here then. I'm sure you know how to research."

"That's a great idea. I've already started a list of what I'm interested in learning about. Everything from distilling to prohibition. Paul brought over all his photos and I've made copies of them. There were some of an old gin mill and a horse-drawn wagon filled with steel barrels and stoneware jugs, so there was no doubt a mill here. There'll be a lot to sort through."

Noah put his arm around Annie's shoulder as they walked away, and I thought they made such a nice-looking couple. It was hard sometimes to look back and remember young love.

I spent about an hour looking talking with the vendors of handcrafted work, and I bought some earrings for Ashley and for Christopher's fiancee for Christmas. Several booths were filled with old cabin décor, and I found some vintage snowshoes and skis, and in another, I bought ski poles and a great old oak box with a pinecone carving on top that was perfect for my father's keepsakes. When I got home, I transferred everything including the revolver, into it, and set it on top of the dresser; there was no need to keep all that hidden somewhere in one of the closets.

I wasn't sure where I'd hang the old ski equipment and decided I'd leave that up to Annie.

I then called Paul, and because it was a night they had entertainment, we decided to eat at the Tudor House. I was looking forward to having a glass of wine and staying afterwards to listen to the group scheduled to play.

"It's R&B," he'd said.

The day finally came to work in my bedroom.

"I know you have all the bedding, and I'm sure it sounds silly, but I'd like to keep my old room looking like it did when I was growing up," I told Annie when she stood in the doorway to my room.

"Honestly, I thought that was what you had in mind when I put everything together," Annie said. "I'd hate to see you lose any of the charm of it."

Annie and Lilly took down all my framed needlepoint and paint-by-number art I'd done when I was younger, and I wiped down the frames. In a drawer I pulled out some old fall leaves I'd hand-painted in patterns of golds and greens, and some dragonflies I'd made from painted maple leaves and twigs.

"These are great," Annie said, laying them out in a pattern. "Do you have any old frames with glass?"

While looking for them, I came across my old sun catcher, and brought it out. Lilly framed my craftwork, and we hung the sun catcher back in the window. Annie rearranged all my old books and pinecones, and hung everything in new groupings, and by the time she was finished with the room, it'd taken on an entirely new life.

"It's like I've never grown up," I said, and my eyes welled up.

"Don't cry," Lilly said, coming to me and giving me a hug. "It looks wonderful. I would have loved to have a room like this when I was growing up."

Two weeks before Christmas, Joseph helped me set up a large tree in the living room where Mother used to put it. He drilled small holes in the trunk's base to add an additional source of water. He and Isobel offered to help me decorate it and we brought in all the boxes of ornaments I'd packed away in the garage cabinets. I knew Annie's friend Lilly could use some extra money, so I asked her if she'd be interested in helping, too.

"This tree is huge," she said when she saw it. "It's really pretty."

The old strands of tree lights were a jumbled mess, and I couldn't remember the last time Mother replaced them, so I bought several boxes of multi-colored lights and Joseph helped us light the tree. And once he was on his tall ladder, he placed the antique angel tree topper at the very top. As a child, I never decorated with any rhyme or reason, and this year, I wanted to keep with tradition. The three of us unwrapped the ornaments and placed them wherever we wanted.

"Look at these silly ornaments I made," I said, remembering how proud of them I'd been. I'd glued ribbon to pinecones and most of them still had the glitter on them. Although we wouldn't light them, there were a number of clip-on ornaments that had seen better days, but I didn't have the heart

to replace the yellowed candles. I wasn't even sure where I'd find any that size today.

"My early gift to you, Carrie," Isobel said, handing me a woven serape fabric draw string bag.

"You didn't need to get me anything," I protested.

"Please, it's for the tree."

Inside the pouch were eight vintage red straw Christmas ornaments.

"These are wonderful," I said. "I love them. Let's each take several and find a place where everyone can see them."

It'd seen its better days, but Isobel insisted she iron the old felt tree skirt Mother and I made years ago. We'd appliquéd felt pinecones, holly leaves and poinsettia flowers everywhere, and I agreed, once it was under the tree, no one would notice its imperfections. Once we were finished, I stepped back and marveled at how well it turned out.

"Mother would have been proud," I admitted.

At that instant, I heard a creak in the wood floor, and turned, certain I would see my mother standing there smiling at us all. Isobel followed my glance, and I wondered if she'd heard it too.

"It's only Sadie," she said, a little sadly.

The next day, Annie called to see if I'd be home. She brought over a lovely wreath she'd made from branches from her trees.

"I can't decide whether to hang it outside on the front door, or above the mantel," I said.

"Either is fine with me. I brought a stand for it, if you decide to set it on the mantel."

"Ha," she chuckled. "We could always hang it around the deer's head."

"What a riot that'd be," I said. "If you decide to do that, I can cut the wreath and we can reattach it around his neck, and I could make another one for the mantel."

"I'd love it. Do you have enough branches? We could use some of mine if you don't."

"If you want to do it now, we can go outside and cut some and I'll make it up for you."

"Oh, Annie, you're the best."

Christopher and his fiancee arrived Christmas Eve, after spending the day with his soon-to-be in-laws, and they took one of the upstairs guest bedrooms. Ashley, her husband and baby daughter Elizabeth showed up right after, and decided if they stayed downstairs, it would be quieter for all of us.

I waited for everyone to get there before I took them on the grand tour.

"The deer wearing the wreath is a crack up," Ashley said.

"Annie and I did it," I said brightly. "I'm glad you like it."

Upstairs, she said, "Your room still looks like you, but more, I don't know, decorated. I like it. And Gram's room is wonderful," she said, picking up the photos of my parents. "I don't remember seeing these before."

"I found them in some of Gram's things. They looked very happy, didn't they? Of course, my favorite is the one with me in it."

"Of course," she said.

"And this old box is interesting," she said, lifting the lid. She unwrapped the cloth and her eyes widened. "Oh!"

My father's revolver was sitting there on top. She set it aside and looked through all his treasures before closing the box back up.

"I had a hard time transitioning," I admitted. "But I'm comfortable in here now. I only hear the floors creaking once a night now." I laughed.

Christopher liked the downstairs the most.

"I like how everything's the same, but somehow different."

We'd finished updating the kitchen, and both kids liked the wood counter tops.

"This is amazing," Ashley said, running her hands over the smooth wood. "Aren't you afraid you'll ruin it?"

"Always so practical," I commented. "If I was a gourmet cook, I might be. But making oatmeal and heating something Paul brings over, isn't really considered cooking."

"So you two are a big deal?" Christopher quipped, raising his eyebrows up and down.

"Knock it off," Ashley said.

"He's okay. And yes, I think we are. Oh, tomorrow I'll have to tell you about my new book..."

When Paul got there, we helped him unload his car. He'd brought everything for dinner that night and for Christmas dinner the next afternoon.

"Tonight we're having lasagna and garlic bread," he announced. "I hope everyone's hungry."

After stuffing ourselves and drinking two bottles of wine, Christopher rekindled the fire, and we all sat around the living room, relaxing. We voted on waiting until morning to unwrap presents, but I wanted Ashley to open one gift for baby Elizabeth.

"Oh, jammies!" she raved. "This is what she'll wear tonight."

I didn't find out until later, she'd already received two other pairs of Christmas pajamas. All that mattered was that the baby wore the set I gave her now.

Isobel and Joseph spent Christmas Eve and morning with their families, then joined us for our afternoon dinner. Isobel brought tamales and flan, and we heated up the prime rib, ham, Brussels sprouts and green beans Paul brought. Chocolate cake and decorated cookies completed the meal.

"Here's to all of us tonight, fortunate to be together at this table, and, to those we loved, who are no longer with us," Paul said, raising his glass.

"Here's to Gram," we all said.

CHAPTER TWENTY SEVEN

Sam and I cut branches from our trees and I made wreaths for each of the cabin doors, and garlands for the fireplace mantels. Because I couldn't find any red and green plaid ornaments, I tied large mistletoe and real holly to red glass ornaments to add color. I made myself a mental note to paint my own for next year.

I put poinsettias on all the cabin porches and went a little overboard with the office; I lined its walkway with more poinsettias and made garlands hung with large red plastic ornaments for the front windows. Inside the office, we had a large multi color lit tree with dozens of multi color bulbs. I wrapped boxes with large bows and set them under it on a large plaid tree skirt.

I hung my handmade garland over the mantle and along the counter, and while I loved it, Noah commented that it looked like I'd thrown up Christmas everywhere.

We got a live tree for Noah's cabin and because he was hoping to fish again in the spring, I decorated it with plaid ribbon, three old fishing poles, old fishing lures and reels, some small scale creels, and some funny fish I'd found in an antique store.

Two days before Christmas, I had a call from Carrie's friend, Paul Larson.

"Carrie's talked me into having you look at the Bracken Fern rooms."

"I'd love to," I said.

"I've started on them, but I now understand they aren't quite up to par. Can we set an appointment for after the first of the year?"

"Sounds great. I'll make myself available whenever you are. I'm really good at working with what you already have, and I'm sure we can get them finished up."

"Thanks," Paul said. "Have a great Christmas."

"You too. And give Carrie a hug."

We spent Christmas Eve at Noah's cabin and had Christmas day brunch, complete with eggnog at Ginny's. We all agreed on only practical gifts again this year, so I framed some old prints of men in canoes for Noah, and since I wanted to convince Ginny to redecorate in a more masculine mountain theme, had some framed for her too. Thankfully, she loved the prints and the theme idea, and because she had a limited budget, I suggested we start with redecorating one section of the restaurant at a time.

I gave Sam a beautiful folding Buck knife I hoped he'd use. And I gave him some shotgun shells more as a joke, but waited until we got back to the cabins to let him open the package. Since he'd come to my rescue more than once, I didn't want him to run out of ammunition in case I got myself into trouble again!

Since I really didn't *need* anything, Ginny and Sam gave me the perfect give; a gift certificate to Ginny's. Noah gave me several pairs of knitted leg and arm warmers, and matching knitted cowls to wear around my neck.

Because we had guests for Christmas, I'd wrapped some custom-made acorn and pine tree chocolates and left them on the bed pillows. The gal who made them for me said she could make them year round, so we began putting those and some wonderful cookies Ginny made in the cabins as our welcome gifts.

Noah and Josh were putting the finishing touches on a room right off the main dining floor at the Tudor House, and since they met the goal of having it open for New Year's Eve, Paul invited us, plus Josh and Bunny, to welcome in the New Year as his guests.

"They'll have live music up on the stage, and a buffet. It's all you can eat," Noah said, thinking that would tempt me.

"Even free food doesn't make me want to spend the evening with Bunny," I said glumly.

"When you clench your mouth that way, you have dimples in your cheeks."

I scoffed and wrinkled my face even more.

"You can sit next to Carrie, and I'll sit next to Josh. You won't even have to be near her."

I thought about it for a minute, my face still set in frustration.

"I suppose that would work."

"I knew you'd come around."

"All right." I sighed.

The evening turned out to be very pleasant. Bunny was three seats away from me, hanging onto Josh's every word, and Noah and Josh could talk when Josh needed a break. As usual, I really enjoyed Carrie's company.

"I still can't get over how much I love the house," she said.

As if she was missing out on a juicy conversation, Bunny quickly got up from her chair and plopped down next to Carrie.

"Babe," she said to Josh, "I forgot my drink. Can you bring it to me?" Then to Carrie she said, "I couldn't hear what you two were saying."

I couldn't give Carrie 'a look', for Bunny would have seen it.

"Annie helped me re-do our home after my mother passed away," Carrie said. "And I was just telling her how much I loved it."

"Oh," Bunny said. Then she must have thought she needed to say something kind, for she said, "I'm sorry for your loss."

Suddenly, the music picked up, and Bunny left us to drag Josh to the floor. Paul appeared and asked Carrie to dance, and then Noah shook his shoulders at me, and we got up too.

We stayed on the dance floor until a slow song came up and Noah pulled me to him.

"See, that wasn't so bad after all, was it?"

"She called him babe, and I don't know if I can ever call you that again."

I knew I was pouting, and he enveloped me in his arms. I felt contentment as I rested my head against the warmth of his body. We fit so well together, and I couldn't imagine life being any better than it was now. I didn't know who said it, but I'd come to believe that after every winter, comes spring. And this was proof.

Time has a way of easing some of the pain we've felt, or in my case, caused. I no longer apologize to Noah for doing what I did. He knows I'm sorry, and that I came back. And he came back to me.

These were the thoughts that were going through my mind as one year ended and another began.

And for now, I was satisfied with that.

CHAPTER TWENTY EIGHT

It was down to thirty degrees out when I woke New Year's Day. I had no actual plan for the day except to stay warm; maybe I'd make a list of resolutions I'd promise to keep, or sit in front of a warm fire and watch the Rose Parade on television. We could make something for breakfast, or go to The Resort for brunch.

We did all three.

We braved the weather and went for brunch, then the minute we got back to Noah's, he stoked the fire and we sat with the dogs, all bundled up in blankets. We watched the rest of the parade, then Noah watched football. I brought out a new notebook, appropriate for new resolutions, and stared at the blank page for what seemed like forever.

Finally, I wrote:

Be a good person.

Do what's right.

Feed the deer and birds.

Cuddle with my cats.

And then I started a new book.

CHAPTER TWENTY NINE

Carrie

"The evening was a great success," Paul said as he locked the front doors of the Tudor House. We were the last to leave, wanting to make sure everything was closed down.

"It's freezing out," I said, making my way to his car. "I hope your heater works before we get home."

"I'm exhausted," he said, "but it was our best New Year's yet. I thought your friends had a good time."

"They did. Thanks for inviting them."

"You'll have to make it up to me. But tomorrow. I'm beat."

We were just warming up when we pulled into my driveway.

"Happy New Year," I said as I opened the front door to my house. "Thank god I turned the heater up before we left."

Morning light flooded through the windows the next morning and woke me by eight. I let Paul sleep as I made my way downstairs to put on a pot of coffee.

I'd bought myself a personal computer for Christmas and had set it up on the dining room table where I could still look out at the lake. While it was quiet, I pulled out my notes and sorted them as much as I could. I was going to write about my mother and Ida Mae.

I began:

After she passed away, I found an old album from when my mother was a young woman. There were photos of her parents standing in front of a small house. Her father wore old boots, wrinkled overalls, a button down long-sleeved shirt and a sweat stained straw hat. Her mother wore a plain blouse, calico skirt, a bonnet and full apron.

Pictures of my mother and her younger sisters and brother were taken at various ages, and towards the end of the album, there was a portrait studio photo of her with a young man. The mounting corners had fallen off, so the photo was loose. On the back, she'd written Lizzie and Jeb, and encircled both names with a heart. On the opposite page was a newspaper clipping, announcing the engagement of Elizabeth Davis and Jeb Carson.

I never knew my mother had fallen in love with a young man before she met my father.

Elizabeth Davis

ELIZABETH

1904–1980

I was born Elizabeth Katherine Davis in a two-room house on our farm in western Nebraska. I was the eldest of six children who lived. A midwife birthed us all, and when I was five, I sneaked into where Ma's mattress was lying on the floor in our bedroom and watched one of my little sisters get born. I'd seen the cows strain to get their calves out, and the only difference between them and Ma was that Ma screamed bloody murder every time she pushed.

We had no electricity or indoor plumbing, which meant we all worked just to survive, and even the youngest of us had chores; milking and feeding our cows, harnessing horses for plowing, cleaning chamber pots, collecting eggs, watering the garden, cleaning stalls and pens and feeding the horses, pigs and chickens.

Ma was in charge of scrubbing the outhouse with leftover wash water, and sometimes she'd add lye to get rid of the smell. Every time I went in there, I was always afraid of bees, spiders and snakes, fearing one would bite me on my exposed bottom as I sat there doing my business. Once Ma told me about a young child who'd disappeared and they found her face down in the outhouse hole. From then on, when I had to go, I held on with both hands.

Once a year, Daddy would muck out the pit and mix our waste mat-ter—or as he referred to it, our shit—with wood ashes and sawdust so we could spread it in the fields and Ma's garden as fertilizer. He'd dig a new hole near the original one and ask another farmer to come lend a hand so he could move the outhouse to a new location.

Until I got old enough to carry a bucket without spilling water, Ma or Daddy would bring the water in every morning. We got to use wash cloths for our faces, but rags for our bathing, which was just a fancy way of saying "washing up." When Ma couldn't stand the stink of us, we all got a tub bath with water heated in the reservoir attached to the wood-burning stove. Sometimes when Daddy wanted a bath, he got his first, then Ma, then us kids by our age, and the water got so muddy, you'd wonder where all that dirt came from. Sometimes, even after my bath, I could wipe my skin with one of the rags, and it'd be smeared with dirt.

I remember Ma telling me another story about a family who bathed this way, and when it came time to toss the water, they accidentally threw the baby out with the bath water.

"Is that true?" My eyes widened in disbelief.

"I don't know. It's just a story that's been passed down. But you never know; we need to keep an eye out for Sissy when we bathe." She chuckled.

By the time I was ten, Daddy had two hired hands that helped him with the wheat crops. They built a shed out a little ways from the house, and that's where they stayed. Ma would cook for them, and we were lucky we had a large dining table, for when they ate with us, there were ten of us in all.

When I was thirteen, one of the hired hands began paying more attention to me than I wanted him to. I didn't tell Daddy, for fear he wouldn't believe me, and I didn't tell Ma, because I knew she'd tell Daddy and he'd end up firing the hand and have more work to do himself. Jack was his name. The problem was, even though he smelled something terrible, he wasn't bad looking.

When it was time to turn in, we all slept in our one bedroom on wall to wall mattresses. Sometimes I'd hear Ma and Daddy doing their sex thing, and I'd think about Jack. But the thought of being with someone that way was overwhelming. However, one night after dinner, Jack took me aside and told me to meet him in the barn after everyone was asleep. When I heard

Pa snoring, I figured I was safe, so I brought my blanket and quietly slipped out to meet him. I was foolish and had not given much thought about what would happen next. And in no time, he had my britches down and with his hand over my mouth to keep me quiet, he hurt me as he thrust himself into me.

"Don't tell your Pa, or I'll lose my job," he said once he was finished.

He pulled up his dirty trousers and went back into the shed, leaving me alone on the blanket. I lay there for a while, and the chill of the night went right through me. I'd had sex with a man, and I felt like I thought the animals must when they mated. I felt nothing. But then shame filled me and I prayed I wouldn't look any different to Ma in the morning.

I crept back into our bedroom, and one of my little sisters looked up at me as I crawled into bed.

"Shh," I said. "Go back to sleep."

The next morning, when I saw the blood in my britches, I panicked. My mother would surely see this, and how was I going to explain it?

"I think I started my bleeding," I said when it was time to do the laundry.

I'd known a girl just a little bit older than me who'd gotten pregnant and shamed her family. While we weren't God fearing Christians, like they were, I prayed every night for about six weeks that I would be spared that same humiliation and disgrace. By the end of seven weeks, I started my bleeding for real and I swore I'd never do anything so stupid again.

When I was fourteen, Daddy let me drive the wagon into town to get our groceries and supplies.

"Take Nellie with you," he said. "She can help."

"Here's the list," Ma said. "And bring them two dozen eggs we collected and see if you can sell them."

Morgan's Mercantile was where we did all our shopping, and they carried just about anything you'd ever want or need. The first thing you saw when you walked into the store, were the candies that filled the glass counter where the cash register sat, and my eyes immediately went to the Baby Ruth bars in a glass jar sitting next to it.

Fruits and vegetables were neatly packed in crates in the middle of the store, and cereals and canned goods were to the left. Brooms and rakes stood in barrels in the hardware department, bolts of fabric were stacked on shelves, and mason jars for canning filled an entire cabinet. Guns and ammunition were in a separate department, along with the camping equipment, cigars, and cigarettes.

I had quite a list of everything we needed; flour, sugar, salt, potatoes, apples, canning jar lids and rubber rings, bags of beans and rice, peanut butter, baking powder, karo syrup, and coffee beans. I gave the list to Mr. Morgan, and while he was filling my order, I went to the fabric shelf and stared in awe at some of the most wonderful fabric I'd ever seen.

I'd never had a dress made from such beautiful material; instead we wore clothing sewn from old patterned flour sacks. I impulsively reached out to touch a bolt and a woman's voice from behind the counter said, "Don't touch that with your dirty hands!"

Startled, I quickly pulled my hand back.

I looked to see who'd said that, and it was fat old Mrs. Morgan, sitting on an upturned barrel, picking at her teeth.

"Get on," she said, as if I hadn't already died enough of embarrassment.

"I'm pickin' up Ma's order," I said, lamely.

Meantime, Nellie was still standing at the candy counter and I could almost see her mouth watering. I wanted to get the hell out of there and never come back, but I also wanted to see if there was enough money left over from paying our bill to buy us kids a treat. Ma hadn't said I could, but she hadn't said I couldn't either.

It turned out we had just enough to buy six pieces of candy or one Baby Ruth bar to share between the six of us. I chose the candies, and I figured I could hide my extra purchase from Ma if the kids would promise to keep our secret.

"Would you like some help loading all this?"

I turned to see young Henry Morgan, and while I hadn't seen him when his mother humiliated me, I still turned twelve shades of red.

"It's turning out to be a pleasant day," he added, not waiting for my answer. I started handing him our purchases, and he and Nellie filled the back of the wagon in no time.

"He sure is handsome," Nellie said as we pulled away.

"Shh," I whispered harshly.

I turned red again, hoping we were far enough away that he wouldn't have heard her. We turned to see if he was still there, and he waved, so I timidly raised my hand in response. Nellie, who was not so timid, turned completely in her seat and waved wholeheartedly.

"I think he likes you," she said, turning back to face the dirt road.

"Just what I need," I said. "Being married to a man with a mother like that."

Nellie had no idea what I was referring to, and I wasn't going to tell her.

It turned out I didn't have to worry just yet about telling Ma about the candies, for half-way home, we saw our brother Tim riding Daisy past us like a bolt of lightning.

"Molly's been bit by a snake!" he called out.

I clicked my tongue and snapped the reins to get our horse to go faster, and all the way home, I couldn't help but think Molly was going to die. I said nothing to Nellie, fearing I'd scare her even more than she already was, but her face had gone pale and I knew she was doing her own worrying.

When we finally pulled up to the porch, Molly was lying in Ma's arms, and they were both crying. Blood ran down Molly's leg where Daddy had cut the bite to let the venom drain. He was squeezing, then sucking and spitting out what he drew out of the wound. Molly started throwing up and crying harder.

"Go get me gunpowder, salt and an egg!" he shouted to me. "And a bowl."

"I'll get the gunpowder and bowl," I shouted to Nellie as she jumped off the wagon. "You get the egg and salt."

Daddy made up a mixture of the three and applied it to Molly's leg. Thankfully, she'd stopped crying and had settled down. Ma held her until she fell asleep.

"That's all we can do until Doc gets here," Daddy said.

"I'll put her in bed," Ma said.

173

About an hour later, the town doctor got there and rushed inside. He took Molly's temperature and let out his breath.

"She's only got a mild temperature," he said. "Looks like she'll be all right. You did a good job fixin' her up."

We all sighed with relief.

"Keep her upright, so's the venom doesn't keep travelin' and come get me if you see any changes. And leave that poultice on her for a few days. If it gets runny, make up another batch."

As Molly slept, Ma put the groceries away and checked her list. Mr. Morgan had given me a dollar for the eggs, and I knew she was going to figure out I'd bought that candy.

"I bought us kids some candy!" I blurted out.

Ma looked at me for a moment, and then her face softened. "Save Molly's for a few days until she feels better."

The next week, Daddy slaughtered one of our cows by shooting it in the head, and after that I made myself scarce. I'd seen him do it once before, and after watching it drop to the ground, decided from then on, I never wanted to watch anyone do that again. We had a calf once that was born lame and Daddy let it live for about three weeks before he killed it, and I ran into our house and cried. He and Tim cut it up and Ma smoked it. Tim was in charge of wringing the chickens' necks and plucking their feathers when Ma wanted to cook one; I couldn't do that either.

We already had a small cellar under part of our house, but in the fall, Daddy, Tim, and the hired hands dug another larger one with a gravel floor and log walls. We had a few more cows and pigs than we needed and Daddy decided rather than sell them to our neighbors, he'd slaughter and dress them for winter.

When I was sixteen, I could sometimes hear Daddy and Ma talk about finding me a suitable husband. Having lived with a house full of children, getting married and having a house full myself, was the furthest thing from my mind. There were only a few prospects around, anyway, young men who'd gone to school with all us kids. And most of them had already quit and gone to work on the family's farms. None of them seemed likely candidates to me, anyway. Henry Morgan, whose parents owned the mercantile, was the only nice-looking boy I knew. And having his mother as my mother-in-law was something I never could have lived with.

A few farmers had lost their wives lately, but they were as old as Daddy and the thought of having sex with someone that old appalled me. Plus, staying on the farm, or anyone's farm for that matter, was never in my plan. And as long as my folks had no one in mind, I was safe.

Canning our foods during the summer months was another chore I disliked. When I could get away with it, I let my younger sisters do the dirty work while I washed and dried everything. One time Ma figured out my strategy, and to prove how unsuited for the job I was, I went so far as to burn my arm once on the canning pot.

"I'm just so clumsy," I cried out.

"It serves you right," Ma said a few days later when my burn got infected.

What I discovered was that I liked working in the garden the best. I'd have Nellie or one of my sisters do the actual hoeing and tilling, and I'd do the planting, watering and picking. We grew strawberries, raspberries, blueberries, tomatoes, peas, onions, carrots, broccoli, cauliflower, beets and collards.

I planted blackberries for jam but also for medicinal purposes like treating an upset stomach or tea for diarrhea. Mixed with honey, we'd use it for sore throats. We also had a small orchard where we grew some apples, peaches and apricots.

"I think you've found your calling," Ma finally said as I brought in baskets of freshly picked fruit.

By my seventeenth birthday, I discovered who my intended was to be. I'd noticed a centerpiece on the dining table one afternoon, and the dinner plates were arranged differently.

"We're having a visitor, and the hands will be eating in their shack."

"Do I need to be worried?" I asked, instantly alarmed.

"No, you don't," she said.

Farmer Buck Carter came to the door with his hair slicked down and a bouquet of flowers for Ma. As soon as I laid eyes on him, I knew I could never marry him, and I intended to let him know it the first opportunity I had. He was polite and smelled clean enough. He made small talk with the kids and talked about farming with Daddy. My mind kept filling with images of Ma and Daddy having their sex and of Mr. Carter naked with the beginning of a potbelly. How would he even find his pecker?

I snickered.

All eyes turned to me.

"Sorry," I said. "I was just watching Sissy doing something silly."

Sissy frowned.

After dinner, Mr. Carter and I went outside, and I made sure we were far enough from the house that curious ears couldn't hear us.

"Mr. Carter," I started.

"Please, Elizabeth, call me Buck."

He shuffled back and forth from one foot to the other, obviously nervous.

"Mr. Carter," I said again. "I'm sure you'd make someone a wonderful husband, but I need to tell you that I have no intentions of getting married and living on a farm. I'm tired of doing chores and just surviving; I want more. And while I know your children are delightful, I've met them, of course, I don't want a family right now."

Buck Carter looked at me like I was a three eyed monster.

"But..."

"So you see, we need to tell my parents there will be no match between us. Either you can tell them you'd jumped the gun since your wife died less than a year ago, or I'll tell them you manhandled me while we were out here. And I'll scream just to prove it."

"Dear God," he stammered. "Please don't do that. My reputation will be ruined."

"Then I think tomorrow or the next day you can talk with Pa and tell him you've changed your mind."

Over the next week, Daddy and Ma apologized to me over and over about the failed fix-up, and I assured them I had no hard feelings for Buck Carter. Honestly, I told them, I wasn't ready to settle down right now, anyway.

A month later, I reconsidered.

Sheriff Wilcox and his deputy came to the house one afternoon in the fall. I was outside collecting the second batch of eggs for the day when they rode up. They climbed off their horses and the deputy began tying them to our hitching post.

"They need water?" I asked.

"Thanks," the Sheriff said.

"Molly, can you take the horses to the trough?"

"How come I have to?" she whined.

"Because I asked you?" I said.

She scoffed, but took the horses over to the trough.

"And you must be Elizabeth?" the Sheriff asked.

"Yes, I am."

"You've grown so."

I was certain the deputy witnessed my face turning red.

"Is your father around?"

"Hey John, I heard someone ride up," Daddy said as he came from the barn.

"This here is Deputy Jeb Carson."

"Good to meet you, son." He and Daddy shook hands. "What's goin on?"

"Well, we've had reports of a drifter out this way and wonder if you've seen anyone suspicious around here."

Daddy scratched his beard. "Can't say as I have. None of the hands have mentioned anything. Are they in trouble? Dangerous?"

"No, but a couple of cows have gone missing lately over at the Jenkins farm. And we aim to keep everything under control around here."

Ma came out onto the porch. "Hey, Sheriff. Care for some coffee?"

"Actually, that sounds great. It's getting cold out."

"Come on in then."

Sheriff Wilcox and Deputy Carson followed us all inside, and Ma indicated they could sit at the table. She poured each of the men a cup, and I said, "I'd like one too, Ma, if I could."

"I didn't think..." she started, then gave me a funny look.

"Well, we'll definitely keep our eyes out. I'll send one of the kids in to town if we see something."

"Thanks," the Sheriff said. "We'd better get back into town before it gets dark."

Nellie was gathering the reins for the horses, and I quickly pulled the one for Jeb's horse out of her hand.

"Ow," she cried.

We walked the horses back, and I walked to the side of his horse where no one could see me.

"Here," I said. I studied his face to see if I could find a gleam of interest in his eyes. And there it was.

"Thanks, Miss Elizabeth."

Maybe I'd be staying around after all.

Jeb came calling that Sunday afternoon with two bunches of flowers.

"What'd you do? Buy the grocer out?" I teased.

I started to call for Ma, but he touched my arm to stop me.

"These are for your Ma, and these are for you. And yes, I darned near did buy them out if you need to know."

I took the flowers inside and found two glass jars to put them in.

"Why, Jeb, aren't these lovely," Ma said. "Why don't you two go out and finish watering the fruit trees?"

I'd watered them the day before, but it was Ma's way of giving us an opportunity to talk alone.

Jeb pumped the water for me, and I slowly poured it around the trees.

"The rocks circling them are to help keep the water in," I said. "Oh, but I guess you'd already know that."

"Actually, I didn't. I've never lived on a farm or had to care for trees or anything like that."

"Where are you from?"

"South Dakota. Deadwood. Famous for the gold rush, Wyatt Earp, Calamity Jane and Wild Bill Hickok."

We kept watering as he talked.

"My parents have a small hotel there in town. The competition is pretty rough, and I knew I didn't want to run it when they got too old to run it. So I left to become a deputy instead."

"Well, if you want to know the truth, I don't really want to stay here on the farm, either. I don't like killing animals, and I don't enjoy having to spend my entire day just doing chores. I've never lived in the city, but that's where I'd like to be, I think."

"Next Sunday, why don't we go to church, and then after, we can go to the potluck dinner."

"I hate to have you think less of me," I said, "but I'm not really a church-going person. But the potluck dinner sounds good."

"I go mostly so's I don't feel guilty having the dinner afterwards," Jeb laughed.

"If I bring a dish, then maybe you won't feel guilty. I'll come up with something."

Jeb came every Sunday from then on, and sometimes for dinner at our house during the week. And every Sunday, either Ma or I would make something I could take with us into town. Sometimes we'd skip the potluck and eat at the corner cafe and go to the movie theater when a new motion picture was showing. There we could sit in the dark and hold hands.

I loved watching the newsreels, for the only time we heard any news was if we went in to town and bought a copy of the newspaper. I learned that Charles Lindberg flew the first solo flight from New York to Paris, Henry Ford produced the fifteen millionth and last Model T and Mae West was found guilty of corrupting the morals of youth in New York.

From the newsreels, I also learned why Daddy and our neighbors had been complaining of having to work harder while they were earning less.

"Farmers Across The Country Continue to Struggle!" *the headline across the screen read. Then the newscaster's voice came on.* **"Farmers, especially those who, before the end of The Great War borrowed**

179

**against their land to increase demanding production, are struggling
now because of overproduction of crops and falling prices."**

*Images of wheat grass and rich cornfields with row after row of stalks
filled with corn blew in the wind. Then farmers on their tractors, or standing with their families, glared across the screen. And the last images were
of empty fields, or ones with very few crops, and wagons that were barely
filled with harvest.*

"Over six hundred thousand farmers have gone bankrupt!"

*Other news filled the screen, but my mind was spinning and I felt sick to
my stomach.*

"Jeb, I need to tell Daddy what we just heard."

It was impossible for me to enjoy the movie, "Robin Hood."

*I was eighteen in the summer of 1922, when Jeb asked Daddy for my hand
in marriage. We planned on living in town, and there was a new department
store being built and I hoped to get a job there. Jeb had gotten a small pay
raise, and with two of us bringing in wages, we hoped we'd be able to save
enough money to buy a small house.*

*Daddy said he'd give us fifty dollars to spend as we saw fit, and when I
told Jeb I wanted to save it towards a house, he was delighted. There was a
retired judge in town, and he agreed to do the ceremony. Jeb's parents would
come out from South Dakota and it would be just our families. We'd have
a reception afterwards in the town hall, where friends and neighbors could
come eat and help us celebrate.*

*"I remember telling poor old Buck Carter I didn't want to get married,"
I told Jeb. "But I couldn't be happier marrying you."*

*A photographer had moved into town and we dressed in our Sunday
best and had three pictures taken. One of us for the newspaper, announcing
our engagement, one of me for Jeb, and one of Jeb for me. On the backs of all
three, we wrote each other's names, and encircled them with hearts.*

*One afternoon, the September heat had broken, and I was sitting on
the porch, working on the list of everything we'd need to set up our new*

household. I was enjoying a glass of tea when I saw a horse riding in so fast it created a cloud of dust behind it. I stood and shielded my eyes from the sun, and recognized Sheriff Wilcox.

"Elizabeth!" he shouted. "Get your Daddy!"

Ma came rushing out onto the porch and called for my father.

"What is it? Who's in trouble?" She counted on her fingers for the children.

Daddy was running. "What is it, John?"

"It's for you, Elizabeth," he breathed hoarsely. "There was a bank robbery just a few hours ago, and they shot Jeb."

I dropped my glass of tea.

Ma grabbed me and pulled me towards her.

My own voice startled me when I could finally speak.

"Is he all right?" Involuntary tears stung my eyes, and I began to cry uncontrollably.

"John?" Daddy asked.

"Jeb's dead. I came to tell you myself."

I would only cry during the day. For two weeks, I wouldn't leave my bed. When everyone laid their mattresses down at night, I turned to face the wall. During the day, I didn't care if it was stifling hot inside, and even though Ma reminded me how beautiful and clear the weather outside was, it was never enticing enough to draw me out.

The times we'd come so close to making love, I wished now I would have opened myself up to him. Welcomed him. Caressed his chest and arms. Held him in my arms. I wished I'd let him show me what it was like to have a man love me.

When I slept, it was fitful and full of dreams. Some were of Jeb and me walking hand in hand, and when I looked at him, I almost burst with love. I'd turn to him a few moments later, and he would be lying in the dirt, cold to the touch and gray, a bullet through his chest.

I'd wanted to see him before we buried him, and I'm sure that's why I could picture him so clearly. The dreams always started with love and ended with death.

Before I met Jeb, I had visions of leaving the farm. And then I knew I could be happy anywhere I was if he was there, too. But now, my only thoughts were of leaving. I couldn't stay there on the farm, where every day I thought about him. And moving into town to find work didn't make financial sense. Plus, every time I saw the bank where he was shot, it would be a constant reminder of his death.

I went into town one last time to buy my bus ticket and to shop for Ma; she'd made her list of necessities, but I saw she'd crossed off her beloved peanut butter and had halved her order of coffee beans. I'd noticed she still gave Daddy his cup of coffee in the morning, but watered hers down to make it last longer.

She made sure I knew to get the less expensive loose tea instead of the convenient new tea bags she'd grown to love.

"I'll go back to making pouches of tea," she said. "I like it better, anyway."

Whether tea bags or pouched tea, she re-brewed her tea so many times, she often ended up with just pale brown hot water.

"And ask if you can get potatoes with eyes; they're older and we can use them to plant. And take some eggs with you to sell."

"Yes, Ma."

"And no candy."

As I turned the wagon to leave, I stopped in front of the bank building and watched as people went about their business like nothing had ever happened. But it had. At least for Jeb and me.

It was then I pictured his cold pale corpse as he lay there in his casket, in a shirt that covered where he'd been shot, his arms folded and his hands placed on top of his chest, no expression on his face.

I actually felt the color drain from my face, and I took a slow, deep breath.

"Elizabeth?" a familiar voice called out to me, but I didn't turn to see who it was

"Elizabeth?" he said again.

It was Sheriff Wilcox, and he had his hand on my wagon. I hadn't seen him approach me.

"Are you all right?"

I turned to look at him and I wanted to scream 'Of course I'm not all right! How could I be all right?'

I clicked my tongue twice, and my horse began to move away.

It was the beginning of winter, 1923 when I left. The entire family crammed into the wagon as we drove to town. Even though I'd told them not to, they wanted to see me off. Ma cried, I cried, and Daddy put the fifty dollars in my hand as he hugged me. With that, and the hundred dollars the town collected for me, I had enough to get me to California.

In the end, I was glad they all came, for it would most likely be the last time I'd see them in a long time.

The trip to Los Angeles was grueling. We filled the seven passenger seats on the motor coach; me, a family of five, and a single man who sat in the back. The three children constantly argued about whose turn it was to sit in the seat closest to the door, and finally, the bus driver took matters into his own hands. He pulled to the side of the road and got up from his seat.

"I need to make a necessary stop, and when I get back in here, you kids need to have figured out who's going to sit where. Give us some peace."

"We'll be on the road several days," I said to the mother. "Why don't you have them take turns?"

Her husband was busy talking with the male passenger and didn't appear to have noticed the driver's comment.

"I'm so sorry," she said sweetly. "I guess I'm just so used to hearing them, I don't even notice. That's a great idea."

She got up and quietly talked to her children, and in no time, they were in place.

"Well," the driver said. "Got it figured out?"

"Yes, sir," the three children said in unison.

Each day, we drove until nightfall, then we stayed in motor lodges, which were buildings with three or four attached rooms. The bus company picked these places because they had a small room off to the side where we could have a warm meal for dinner and muffins for breakfast.

It would be three firsts for me; one was that I'd sleep in a bed by myself without being cramped into just one small section of a mattress, and the other was comprehending what it was like to not have seven other people in the room with me. It was eerily quiet until I heard the family in the room next door as they tried to stop the children from jumping up and down on their bed. Then it grew quiet again.

Until later, when I heard the husband and wife having relations. I couldn't help but think of what sex with Jeb would have been like, and I put my pillow over my head to block out the noise.

The third, and most glorious, part of it all was the bathtub! I had to go to the office and pay ten cents for hot water, but I thought I'd died and gone to heaven soaking in that warm clean water. I even washed my hair.

Throughout our long trip to Los Angeles, I came to know my traveling companions better each day. Mary's husband was a pharmacist in Nebraska, but had a dream of traveling to the west. He found a position with a new chain of stores, Thrifty Cut Rate, in Los Angeles.

"The drugstore is paying for our travel and three months' lodging when we get there," Mary said. "Otherwise, we wouldn't have been able to afford to take the risk of Fred finding a job."

"You're very fortunate," I said.

"What will you be doing?"

"I'm not sure yet." I told her about Jeb. Her eyes filled with tears, and she reached across the aisle space between our seats and gently touched my arm.

"I'm so sorry for you," she said, sadness in her faint smile.

"Sometimes I feel like it's the end of my world, but I know I'll be all right. I just want to be somewhere where no one knows me. I don't want their pity."

"I understand. I hope you find what you're looking for."

"Me too."

The next day, Mary leaned in to talk to me and said, "I think I may have a solution for you, even if it's a temporary one. I told Fred that you'd be looking for a job when we arrive and he is certain there will be something for you at the new drugstore. It may not be glamorous, but I think you should look into it."

When we finally got to Los Angeles, I followed them to their eventual destinations; the store and then an apartment. They originally offered me a job stocking shelves, but then the manager told me they were opening up a new department called cosmetics, and they needed someone who could sell.

Mary offered me their divan, and the six of us crammed into their one-bedroom apartment. I offered to pay rent, but Mary refused.

"Just chip in for groceries, and we can alternate cooking and looking after the kids," she'd said.

It was a madhouse at bedtime; the youngest child pulled his small mattresses out of the closet and slept on the floor in the bedroom with Mary and Fred, and the two others slept on a mattress near me on the living room rug.

"Just leave me room to get to the bathroom without stepping on you," I'd remind them.

Night time was the worst; that's when I'd think of Jeb and the life we could have had. My days were filled with work, and I had little time to think, but at night, once the apartment was quiet, was when my mind wandered. I'd try to focus on one of the children, listening to their deep peaceful breathing, relaxing myself to sleep. Most of the time it worked, but sometimes when I just couldn't stop the jumble of thoughts going on in my head, I'd get up and sit at the kitchen table and read until my eyes drooped shut. When that happened, I paid for it in the next morning. Sometimes I slept through everyone getting up and getting ready and then one of the kids would come shake me awake.

"I'm thinking about getting a job at the Thrifty, too," Mary said not long after we settled in. "Or if they have nothing that sounds interesting, I'll try the department store across the street."

It was the largest store I'd ever seen, and it was called The Broadway. I was eager to earn more money, so on my days off from the drugstore, I worked there in the cosmetics department. It was harder work, for I had to convince women they needed new perfume or a make-over. I applied the basic skills

I learned from Thrifty and quickly stepped it up for the more sophisticated Broadway customer.

Within three months, an apartment in our building became available, and I was finally making enough to get a single apartment of my own.

One day I decided I deserved to splurge, and I had lunch at a diner down the street from the stores. I sat at a table in the window and ordered a grilled cheese sandwich and a Coke. I watched people walk by, couples arm in arm, men in suits, and women by themselves or pushing baby strollers. Then a very attractive woman came into the diner, looked around, took a deep breath, and straightened her shoulders. She went up to a table where two older gentlemen in suits sat absorbed in their conversation.

"Miss Crawford," one man declared as he stood. He pulled out a chair as the other man stood.

It was the actress Joan Crawford!

"Gentlemen," she drawled.

"I hope you don't mind meeting us here; we have another meeting just across the street."

"No, this is fine. I just love these diners," she said without a hint of sarcasm. "I'll have an iced tea with lemon," she told the waitress.

I couldn't hear their conversation, and I tried not to stare as I watched them. I'd finished my lunch before Miss Crawford left, but I waited a few minutes, and when she finally got up, I paid my bill and went over to the table where the gentlemen were. I saw a once in a lifetime opportunity that I couldn't pass up.

"Excuse me," I said. "I couldn't help but notice that was Joan Crawford, so I'm assuming you have something to do with the movie industry?"

The men looked at each other, then back at me.

"Yes."

"Well, I was wondering what it would take to get into the movies?"

They looked at each other again and chuckled.

"A pretty face, and a lot of luck," one of them said. "You have the face. Here's my card. Call me and we can do a screen test and see if you have any talent."

I stood there and read his card.

"Now, if you'll excuse us, we need to be off," he said.

"Oh," I said, stepping back. "Thanks. I'll call you. My name is Elizabeth Davis."

I hadn't intended to become a Hollywood actress when I came to California, but now I suddenly believed it could be a possibility. I'd heard of young women being discovered on street corners, or in cafes, and I felt I stood just as good a chance at being noticed as anyone. When I told Mary, she insisted I get a current haircut, so the next day I asked one of the girls in the cosmetic department where she got her hair done and it was just around the corner.

On my lunch break, I stopped at a newspaper stand near the Thrifty to look at movie magazines to see how the stars wore their hair and I must have lingered longer than the newsstand operator wanted, for he brusquely asked if I planned on making a purchase. I bought one magazine and didn't give him a tip.

I wouldn't call for the screen test until after I saw how my new look turned out.

"I want to look like Joan Crawford," I told the beautician. "With a combination of finger waves and more relaxed curls below my ears."

I winced as I saw my long brown hair fall to the floor, but it had to be if I was to change my look.

"If you want to look like Crawford," she said, "you'll have to do your eyebrows darker. I'll show you how it's done. And are you shaving your underarms?"

I was astounded by her frankness, and must have blushed to purple.

"I can see the answer is no. I can help you take care of that, too. No movie studio wants hairy legs or armpits."

After my appointment, I stopped in the Thrifty and bought the latest Milady Décolleté razor by Gillette. When I got home, I stopped at Mary's and got her approval of my new look. I showed her my shaver and said, "You can use it too, if you want."

The next day, I made an appointment for the screen test.

I could tell from the first words I spoke, I wasn't doing well at the audition. I'd been given a page to memorize, which I immediately realized wasn't one of my strong suits. I was nervous, my voice was stilted, my hands shook, and my face perspired. I kept apologizing for forgetting my words, and suddenly my sense of confidence was shattered.

My shoulders sagged.

"I think I need to stick with selling cosmetics." I turned and walked out of the room, knowing I'd just completely made a fool of myself.

I barely made it outside before I burst into tears.

"You're such an idiot," I said aloud, jostling my way in a crowd of people crossing the street.

"Hey, watch it," someone said, rushing past me.

As I stepped up the curb, someone bumped me and I felt myself falling face first onto the concrete sidewalk. Instinctively, my right arm extended and cushioned my fall. An older man stopped and reached down to help me up.

"Are you okay?" he asked, helping me up.

"I think so. I don't feel like I broke anything, just bruised my ego."

I'd stopped crying, but now I was limping. I finally made my way back home and climbed the stairs to my apartment. I opened the door and just stood there, taking in the single bed, kitchen table and lumpy sofa that came with the place, and I hated it.

Had I made a mistake coming to California? I was trying to start my life over, and now I'd failed at something I thought I could do. I tried to think about all the positive things that had come my way; I'd met Mary and her family, I had two really good jobs, and I was making enough money to periodically send something home to my parents.

Our apartment building had no central lobby, but each floor had its own telephone, and unless you could afford your own phone, this was the number you gave out. There was a notepad and a pencil hanging on a string next to it, and if you were home and you heard the phone ring, you were expected to answer it and take a message. There was a bulletin board organized into squares—one for each apartment—and this was where your messages would be pinned.

I'd never had a message before, so the next night after work, it surprised me when I saw a note tacked up for my apartment. I thought at first it must have been a mistake, until I read my name.

"Elizabeth Davis," it began.

"We think we might have something for you. Stop by our offices tomorrow at 2 pm.

Alfred Adler"

As soon as I read the note, I pounded on Mary's door.

"I think I might have a chance at becoming an actress after all," I blurted. I hadn't mentioned the failed audition or my fall the previous day.

"That's so exciting!" Mary hugged me.

"Ow," I said, wincing. "I can't believe it," I said as I rushed off. "I'll let you know how it goes tomorrow."

I was on cloud nine. That night I treated myself to dinner at the diner where I'd met Mr. Adler and imagined myself a famous star that everyone would recognize as I had Miss Crawford. I was so nervous, I barely ate, and had the waitress wrap the rest of my dinner in foil; I'd drop it off at Mary's, where someone was always hungry.

I laid out my outfit and set my hair in pin curls. I then realized I didn't have a way to reach the drugstore to tell them I wouldn't be in the next day, but then cast the need aside.

'Cast,' what an appropriate word. I was going to be an actress and soon I wouldn't need to worry about either of my sales jobs.

I lost my job at the Thrifty when I didn't show up for work that next day. And becoming an actress was not what Mr. Adler had in mind for me. I wasn't being offered a movie career, but something else "more profitable and more important."

"There's a famous hotel in town where movie people and some very influential individuals come to stay," Mr. Adler said.

It was still 1923 when I moved from my apartment into the Hollywood Hotel.

I was to do make-up for the young ladies who also stayed there, and become a personal assistant to a woman named Virginia Hill who had a suite there. My salary would be two hundred dollars a month!

I shared a room with another girl, a very pretty southerner from South Carolina. Her name was Linette, and she was an escort.

"When gentlemen stay in the hotel and have somewhere important to go, they like to be accompanied by a pretty lady," she explained. "I get to wear beautiful clothes, go to fancy restaurants, meet interesting people, and the best part is I make $25 for the evening."

My mouth dropped open.

From Linette, I learned movie moguls and screen stars like Rudolph Valentino and Ethel Barrymore had stayed in the hotel.

"Have you seen them? Any stars, I mean?"

"Of course, silly," she responded, surprised I'd ask such a question. "All the time. I've even met Louis B. Mayer."

The day after I moved in, I met Virginia Hill.

"Discretion is the key to your success," she told me in our interview. "You will be flexible, meaning sometimes I'll need you after hours. It's necessary that you have diplomacy. You will organize and maintain my diary and make appointments, screen my phone calls, and handle them when appropriate. And most important, you will be discreet and trustworthy. Is that understood?"

"Yes, Ma'am," I said.

"And my name is not Ma'am. It's Miss Hill. If you have any questions, you will direct them to only me. Do you understand? You will tell no one what you're working on. You will report only to me unless I instruct you to do otherwise. Is that clear?"

"Definitely, Ma...," I stuttered. "Miss Hill."

"I'm sure there will be other things for you in the future...you're a beautiful girl."

"Thank you."

"Your desk is in the office outside mine. When my door is closed, that means you are to knock first and you will not enter unless I call for you. There must be absolute discretion...need I say more?"

"I understand," I said. "I'll be happy to help you in any way I can."

"Thank you. Now, I understand you're going to be wearing several hats when I'm not here."

"Are you referring to the make-up, Miss Hill?"

"Yes."

"I'll most likely be doing that in the afternoons, unless you need me. I'll be happy to do what you need."

"That's what I want to hear."

The girls made appointments to have their makeup done, and I got to where I could do one every ten minutes. Within a month, they gave me my own suite, and we set up the make-up table and an area where the girls could change into their evening clothes. They came and went all hours of the night, and sometimes I had a difficult time sleeping for all the noise they made.

I loved hearing their stories, about how handsome—or awful—their date was, where they went for dinner, who they met. And most interesting of all, was hearing about what they did afterward. At first, I thought my hair would curl just listening to them, but then I got used to it, and I'd laugh with them when they told some incredible stories.

"You should think about it, Elizabeth," Linette would chide. "You could make a lot more money being an escort than doing our make-up."

I had to admit I thought about it sometimes, especially when I heard the girls talk about how they sometimes made fifty dollars and more per night. But I was satisfied with what I was doing, and I couldn't imagine having sex with a man I didn't care for.

From the girls, I learned more about Virginia Hill. She'd quit school after eighth grade and got married. The marriage didn't last and after her divorce, she got a job in Chicago waitressing at a restaurant owned by the mafia. She got involved in Chicago's organized crime and was a bag girl—a courier—and later became a madam. According to Linette, she was known as the "Mistress of the Mob."

I also learned that there was such a thing as organized crime in Los Angeles.

"It's coming here more and more," the girls would say. "Hell, that's ninety percent of where my clients come from."

Just before the end of the year, I received a letter from Ma.

> *"Dear Lizzy,*
>
> *You can imagine how surprised I was when I opened your letter this afternoon! I'm conflicted about you sending your hard earned money, but at the same time, you couldn't have sent it at a better time. We'll use it for Thanksgiving dinner and we'll invite some of our neighbors.*
>
> *I hope this finds you well.*
>
> *It seems like everything is changing here since you left. Even though it's winter, we still haven't had enough rain and our crops are not producing. All our neighbors are having the same problem, though, so we know it isn't because we're not trying. What little water we get goes towards our garden first, so that no matter what, we'll have enough to eat.*
>
> *I miss you terribly, but I think you did a wise thing moving to California where there are so many more opportunities to make a living. I'm sorry you didn't get a part in Hollywood, but your work at the hotel sounds promising.*
>
> *Nellie has taken over driving into town to get what supplies we can afford. She remembers when you got that candy for all the kids and hopes one day we'll have enough grocery money left over to buy some again.*
>
> *Everyone says to say hi! The little girls, and even Tim, miss you dearly. And so do Daddy and I. Please write and let us know how you're doing.*
>
> *With love,*
> *Ma"*

It didn't take long to save another fifty dollars, so I wired half that back home. As soon as she got it, she sent another letter.

> **"Oh, my gosh, Lizzy! Things must be so good for you in California...I can't believe you have money to send home again. While we certainly can use it, I didn't mean to imply in my last letter that we were struggling so. But I definitely will not complain.**
>
> **I immediately made out a shopping list and sent Nellie in to town in the wagon. She nearly filled it up, and I'll have you know, she brought back five candies for the kids.**
>
> **I'm so proud of you and your success.**
>
>

Love,

Ma"
>

For the holidays, I sent her a hundred dollars.

> **"Lizzy,**
>
> **I don't know what to say. We'll have enough money to buy a turkey, and you remember the Jones' and Jessop's? They'll bring side dishes, and we'll have a huge potluck dinner for Christmas. It'll be the finest ever. And even the farm hands will fill their stomachs.**
>
> **I drove the wagon into town and Mrs. Morgan at the Mercantile was her usual bad-tempered self, but she let me look through her Sears catalog. I put enough money in an envelope, along with an order for Christmas, and sent it off. I'm hoping we'll get it in time, especially shoes, but if not, I'll find something to wrap and put under the tree.**

> ***We miss you dearly, and beyond hope, we're
> wishing for a white Christmas. We haven't had one
> in so long, but we can always hope.***
>
>
>
> ***Love,***
> ***Ma."***
>
>

The Hotel had two ballrooms, and they decorated both for their New Year's celebrations, complete with their own rotating mirrored ceiling balls. In one, regular guests would be greeted by the hotel staff, and served a four course meal along with sparkling cider. Virginia Hill was in charge of the other gala; the one for special invited guests only. They'd have the same four course meal, but liquor and champagne would run freely.

"Want to make a little extra money tonight?" Linette asked me as I did her make-up. "The escorts mingle and draw in any unattached men. Some of the popular girls have been assigned to the important bosses."

"I don't think so," I answered. "Although I have considered talking to Miss Hill about it."

"I don't see why you can't keep your job and work at night sometimes," she said.

"I'll see what she says. I don't want to jeopardize my job, but I could use the extra money."

"Ask her if you can come tonight to see how it works."

"Hmm," was all I said.

Miss Hill had no objection to my attending and told me to find a suitable gown.

"Have a plan, though, in case any of the men show an interest in you."

"I'll think of a polite way to say 'No'."

They had elaborately decorated the large hall with multiple layers of fabric on the tables, the finest china and silverware, champagne and wine glasses, and cups and saucers for coffee afterwards. Each table had an elaborate centerpiece with candles that would be lit before guests started arriving.

Miss Hill and I stood on either side of the wide-open doors and greeted everyone as they came in. Most men knew Miss Hill and gave her a quick air-kiss as they approached her.

"*Virginia.*"

"*Good evening, sir.*"

"*Miss Hill.*"

"*Good evening, Miss Garbo.*"

"*Good evening, Mr. and Mrs. Raft,*" *I said.*

"*That was excellent, Elizabeth. I'm impressed,*" *Miss Hill said, closing doors. "I think most everyone has arrived, and I'd like a drink. How about you?*"

"*Shall I get you something?*" *I asked.*

"*That would be marvelous. I'll just be over at that table,*" *she said, pointing to a table with an open setting.*

As I stood in line at the bar, I looked around at all the glamorous people. Some I recognized as movie stars, and some looked like tough men stuffed into tuxedos.

"*Good evening,*" *a man's voice said behind me.*

I turned to see a handsome man with thick dark hair and a mustache standing there. Had he been watching me as I took everything in? Had I made it so obvious it all mesmerized me?

"*Are you new?*" *he asked.*

I'd rehearsed my line and casually said, "I'm assisting Miss Hill with the event."

"*I see.*"

"*I've been here about a month.*"

"*And what is it that you do to assist Miss Hill?*"

Was he toying with me?

"*Actually, I do several things. During the day, I help with whatever she needs, and after that, I do the make-up for the girls.*"

"*The girls?*"

Before I answered, I eyed him suspiciously.

"*The escorts,*" *I corrected.*

"*And are you one of the girls?*" *he asked.*

"*No, I'm not,*" *I snapped.*

"*Sorry if I offended you,*" *he said apologetically. He held his hand out to me. "My name is Thomas.*"

"I'm Elizabeth." I caught Miss Hill's eye, and I could tell she was getting impatient. "I need to get Miss Hill's drink. Nice to meet you."

"Nice to meet you too," he said, his warm hand still in mine.

"It's about time," Miss Hill said as I handed her her drink. "And I see Thomas is enchanted with you."

My cheeks burned. I turned to see he was still watching me.

"Don't be embarrassed," she said, laughing boldly.

I saw Thomas again that night sitting at a table with a group of men; he was sitting back in his chair, his coat open and his arms dangling behind him. My eyes widened, for it was the first time I'd seen a shoulder holster, and I didn't look away quickly enough to escape his smile. He sat straight in his chair and pulled his coat closer, but his eyes never left mine.

I stayed until midnight and the countdown, and watched as confetti fell from the ceiling, covering everyone on the dance floor. Couples kissed, and I felt the yearning for romance. The crowd started thinning as some of the men were leaving with their escorts to rooms the hotel had made available.

I saw Linette leave with an older man and watched as she casually moved his hand from her backside. I watched another couple kissing as they still danced, and I suddenly felt miserable. I'd been so busy helping Miss Hill today, I hadn't thought about Jeb and I felt a twinge of guilt. It was the beginning of a new year, and yet I didn't feel like anything had changed. I wondered if any good would come my way.

Two weeks later, Miss Hill set up my first date. I was going to a movie opening.

"Mr. Navarro is a homosexual," Miss Hill shared while she was prepping me for the evening. "Yes, Hollywood has them," she said. "The public isn't supposed to know. The studios, for sure, want to keep their little secrets. Your job is to hold his arm as he reaches for you to get out of the car, and to smile. You're his date. Act like one. You'll be safe with the movie screen's latest Latin lover."

When the large black limousine pulled up outside the hotel that night, the bellman, in his gray livery, stepped forward and opened the rear door for me to get in. A pleasant-looking man with trimmed hair and a pencil-thin mustache greeted me warmly.

"Good evening," he said with a very strong Spanish accent. "I am Ramón Navarro."

"Good evening, Mr. Navarro," I said. "I'm very pleased to meet you."

He took my hand and gave it a cool kiss.

"I saw you in Ben Hur," I quickly added, and immediately regretted sounding like a young fan, although he wasn't much older than me.

He smiled, no doubt recognizing my inexperience. "Thank you," he said.

"I've never been to an opening," I said, again realizing I wasn't being very professional.

"That's all right, Miss Davis. I've never been with an escort."

"You haven't?"

"No. So we're both new at this…"

The crowds that waited behind velvet ropes to see the movie stars as they got out of their cars dazzled me, as did the photographers and their flashes. I held Mr. Navarro's arm as we smiled for the cameras.

"Mr. Navarro!" a young woman called out. "Mr. Navarro."

After the screening, we went to the Brown Derby restaurant for dinner and cocktails.

"Just watch me," Mr. Navarro said when he saw me looking at all the different silverware at our place settings. "Start from the outside, in. I had to learn it too. Continue to watch and learn from others. And please call me Ramón."

When the limousine brought us back to the hotel, he walked me inside to the lobby. As he gently kissed my hand, he slipped me an additional fifty dollars.

"Thank you for a wonderful evening," he said.

"Thank you, too…Ramón."

Over that year, I had several more 'dates' with Mr. Navarro before Miss Hill arranged an evening with a man from out of town. She later told me she was planning on scheduling Linette, who was more experienced than I was, but Linette had to fill in for another girl that night.

"I'm sure I'll be fine."

"If he does something you don't like, kick him in the nuts and run," she said.

While I was waiting in the lobby for our car, a man touched my arm. I turned to see it was Thomas.

"Good evening, Miss Davis," he said. His smile widened. "You're looking exceptionally lovely tonight. I understand you're now testing the waters in the circuit." He grew serious. "You need to be careful. You'll see Mr. Navarro has spoiled you."

"I appreciate your concern, Thomas. I grew up on a farm and I can pretty much take care of myself," I said. "And yes, this evening I'm going with a man called 'Junior', which is a funny name for a grownup."

Thomas tensed slightly, and his smile disappeared.

"Where will you be going?"

"I'm not sure. I know for dinner and then drinks, I think. He's in town with a new camp of men who would like to start supplying your liquor, I hear. Miss Hill said they'd already had one meeting, and have the night off."

Thomas's eyes never left my face.

"You're making me a little nervous, Thomas—is there something I should worry about?"

"I don't know them personally, but just be careful."

"I will. There's the car now. Thanks for the advice."

The driver had opened the car door and was waiting for me as I came outside.

"Good evening, Miss," he said.

"Oh," I said as I stepped inside the car and saw there were two men in the back seat.

"Sit here," one said as they made room for me between them.

"Junior," the man on the left said.

"Willie," said the other.

In a gown, I was overdressed for where we ended up having dinner; a well-known deli, Philippe's, famous for its French dip sandwich. I sat at a wooden table waiting while they ordered our meals at the counter and customers stared at me. I tried to pretend I didn't care.

Junior hadn't finished swallowing his last bite of sandwich when he crammed fries into his mouth. "Hey, isn't this the best?"

"Yeah," Willie said, licking his fingers.

"What say when we're finished, we go back to our room at the hotel?" Junior said, wiping ketchup from his mouth.

I hadn't touched my meal, and while I'd felt uncomfortable with the two men, I now felt frightened. I didn't want to come out and say that an evening in their hotel room was not in my plans and I didn't want a scene in the restaurant.

They made me sit between them on the way back to the hotel, and before I had a chance to ask the driver to take me to the front door, Junior jumped out of the car and took my arm.

"Feeling okay now, dear?" he asked. "Let's just get you inside."

Willie followed as Junior grabbed my arm tighter and pulled me towards the elevator. I saw him look around the lobby before we got in.

Where was everyone?

Junior told the elevator operator to take us to the sixth floor, and it seemed like only seconds, before the door opened and he was pulling me out. I knew better than to scream, so I clenched my mouth tight.

Why didn't the elevator man do something? He just stared straight ahead. I turned to look for him, but the metal door had already closed.

When I came to, I saw Linette and Miss Hill before I saw the two bodies lying on the floor. Each had gunshot wounds to their heads, and blood was everywhere.

"Everything changed to slow motion," I told Miss Hill. "Junior unlocked their door, and Willie dragged me inside. Junior undid his pants while Willie struggled to keep me from pulling away. Then Junior held me until Willie could pull his pants down. When I tried to fight them, Junior slugged me in the face."

"Linette," Miss Hill said. "Wrap another towel with ice for Elizabeth's face."

"How did you even find me?" I asked. Humiliation defeated me and I cried. "Ow." I didn't know what hurt worse; my fat lip, my swollen eye,

or my pride. I'd been so sure I'd be able to take care of myself, but I hadn't expected anything like this.

Linette said, "The minute George saw you get into the elevator, he knew you were in trouble. He came back down and looked for Miss Hill. She wasn't in her office, so he rushed to the dining room and found Thomas having his dinner."

"Looks like they won't be getting that liquor contract," Miss Hill said, lighting a cigarette.

I went back to doing make-up and working for Miss Hill. For some reason—I think the mob god was looking out for me—from then on, they only sent me out on Hollywood assignments. For that, I was grateful.

"She's too valuable to me and the girls," Miss Hill had told her boss.

I stayed in the suite and was making enough money to send home two hundred dollars a month. Ma's latest letter told me things were getting worse for all the farmers back home. There was still a drought and wheat prices were lower than ever. Even worse, a swarm of locusts had descended on the farmland and they had devastated the few crops there were.

"They exploded," Ma wrote. "They hit our bodies and clung to our clothes."

She told me Daddy had used some of the money I sent to rebuild their windmill, which pumped their water. She hoped I wouldn't mind that they helped two of their neighbors repair theirs too.

I wrote back that the money was theirs to do with as they saw fit. If they could help a neighbor, then I was happy too.

There had been a rumor among the girls about a private club that opened up in the San Bernardino Mountains. It offered women liquor and gambling. I'd never met him before, but a man named Benjamin Siegel came to the hotel in the fall of 1929 and began having meetings with our boss and Miss Hill.

While I did their makeup, the girls voiced their opinions.

"I hear they're looking for girls."

"Why would anyone want to go up to the mountains where it snows?"

"If they ask, I'm not going. I like the weather here."

A few days later, Miss Hill left a note on my desk. "When Mr. Siegel gets here, please accompany him to my office."

"Here's what's going on," Mr. Siegel said to me. "We have an opportunity to get this club turned around, but we gotta jump on it now before customers get disenchanted, shall we say? There are two girls up there now, and we have a couple more ready to go. We have a housemother, if you know what I mean, but things have to change. So, since you seem to do a good job managing things for Miss Hill, here, you are what we're looking for. To run the place." He let this settle in.

I hadn't expected this, and I looked towards Miss Hill for her reaction. She only gave me a slight nod.

"But who will take my place here?" I asked, looking again at Miss Hill.

"We'll find someone. Of course, she won't be as efficient as you," she answered.

"Oh," was all I could think of to say.

I had a million questions.

Where would I live?

What would my responsibilities be?

How would I be paid?

Would I be a working girl?

I was not really in a position to say anything other than 'Yes, I will go,' but I was leery of asking Mr. Siegel if I could think about it.

"I enjoy my job here," I said.

"Well, you can do the same, but have more autonomy," Miss Hill said. "You'll take care of the girls and make sure the club is the best it can be. I have confidence in you, Elizabeth. And to answer your question, yes, you will be hard to replace." I believe it was the first time she'd ever smiled at me.

After Mr. Siegel left, she said, "They need new management. You'll no longer be an escort or one of the girls in the old sense of the word. You'll be taking the place of the current woman who's gained the favor of one of the big bosses and is going into retirement. Plus, I think you're the better candidate for the job," Miss Hill said in confidence. "And you'll make more money."

I would now work closely among the mob and the Hollywood elite who came up for gambling and the gin. It would be good timing for the transition, for business tended to slow down in the colder weather and it would give me time to resettle.

"You'll have a little time to learn everything about the club, from bookkeeping to managing the girls," she added. "And you'll need to choose several outfits from the rack. You'll need to dress properly."

I'd thrown away my old suitcase when I arrived, so that next week I bought something new, something more in style. Miss Hill gave me an allowance to buy a warm coat, and I packed my few belongings; dresses, bras, underwear, shoes, and said my goodbyes to the girls. Although I was ready to go, I felt as if I was leaving my family again. Linette had become my friend, and Miss Hill, my teacher. I was up for the challenge, but my heart would still be in Nebraska and now Los Angeles.

Before the first snowfall of 1929, and after a two-hour drive up a winding mountain road, I arrived at Club Arrowhead of the Pines in style—as a passenger of Thomas' 1929 Packard. Mountains to me meant green, and I was surprised as we began the climb up the winding road. The land was brown; the shrubbery was brown, and the only sign water ever fell there were the random pockets of wildflowers providing the only color. Dreary was a good word, and it wasn't at all what I expected.

We talked little as I sat in the back seat, but I'd catch his eyes looking back at me in the rearview mirror. I couldn't tell if he was analyzing me or not, but I felt a charge flow through me every time our eyes met. I'd turn away, knowing I was blushing. After all, I was assuming he was the one who took care of Junior and Willie, and he'd seen me without my clothes on, as no other man had.

As we climbed the winding mountain road, more greenery appeared, and eventually the roadside was dotted with trees. I wondered what fresh adventures the mountains and change of scenery would bring. Although the chances of me leaving this new world I'd fallen into were slim—I'd already conceded that—would I eventually find love? I hadn't given up on dreams of maybe having a family.

The air cooled as we drove, and by the time we reached our destination, it was almost twenty degrees cooler than it was in Los Angeles. I was glad Thomas reminded me to leave my wool coat out of my suitcase; I wasn't sure if the mink collar would be too much for my new lifestyle, but I left it attached, anyway.

Thomas came to my car door and opened it, waiting until I finished gathering my things before I got out. He held his hand out to me like I was a proper lady, and of course I totally blushed again. He had that way about him.

I looked around the property and I could tell the grounds were handsomely kept. I could see there was a large swimming pool and potted trees filled in around the outdoor furniture surrounding it.

He brought my things to the main double door entrance of the large Tudor style building first, and I waited outside while he checked to see where I'd be staying. We then crossed the road to "The Market," which was a butcher shop and a soda fountain. Down in the basement, they stored the ice, and above the market was the brothel, also known as "The Crib," where a hand selection of starlets were brought up to entertain guests. That was where I was to stay until other arrangements could be made.

I followed as Thomas brought my luggage up the stairs, and I was out of breath and a little dizzy.

"Oh," I muttered.

"It's the altitude. Are you okay?" he asked.

He'd taken my arm and led me to where some chairs sat by a window. I breathed deeply. "I'm better."

It was very cold and there appeared to be only one unlit fireplace to keep the entire floor warm. Even the heat of the sunshine beating in didn't make me feel any better. I felt such a foreboding and an inability to escape it. I obviously hadn't bettered myself by coming up here and I closed my eyes and whispered, "I'm better."

He was holding my hand when I recognized comprehension in Thomas' face and he said, "You'll be all right."

I knew he was a man who'd seen plenty, so his tenderness surprised me.

I tried to gather my wits before I blurted out something I'd regret. After all, he would most likely tell his boss how I'd reacted, but I couldn't help myself.

"I'm not all right! Can't you see what I've done?" I cried out, pulling my hand from his. I looked around and saw that they'd sparsely furnished the little lobby where we sat with worn chairs and threadbare rugs. I closed my eyes and wanted to weep. But instead, I did what they had trained me to do, which was 'always keep an even keel'. I took a deep breath.

"If I'm to be here, then this place needs to be upgraded," I said bravely. I straightened my shoulders and held my head high. "I don't want to live here, and neither should the rest of the girls. And clients deserve girls who are happy. Who do I need to talk to?"

Thomas sat back and said calmly, "I'll find out."

There was no phone in the building, so he would have to walk back to the lobby and talk with someone. I would go with him. He raised his hand to suggest I stay where I was, then realized I was going to go with him anyway, so he shrugged his shoulders and led the way back.

The speakeasy lobby was another surprise; two girls were standing by the bar, and the room was shabbily decorated, with old chairs, rugs, and lamps. It smelled of stale cigar smoke, and my first thought was that this was not a place that would make customers want to come back to. Not if you compared it to the hotel in Los Angeles!

Thomas found someone who would talk to me, and in a few minutes, they both returned.

"Miss Davis," the man said, offering his hand. "Benny Hofman."

I sat, which surprised them. So they sat as well.

"I'm finding the accommodations quite unsatisfactory, Mr. Hofman."

"Call me Benny."

"Oh. Okay. If you want your girls to be happy here and not feel like they're living in hell, then something needs to be done about the décor in the rooms."

Both men looked at each other, then at me.

"And upon entering this establishment, I find it also in a state of disrepair, and to be honest, it's awful. Why would gentlemen want to visit here when it looks like this?" I spread my arms out to emphasize my point.

Thomas just sat there with the beginning of a grin on his face, while Benny sat pensively. I thought, 'you've done it now,' and just looked him evenly in the eye.

Eventually, he leaned forward in his chair and said, "Miss Davis."

"Yes, but you can call me Elizabeth."

"Miss Davis, you've only been her for what? Less than an hour?"

While I may have turned red, I faced him directly. If I was to be reprimanded, then so be it.

"That sounds about right," I said, with confidence I hoped wouldn't dissolve as I sat there.

"It seems like you have a keen eye. You see things with, shall I say, vision?"

I tried not to show my surprise at this response.

"If I talk to The Boss and if he feels this is something he'd like to pursue, is this something you'd be interested in handling for us?"

I tried not to swallow as hard as I did, for I didn't want to show any signs of weakness, but I knew I could make some positive changes around there that would make a world of difference. I didn't want to live the life I'd ended up accepting, but if I could make it any better or easier for myself, then I'd do whatever it took.

"Absolutely," I said with a slight tilt of my head—like I knew what I was doing.

I excused myself and made my way back to where I'd be staying. I looked in all the rooms and it appeared only a few were occupied, so I chose one I thought I could live with until we saw some improvements. I put what looked like a clean set of sheets on my bed and lay down. I was exhausted, but I couldn't sleep.

That night, I went back down to the main lobby and asked about dinner. I was famished.

Thomas left that next morning. I watched his Packard drive away, and for some reason I felt a part of me was being left behind. I decided to make the *best of my situation, so after having breakfast, I walked the grounds. The property included the brothel and market, a private gambling club, luxury guest quarters, a speakeasy, tennis courts, a barbershop, a gas station, stables, a pulley ski lift, and an Olympic-sized swimming pool. Of utmost importance, I could see, was the privacy the wooded area provided its members.*

I spent the next week in a cramped office off the speakeasy kitchen, going over the books and trying to make sense of it all. There were stacks of invoices, both paid and due, file cabinet drawers full of paperwork that needed to be sorted and filed, and a checkbook buried under a ledger filled with clients' names computations. I found four sets of books; one for the kitchen, including purchases of food and supplies, and another for income from meals and liquor, a third for gambling and betting, and the fourth for the market. I had little experience with bookkeeping, but even I knew that we needed to separate the liquor and our general maintenance and supplies. It was more than I could manage if I was to make changes and run the business, so I began a list of what I thought we needed to do. First on that list was to hire a bookkeeper.

A week later, Thomas pulled back in to the gravel parking area of the club, and my heart skipped. I knew there wasn't a logical reason, but while he was here, I hoped he'd look for me. He did better than that; when I wasn't in the speakeasy, he came up to find me. Beyond all hope, I was thinking he'd come to see me personally. But that wasn't to be the case. He asked me to pack enough things that would keep me for a couple of days. He was bringing me back down to L.A. so I could shop for everything I thought was needed to bring the place up to the standards it deserved!

All the way down the mountain, he would again look at me in the rear-view mirror, but instead of shying away from him, I could now look at him without trembling. In fact, I dared him with my eyes to look at me.

I asked him to stop when he could so I could use a restroom, so when we came across a small diner, he pulled into the parking lot. As before, he got out and opened my door, and helped me out of the car. This time, I stood there for a moment, just looking at him, and I could tell he was interested in me.

I went inside, and from the small restaurant window, I watched him for a few minutes before I made my way back to the Packard. He was waiting for me, leaning against his car, his ankles crossed, and I took in his brown wing-tip shoes and his argyle socks, which showed slightly. His fedora hat was tilted just so, and he was looking at his gold pocket watch. He closed it and put it back in his vest.

I then did something I never thought I'd ever do; I walked up to him, and as he straightened, I stood on my tiptoes and kissed him. His lips were warm, and his mustache was soft against my face. He was hesitant at first, but then he gently took hold of my upper arms and kissed me back. When I pulled away, his hand went to my cheek, and he caressed it. It was the first time I'd noticed his wedding ring, but I didn't care.

The rest of the trip back was again in silence, with our only contact in the rearview mirror. I'd never felt this way about anyone, even Jeb, and my heart was burning inside. I trembled then, but he never saw it, as he only saw into my eyes.

He brought me back to the Hollywood Hotel, but instead of me being brought to where I'd originally stayed, in one of the working girls' quarters, I was taken to a room such as I'd never seen the likes of. It had a gigantic bed with lush bedding and matching draperies, a large chandelier, a large marble bathroom with a sunken tub, and its own hanging candelabra. There was more closet space than I could ever fill, and when I looked inside one, there were several beautiful evening gowns and daytime outfits befitting a genuine lady. There was also a door that, if unlocked, would lead to another room.

"This must be heaven," I said to the porter. "Here," I said, handing him a dollar.

I was told I'd be having dinner with Benjamin Siegel; he was the one who had authorized the purchase of furniture and décor to make the club as welcoming as the hotel. Of course, the Hollywood Hotel was much grander than the club, but he understood what I wanted.

Thomas also joined us for dinner, and I had to catch my breath when I first saw him. They both stood as I made my way to our table, and I could tell by the way they looked at me, I'd dressed appropriately. I wasn't afraid of Mr. Siegel, so I'd be able to speak my mind. I could see the hunger in Thomas' eyes. Mr. Siegel noticed it too, for he glanced his way.

"So, tell me, Miss Davis," Mr. Siegel said, lighting his cigar. He lit Thomas' as well. "I understand you think we need some glamorizing at the club."

"I do. If your plans are to make the club a place where gentlemen want to visit, then it needs some of the glamour that comes with it. The speakeasy itself is dingy, and the rooms where the girls stay are appalling. I realize this is not where the gentlemen are expected to visit, but they're not the least bit decorated. We want the girls to feel like they have a special place to unwind and relax in. They just need to be decorated."

I took a sip of my cocktail.

"Delicious," I said to no one in particular. "I know the property is new to you, but it really needs help. No hand-me-downs."

"Well," Mr. Siegel said, "Thomas has brought you down to buy what you think we need and then we'll have men and a truck take you back up and you can decorate to make us the success we wish to be. There are several warehouses around here that have plenty of merchandise to choose from, so you shouldn't have any problem finding what you want. Just tell them to bill me, and I'll take care of everything."

"Do I need a budget?" I asked. Even though I was being given the opportunity to do this, I was sure there was a limit to the spending.

"Will twenty thousand do?"

"That sounds great," I said confidentially, however, I'd never seen that amount of money before and I did not know how far that would get me. "Do you have someone to drive me to these places?"

"Thomas has offered."

"Great," I said, as our dinners were being served. I caught Thomas's eye once, then I avoided looking at him for the rest of the evening.

"I'd also like to recommend hiring someone to be our bookkeeper. The office is a mess, and I think we need to keep better track of our expenses. I won't have time to organize it and set it up, but I can oversee it."

Mr. Siegel pursed his lips and looked at me as I told him what I'd discovered.

"I see. Do you have someone in mind?" he asked.

"No, but I think I can find someone up in the mountains. I'd train her, or him, as Miss Hill trained me. Discretion being the key."

Mr. Siegel nodded.

After dinner, Thomas escorted me back to my room. He knew exactly where it was, which in a way didn't surprise me. I expected him to kiss me goodnight, but what he did instead took my breath away.

He opened my door, and he pressed me against the wall as he kicked the door closed. His mouth covered mine in almost savage kisses, and my knees were so weak I thought I was going to slide down until I reached the floor. Thomas unzipped my gown, and it dropped to the floor, leaving me exposed in only my garters and stockings.

It seemed to take him forever to get his cuff links undone, and I thought he was going to rip his shirt off. But then he unzipped his trousers and his pants fell and I could tell he was ready for me.

Thomas made love to me all night. He made sure I was satisfied before he entered me again and again, and I'd never known the act of love could be so beautiful.

He would look into my eyes and then kiss my face tenderly; first my cheek, then my closed eyes, then under my chin and down my neck. He'd kiss my breasts, then my abdomen until he'd make his way down to the place only he knew how to find.

Thomas "Tommy Gun" Meyer became the love of my life. I had an idea what Thomas did for his bosses and it never ceased to amaze me how a man could so easily take another man's life, yet be so passionate in lovemaking.

I used to wonder if he'd felt the same way about his wife as he did about me, but we never spoke of his other life. She wasn't here, but back in Chicago and I knew he had no children.

We spent three days searching through enormous warehouses of antiques to find everything we needed to furnish all the girls' bedrooms and the speak-easy. We'd spend the nights having romantic dinners and then making love.

Because he got up earlier than I did, I'd lie in bed and watch him dress; he'd lay everything out on the dresser in the order he'd use it. Underwear, socks with garters, pants with a perfect crease, white shirt, gold initialed cuff links, a bold tie with his diamond stickpin, his shoulder holster with his .32 Colt pocket automatic pistol, his diamond lucky horseshoe pinkie ring, and then his jacket. Everything he did was a work of art, and I often thought that was how meticulously he carried out his orders.

Thomas would go downstairs and have breakfast with the guys, and then, when I was ready, I would join him. While I was certain they knew we were together, it was best if it looked like I was coming to them ready for the day's shopping.

We made arrangements for everything to be loaded into the truck, and it would follow us up the next morning. When we made love that night, I couldn't help but start to cry, and I was angry with myself for letting Thomas see that I was unhappy. This had been the happiest few days of my life, and it was coming to an end! He wiped away my tears, and gently said, "You have me forever," and that's when I really cried.

On the trip back up the mountain, Thomas insisted I sit in the front seat with him, and I snuggled as close to him as I could get. About half way up the mountain, he took my left hand in his and kissed it, and I wanted to cry again.

He could see the look in my eyes and said, "Don't. I'll see you as much as I can—and I promise you'll stay off the floor. You'll manage only."

Thomas had to go back down the next morning, so we stayed in one of the guest rooms instead of my room in the brothel. Immediately, it had become clear to the staff that my status had been upgraded. As before, when I watched him drive away, I felt a part of me was being ripped apart. I bit my tongue to keep from crying and decided the best thing to do was to get busy unloading the truck.

I had the girls decide which rug and bed went into each of their rooms and they took all the new linens we'd brought up and made the beds. I'd included a new wringer washing machine in my updating and had instructed the handyman to begin building us a new wash-house while I was away.

The speakeasy ceilings were tall and arched, resembling a cathedral. The floors were oak hardwood, and we brought in the largest rugs first. Without them, the room would be too loud and that wasn't the atmosphere we wanted. Next the chairs and sofas came in and were grouped in to conversational clusters, and then the coffee tables and end tables with lamps. Electrical advances had brought in the ability for floor plugs, so we had lighting throughout the enormous room. Artwork was hung, accessories and plenty of ashtrays were placed on the tables and books filled the one library wall by the fireplace.

We brought new iron beds, nightstands, lamps, artwork and rugs into the guest rooms. I ordered a second washing machine to double laundry productivity, and I brought up enough sheets and towels to eliminate the need to have to do guest room laundry every day. I brought up one of the laundry carts from the hotel, which would make housekeeping go more efficiently. We re-organized the storage upstairs, and that's where we stored the extra towels and linens.

I could hardly contain myself when I gave it all the last look. It looked incredible! I then went over to see how the girls were doing, and it was like we had given them a new lease on life; they were chatting about the fresh look and had taken it upon themselves to get everything finished. The bedrooms looked great, and the small lobby with its new furniture was very cozy. The bonus was that all of it came in under budget!

Word got out that we were the place to go to if you wanted women, gambling, and liquor. There was a sweet natural spring on the property which provided water to make gin. About twenty-five percent of it stayed up here for the guests, and we brought the rest down in our truck, which had been fitted with extra "gas tanks."

Hollywood celebrities like Clark Gable, the Marx Brothers, and Jack Benny drove up to party and vacation. Several of their vehicles were also outfitted with extra tanks to transport our gin back down. The outlying cabins became part of a membership for those who paid two hundred fifty dollars for an annual two-week vacation, including all privileges.

We built a guard gate that everyone had to pass through, and if you weren't on the guest list or famous, then you were turned away. We set up a system with the local sheriff, who'd alert us if he got wind that someone in law enforcement or government wanted to investigate. It gave us time to alert our patrons and close up the basement gaming area; we'd use the underground tunnel to go from the speakeasy to the 'Market' where everyone hid until the coast was clear.

In no time, we needed more girls. I made the request, and one afternoon, they brought three new girls in from Los Angeles. They called one Ida Mae; she was pretty, with shoulder-length brown hair, large brown eyes and painted red lips. Violet, a redhead, held on to her young son's arm as he pulled at her to go see the horses hitched to a wagon nearby. With red curly hair himself, he was probably five or six. It surprised me there was a child.

I didn't hear the name of the third girl at first, but Violet called out to her for help in restraining her son. Her name was Norma. She was pretty too, with bleached blonde hair and beautiful blue eyes. They were all very slender, including the boy, and needed to put a little weight on. I'd take care of that.

I stood at the front door of Bracken Fern Manor, as the 'apartments' were now called, and watched for a few minutes while the men unloaded their suitcases. I covered my eyes from the bright sun as I went to greet them. A cool breeze whipped Violet's hat off, and her son ran to pick it up.

"Come see your rooms," I said.

That next spring, Ma sent a letter telling me my sister Nellie was getting married to none other than Earl, the son of the Morgan's Mercantile family. Since the Morgan's knew just about everyone, it was going to be a big wedding and reception.

"We've set aside some of the money you've been sending, and we're hoping you're okay with us using it for Nellie's wedding. Being the parents of the bride and all, we're expected to pay for everything. We had a

social visit with the Morgans and since they think the wedding will be good for their business, they want to invite some of their customers. Mrs. Morgan offered to chip in for the expenses.

You know it's been known to rain in spring, so they're paying to set up one of those huge revival type tents just in case. Mrs. Morgan is looking forward to having a daughter-in-law who can help in the store, although I don't think that's what Nellie has planned. She reminds me of you like that. Havin' a mind of her own.

Love,
Ma"

I wrote Ma an extra check, and tucked it in a large envelope, along with a hand painted card with two hundred dollars inside for Nellie. I knew they'd be getting almost everything they needed at their reception, but this way, Nellie could buy something special for their new home.

Thomas came up every week, and we'd stay in one of the guest rooms at the club. It was his suggestion to look for an outside cabin to rent, so we'd have more privacy. I thought it was a great idea, so I found one in an area off the highway. One of the Hollywood production companies had built a series of seven cabins in the mid-20s, and after they completed the filming, they sold the cabins to a couple who wanted to use them for rentals. When Thomas approached them about letting us rent one cabin full time, they welcomed the idea.

I remembered the cabin, number three, for it had a larger porch than the other cabins, and the natural sunlight flooded through the front windows. We set chairs out there to sit in the early evenings and I added pots with flowers and hung a bird feeder on the post.

Sometimes, if Thomas was out of town, Ida Mae would come spend a night with me in the cabin. I'd made it a rule to avoid personal relationships with the girls, but she and I hit it off from the beginning. We'd either have the kitchen at the Club pack dinner for us and we'd sit in front of the fire and eat, or we'd bring home the fixin's and stuff ourselves with sandwiches and eat potato chips. Once, when she got roughed up, Ida Mae stayed in the cabin for a few days so she could nurse her bruises.

During the summer, when Linette from the hotel came up to see what the Club was like, she sunbathed at the pool, we had a steak dinner at the Club, then we stayed in the cabin, and drank so much wine, we both had hangovers the next morning.

Even after Thomas and I moved to the lake house, we kept the cabin for emergencies with the girls, or for clandestine affairs. The mob bosses didn't hide their dalliances, but the Hollywood crowd did. Occasionally one of the girls would get roughed up, and cabin number three became a haven for them if they needed to step back for a few days.

In early 1930, worried the Great Depression was going to affect us up in the mountains, Thomas saw it as an opportunity to invest some of his cash. So he purchased a large cabin on the lake. It had sat unfinished, so he hired workers who were there every day, and who were grateful for the work.

Little did I know it at the time, but he put the property in my name so I'd have something of my own. And when I saw the house completed, the proof of his love overwhelmed me.

"You can now fill it with whatever you want," he said, taking me into his arms.

"Oh Thomas," I said, finding it difficult to speak, "this is beyond incredible."

The first thing I did was set the freshly painted red chairs and the potted flowers from the cabin on to the porch. I'd thought about leaving the bird feeder, but knew no one would keep it filled, so I took it down and hung it from the porch roof beam so I could see it when I sat out there.

"This is just the beginning," Thomas said. "I want you to start buying houses. People will always be looking to rent and when you're old and gray, you'll have quite a nest egg."

When I frowned, he said, "There are going to be some tough times ahead for some people, so this is the time to buy. You will always have tenants. Trust me," he said, holding me tightly. "Now let's go inside."

If Thomas was only going to come up for a day or two, we'd stay in a guest room at the club so I could still manage the girls, but if he knew we'd have more time than that, we'd stay in the new cabin. It felt funny calling it a cabin since it was so large; four bedrooms, two bathrooms, a large den and living room, and a large kitchen.

It wasn't long after we moved in that I discovered I was pregnant. In some respects, it was only a matter of time before it happened, for we made love often and weren't always careful. Thomas disliked the thought of me using a diaphragm, which was the popular form of contraception then; plus, it was only about ninety percent effective. Instead, we tried to practice the withdrawal method. However, Thomas wasn't always good about pulling out before he spilled his seed.

When I told him, I was a little unsure how he would take it since children could complicate our relationship. But instead of being unhappy with me, he took me into his arms and said, "I love you, Elizabeth. I'll make sure the two of you are taken care of if anything ever happens to me."

At first, I felt almost euphoric, and then I realized the possibility that one day something could happen to him. He was in a very dangerous line of business. He never smelled of death or fear, but more than once I'd noticed blood spatter on his shoes. I'd wait until he fell asleep to clean it off.

Thankfully, I had very little morning sickness, so I could keep up with my work at the club. If I needed something lifted, I'd ask one of the men to help, and the girls did what they could to make life easier for me.

About six months into my pregnancy, two terrible things happened at the club. Norma's little boy somehow got into the stables and was accidentally killed by one of the horses. It was awful to see his battered body being carried out, his red hair matted with blood. And it was even worse to see Norma. Her grief was unbearable and I could understand why. Until I'd become pregnant, I thought of children as more of a nuisance than anything. But I now knew that a child's death could tear a mother's heart out.

They buried her son in a small mountain cemetery, and only a white cross marked his grave. For days, you could find her lying on his grave and when she continued to refuse to eat, she grew weak. One morning, the girls found her in her bed, unable to get up. We called for the doctor, who could find no physical problems, other than a stressed heart.

Norma died the next day.

"She's most likely died of a broken heart," the doctor said. "That's what I'm writing as cause of death: Heart."

We buried Norma next to her son.

Almost two weeks later, Violet shot and killed herself in her bedroom. Thank god Thomas was up and he handled the clean-up. The doctor came again and wrote out a death certificate, listing suicide as cause of death. We had to paint the walls and replace the mattress and bedding, and put in a new carpet.

We all knew she'd fallen in love with the bass player at the club, but Mr. Siegel had taken a fancy to her and was jealous of their relationship once he discovered it. The bass player disappeared. Violet refused Mr. Siegel, and she was scheduled to be sent away.

They buried her next to Norma.

Years later, people swore that Violet's perfume still wafted through the rooms upstairs…and I've smelled it too, so I know it's true. It was her violet fragrance that followed her everywhere.

Not long after that, Mr. Siegel became interested in Ida Mae. I'd seen him with her, and she'd seemed truly interested in him. He pulled her from rotation, and she became his 'Lady'. They'd stay in one of the guest rooms when he came up, and when she became pregnant, he set her up in cabin number three until he sent her away. He didn't want the publicity surrounding him having a child when he had a family back east.

We were experiencing a shortage of girls, so I sent word down the next time Thomas went down. Within a week, I greeted six new girls.

I hadn't heard where Ida Mae had gone, and I was happily surprised when I got a letter from her about a month before her baby was born. Correspondence was discouraged for fear the club's true nature could be jeopardized, unintentionally or otherwise. There was no door-to-door mail delivery in the mountains, for it was too rural, so every other day one of the custodians would go to the post office and bring me the mail.

"Dear Elizabeth,

Benjamin has bought me a lovely ranch just out-side San Diego, in Rancho Santa Fe. When the house is finished, it will be a wonderful place he can visit without reporters finding him. I've always envied the life you have with Thomas, and now I have that life, too.

I hope one day to see you again.

Ida Mae

P.S. The baby is due soon. I only pray it's healthy."

We named our daughter Carrie Rose after Thomas's mother. We had almost five perfect years together, taking the boat out on to the lake in the summer, and playing in the snow in winter. We filled the house with things we loved, and we had photographs taken of us with Carrie every year. I hung them in the hallway upstairs.

The day before Carrie's fifth birthday party, Dottie, one of the girls from the Club came to help me clean the house. There weren't many children her age in the neighborhood, so we invited the entire kindergarten class and most of the mothers had responded yes, they'd be there. I left Carrie with Dottie and went into town to pick up a few more decorations and an enormous teddy bear I'd had wrapped. Carrie loved bears, and I'd found a bakery in town that decorated the most wonderful cakes. Carrie's was green with brown frosting trees, candy rocks, and a chocolate brown bear wearing a colorful hat and holding a gift.

I brought the cake in and hid it in the pantry, and I put the wrapped bear in the downstairs closet.

The next day, as soon as Carrie took her nap, I set the hamburger patties and hot dogs on a tray, and found bowls for the chips. Thomas was planning on being home for her birthday, and when I heard a car pull up, I waited a few minutes to call out, "The door's open!"

When no one came in, I looked out the window and saw Mr. Siegel's car parked in our driveway. My blood turned cold as I immediately knew this would not be a social visit, but the one I'd dreaded for years.

"There was an ambush. A rival mob family has killed Thomas," he said the moment I opened the door.

My knees buckled, and he instinctively grabbed my arms. It was déjà vu. In my mind, I clearly saw Sheriff Carter coming to our farm years ago and telling me Jeb had been killed. I felt like my heart had been ripped from my chest.

To the outside world, I held my composure, but when I was alone in our cabin, I felt total despair. I tried unsuccessfully to hide my pain, and I cried continually. To say I missed Thomas was an understatement; I missed everything about him that was comforting, and I longed for him to hold me and tell me everything was going to be all right. I was facing a life of loneliness and even though I had Carrie, she couldn't possibly fill the void I now had in my heart. And when I looked at her, I saw Thomas. It was almost unbearable.

I found someone who could stay in the cabin with her while I devoted all my waking hours to improving the Club. I had the speakeasy cleaned from top to bottom; we got new mattresses for the girls, and even that didn't make me feel any better.

I spent a lot of time on our boat, going early when no one else was on the lake and the solitude comforted me. I'd made up a mixture of sunflower seeds, chopped peanuts and dried fruit for birdseed, and pulled into the dock area at the Village where I could toss it to the ducks.

About two weeks after Thomas' death, I found an envelope hidden on my porch, and inside was his watch, tie tack, money clip, pinkie ring and his revolver. There was also five thousand dollars. For a year, I'd receive that same monthly payment, and I tucked it away in my desk drawer.

Carrie was acting out and suffering because I wasn't home with her, but I could barely stand it when I was there. Every time I looked at her, I saw Thomas's eyes and my heart would break all over again.

One evening, it was dark and wet outside, and the sky was multi shades of charcoal gray. Carrie and I cuddled under a blanket on the sofa facing the fireplace, and the flames rose, the fire crackled, and her face glowed in the firelight. She was beautiful, and I knew I would have to get a grip on my life or I would ruin the life of my child. After six months, I resigned myself to my fate again, which meant I had to take care of my daughter. We were going to have to work this out.

Even though Prohibition had ended, the mystique of the club carried on. However, in 1941 the Japanese bombed Pearl Harbor, and that started the downfall of the Arrowhead Club in the Pines. While the movie stars and local mob members still frequented it, men were going to war, and we were losing customers.

By 1946 Mr. Siegel had found other opportunities and in late December he officially opened the Pink Flamingo Hotel and Casino in Las Vegas. I was never close to him, but he always treated me fairly, so it saddened me to hear that things hadn't gone well for him after that. Although the well-known singer and comedian Jimmy Durante opened the show, the weather in Vegas was terrible that week, so a lot of Hollywood guests didn't show up. I heard the casino lost three hundred thousand dollars the first week.

Two weeks later, the Hotel and Casino closed. And in June 1947, Mr. Siegel was found dead in the Beverly Hills mansion of his current girlfriend, Virginia Hill. His murder was never solved.

Using Thomas' suggestion, I kept buying homes as a way of building our future. I now had eight homes in the mountains, which brought in enough for me and Carrie to live comfortably, so I retired. Not long after that, the Speakeasy closed down.

I never told Carrie the truth about who her father was; not that I was ashamed of him, but I thought she'd carry an unnecessary burden with her throughout her life if she knew. So I maintained the story Thomas was killed in an automobile accident. She was too young to remember much, and she accepted that as a fact.

I knew I hadn't been there for her after Thomas died, but once I realized I had to pull my life together, I did my best to be a good parent. I made sure there was always someone there for her when she came home from school. I took her shopping and tried to find things she could do that interested her.

One summer, I took her home to see my family. My father had died several years back, but everyone else was still there. Somehow, they'd kept the farm afloat and raised enough cattle and wheat to provide for all of them.

"When we get your Western Union, we buy another cow," my brother said. "Or we buy more chickens."

Nellie had two children, a boy and a girl, and Tim had three kids. Ma looked happy, but deep lines and sun exposure had ruined her once soft complexion. Her hands were rough and dry, and covered in brown age spots. And when I hugged her, I could feel how slender she'd become. She'd never been heavy, but age and hard work had taken its toll on her.

Ma died just before she turned sixty, and I went back home for her funeral. My nieces and nephews had grown up, and Nellie and Earl ran the Mercantile in town. When Earl's parents died, Earl sold their home and bought Nellie a newer one.

"I didn't want to live in his mother's house," she confided.

"I don't blame you. I don't know how you tolerated her all these years," I said.

Carrie eventually went down to college and ended up marrying a professor and having her children. She became the teacher she always wanted to be, and when she divorced James, she stayed down in L.A. for the kids. They all came up during the summers, and I loved having her here, even if we did nothing but sit and look at the lake.

Her passion had always been to write, and that's what she eventually did. She became a well-known author and loved it. Several times she'd say, "Mother, your life would make a great story. Tell me something."

I told her about growing up on the farm with no bathroom or running water, and how my parents had thought to marry me off to one of the farmers, but I never told her I'd lost my fiancé before I came west. I wasn't sure why; maybe it was because I didn't want her to know I'd loved someone before I met her father. Of course, I couldn't tell her about everything else, so I made up stories as I went along. She seemed happy enough.

Carrie's come home to live with me and I've tried not to burden her with my care. I've been diagnosed with Parkinson's and while it's a nuisance, I know I won't die of it; I try to keep my shaking hands from shaking, but it doesn't work. I don't let on, but I see Carrie looking at me, watching out for me. My bones ache with my arthritis and sometimes I can't recall when they didn't hurt. I've been in these mountains now, for over forty years, and I'm tired. But there's nowhere else I'd ever want to be, for in this house, Thomas is still with me.

Isobel's husband comes over and plows the snow, clears the berms, rakes the land and fixes anything that needs fixing. Isobel comes during the week to help me get around. She's the only one I tell when I lose my balance and she's promised not to tell Carrie. My cane has become my constant companion.

Linette, whom I hadn't spoken with in years, sent me an L.A. Times newspaper article about actor Ramon Navarro, my first escort assignment in Los Angeles. He'd been murdered in his Laurel Canyon home by two brothers who'd contacted him for sexual favors. He had, in the past, hired prostitutes through an agency, and the brothers got his number from a previous guest.

Mr. Navarro was always very kind to me; not only was he a gentleman, but I remember he always gave me a fifty-dollar tip.

I folded the article and put it in my sweater pocket. I planned to put it in my dresser with the rest of my memories. I thought about going upstairs, but when I looked out towards the lake, it was so beautiful I decided instead to go sit in my chair on the porch.

I watched as my birds landed on the feeder, poking for their food, and then the most miraculous thing happened. I heard the slightest snap of pine needles in the near distance, and within moments, I saw a deer with her fawn. They were eating apples from the basket I kept at the base of the tree. I didn't move. I didn't even want to breathe.

The deer raised her head and sniffed the air, then turned to where I was sitting. But she didn't sense danger, and she went back to eating. When they had enough, she led her baby away, back into the trees.

I'd been blessed with a sight I'd never seen before.

And that's when I thought of Thomas, for I'd been blessed with him, too. I slowly rose from my chair and went back inside. I patted Linette's letter in my pocket to make sure it was still there, and then I started up the stairs.

Once in my room, I sat on my bed, trying to catch my breath. After a few minutes, I went to my dresser and opened the drawer. I picked up my old mother-of-pearl compact, and when I pulled it out, its contents were so dried and dusty, powder spilled everywhere.

"Damn it," I said sharply.

I could feel the color flare in my cheeks from anger. I closed the drawer and opened the second one, which was filled with Thomas's things; I sorted through his ties, tie tacks and cufflinks until I found his pocket watch and fob. I recalled the first time I'd seen it; he was waiting for me at the diner and he pulled his watch out to check the time. His 1898 silver dollar money clip still had several hundred-dollar bills in it, and I put his lucky horseshoe pinkie ring on one of my fingers. In a soft cloth was his pearl handle revolver, and when I unwrapped it, I breathed in the smell of the metal barrel.

I touched all our old letters. I'd always loved receiving his, and I'd stop what I had been doing and write back. But I could never send them; first I never knew where he actually was, and second, I knew he had another life somewhere else.

It was the newspaper clippings and death certificate I wanted to find most.

I used to think I wouldn't care if anyone learned the truth about my life. And I thought if they found all this, it probably wouldn't make any sense to them, anyway. But now I'd changed my mind.

The newspapers were from up in the mountains, and there were photos of Bugsy Siegel and well-known actors standing in front of the Tudor House.

And then between the newspapers was a death certificate.

Deceased: Thomas Meyer
Residence: State of Illinois
Date: November 3, 1934
Place of Death: Los Angeles, Ca
Married
Husband of: Maryann Goldmann Meyer
Cause of Death: Gunshot injury, catastrophic injury to the head,
   damage to the brain

I set all this in a pile on the bed and put everything else back in the dresser drawer. I took a deep breath and started down the stairs, where I'd start a fire in the living room fireplace and burn it all.

Somehow, between holding my cane, the papers and the railing, I lost my balance and tumbled to the bottom of the stairs.

It was Isobel who found me. My entire right side burned with pain, and when I tried to move, I cried out.

"I've called the ambulance," she cried. "Oh, Miss Elizabeth."

"Take the papers!"

"What?"

"Take the papers and burn them in the fireplace."

Isobel wanted to sit with me, but I insisted again. "Burn them!"

I could hear the faint wail of the siren as I saw Isobel look towards the fireplace. And then I relaxed my head.

I can tell my time is near. I sleep downstairs in a hospital bed now, for I've broken my hip and arm. My entire body hurts, and it's been getting harder for me to breathe. They say I have pneumonia. In all these years, the altitude never bothered me, but it seems to now. I've asked that I be able to die in my home; I don't want to lie there in a hospital with all the smells and noise. Carrie has promised me, and I find peace in knowing this. She's been with me these last years, and I'll cherish her until my last day.

But until that day comes, I'll continue to lie in my bed, tilted up and facing the lake. It's the end of fall and it's turned cool. There aren't many boats out, but when one does go by, I can understand the peace the lake brings to those who are out there.

The Cabins

Map

Carrie's Living Room

Carrie's Master Bedroom

Carrie's Den

Carrie's Kitchen

AUTHOR'S NOTES

Again, I need to thank my wonderful husband, **Larry Braun**, who is still, as Bette Midler sings, the wind beneath my wings. Book two's final editing came about when, by chance, I was diagnosed with ovarian cancer and underwent chemotherapy. Even though I knew I was going to be alright, I admit now, I sometimes drifted from my goal to finish the trilogy; but with support and constant reinforcement from Larry and friends, I kept at it. And as you can see, book two is done, and the good news is, book three will be published soon too.

Halfway through my chemo, I had a hysterectomy and the great news was, there was no more cancer! I've completed the treatments, just as a precaution, and I'm looking forward to finishing the other books I've started.

I'd like to insert here how important that women continue to get their mammograms and, if you still have your "lady parts", ask your doctor for a periodic ultra sound; they aren't normally part of an annual exam, but I truly believe having one saved my life.

I got the idea for this book one night when we went to The Tudor House, which is a real place in Lake Arrowhead, to have dinner and listen to a group playing music. I only knew it had once been a speakeasy and that the mob was somehow involved in the twenties and thirties. The next day, I searched for its history and I was intrigued.

Details I didn't include in the story:

Bugsy Siegel was only forty-one when he was killed.

He wasn't the originator of the club, but came onto the scene later. All the "ladies" except Violet are a product of my imagination. And to my knowledge, Bugsy didn't have an illegitimate son.

Sometimes when I'm researching something for my books, I lose myself in some interesting facts that don't quite fit in with the storyline but are noteworthy. For example, in 1980, Carrie is buying coffee beans and, not being a coffee drinker myself, I went to Mr. Google to look up when households had modern coffee grinders. It turns out I was accurate with my date, but I came upon a story about Abigail Folger, heiress to the Folger's coffee fortune. On August 8, 1969, she was an unfortunate guest at the Sharon Tate and Roman Polanski home in Hollywood Hills, and was murdered by the Charles Manson Family.

And Bugsy Siegel's murder was never solved, but his girlfriend, Virginia Hill, was conveniently out of town when it happened. It was rumored he'd fallen from grace and needed to be disposed of.

Again, I'd like to thank all my support team for help in getting book two off the ground.

Gary Marsh sketched the rooms Annie worked on, and web/graphic designer **Susan Leinen** formatted the images for the book. My friend, **Susan Newman Harrison**, also a graphic designer, originally painted a cabin that inspired the first book and also kept reminding me I had a finished product ahead of me.

After book one, **Tim Novak**, my best IT friend, didn't have to help me with as many dumb questions about saving my work. Thank goodness.

My editor, **Pam Sheppard,** is so encouraging; she helps point out inconsistencies, and made suggestions about one character who didn't seem to be pulling her weight.

And my early readers, **Myrt Perisho**, **Susan Denley** and **Pat Aldridge,** give me not only a reader's point of view, but gently pointed out anything that didn't make sense.

And finally my proofreader, **Sue Jorgenson**, hopefully found most of the typos, and helped me get my timeline back in gear.

Even with so many sets of eyes on the text, I'm certain you'll find something that slipped through; so please let me know if you do, and I can correct them with future printings.

Places

The Tudor House is an actual place, originally called Club Arrowhead in the Pines. There was a working girl there called Violet, who committed suicide, and for years, people have claimed they can still smell her perfume wafting through the air.

Purchased in 2013, it's undergone major renovation and updating, and offers fine and casual dining, a dinner theater, a concert and wedding venue, a microbrewery, and a great Sunday Brunch. You can also stay at Bracken Fern Manor.

Cedar Glen is a small town "in Lake Arrowhead" founded in the 1880s. I wrote the history of the town based on information I've read, and is as accurate as possible, but I took some author privileges about some of the businesses located there. When we had our second home in Lake Arrowhead, we frequented these and everything here is accurate as of the publication of this book.

Cedar Glen Inn was one of our favorite family-run restaurants. Their breakfast is huge, and their prime rib on the weekends is delicious.

Cedar Glen Trading Post was where everyone bought hunting and fishing supplies, paint, small tools and had spare keys made.

Timberline in the Glen is truly a favorite home décor store. It reminded me of the store we had in Orange County called Designing Whims. We bought some unique furnishings for our home, and I never could get out of there without buying something I treasured.

Wildhaven Ranch is a wild animal sanctuary, education and visitation center for endangered and indigenous wild animals. It is operated by the San Bernardino Mountains Wildlife Society, a 501(c)(3) nonprofit organization. If you love animals, consider becoming a donor: contact them at info@wildhavenranch.org

Mission Inn, Riverside Ca. Although I've used the Inn in 1981, it technically hadn't reopened until 1992, after the Roberts family purchased and reopened it.

If you go to chrysteenbraun.com, you can see the two homes we had in the mountains. They fulfilled all my dreams and fantasies about having a second home.

Also, the greatest thing you can do for an author is to recommend their books to others, and to leave a review on Amazon.

All you have to do is:

- Log in to your Amazon account
- Go to the product page for the book, then select the book format
- Scroll down to the Customer Reviews section and click on "Write a Customer Review"
- Rate the book (hopefully with lots of stars)
- Write your review and "Submit
- You'll see "Thanks for your review"

I'd love to have you consider my books for your book club and if you write to me, I promise to reply. chrysteenbraun@gmail.com

Sign up for Chrysteen's newsletter at chrysteenbraun.com

Turn the page to read

the prequel and first chapter of

The Starlet in Cabin Number Seven,

the final book in The Guestbook Trilogy.

Celeste 1980

I knew I had a purpose for standing here in my closet, but I had a splitting headache, and the reason was escaping me. When I saw the tall jewelry box, I went to it and stood there for a few moments, and then I remembered. From the top drawer, I took out my wedding rings; the first was from Joseph, and the second from Andrew. I hadn't worn either in years. I skipped the second drawer, which was filled with the costume jewelry I'd worn in my movies, although now I couldn't recall which pieces I'd worn in which movie. But it didn't really matter. It was the third drawer I was most interested in, and I found what I wanted. Under one of my mother's embroidered handkerchiefs, I found the gold necklace with the locket and the diamond watch my grandmother left me when she died.

I wrapped them in the handkerchief and put them in my purse. I carried my suitcase downstairs to the entry, and set it next to the small painting I'd chosen to take with me. I'd forgotten I needed to wrap it and pack it safely in between my clothing. I would do it after I called my travel agent to book my flight.

PROLOGUE

Annie
Today

I've fallen again, this time as I was coming down our stairs, and I've cracked three ribs. There's never anything they can do for you when that happens besides give you a brace and wait for the ribs to heal. I'm wearing it now and it's hard for me to breathe.

I'm staying in our downstairs guest bedroom and I'm actually sleeping better down there. We've never had guests, which is just as well for me; for some reason, I've never really felt comfortable having someone stay in my house. I'm actually sleeping better down there. I'm not awakened by my husband's breathing machine when the mask moves away from his nose and the hissing air wakes me. It's usually in the middle of the night and I can't get back to sleep.

I must sound like the crotchety old woman I've become.

I'm growing more tired, and I've thought about not finishing my third book, but I actually feel comfortable sitting at my desk when I wear my brace. I haven't told my husband, but I'm beginning to forget where I've left off, and I often have to reread what I wrote the day before. I've started keeping detailed notes so I can easily go back to edit.

My sweet neighbor just brought over a vase of flowers she'd cut from her beautiful garden, and I've set them on my desk where I can enjoy them.

A friend once told me I'd live to be eighty-six and I'm now eighty-two. If I fall again, it might be a hip that gets broken...or worse. I could hit my head and die from internal bleeding like my father did so many years ago.

This afternoon I had a phone call from my stepson, sweet William. He wanted to let me know he'd become a great grandfather. How on earth did that happen, I wondered? But then I count back the years, and if I'm eighty-two, that makes him seventy-two. Yes, that's hard to believe, but he was only ten years younger than me when I married his father, David.

"They've named him David," he said, somewhat cautiously.

"Oh," I said.

"It was on Dad's birthday."

"What was?"

"When David was born. Yesterday."

"Oh," I said again. I'd long ago forgotten dates that were at one time so important to me. Especially those from so long ago.

"And his middle name is Andrew. I thought of it; after you, after Annie."

"Oh!"

"I hope you don't mind."

"Oh, of course not. I'm actually quite thrilled. Although I've never been called Andrew," I said, chuckling.

I told him about my fall, and about the lovely flowers on my desk. He asked how I was doing otherwise, and when I thought about it, all the complaining I'd recently done was mostly because I didn't have anything else to do.

"Let's see," I said. "If your father was alive, he'd be..." I had to take a moment to calculate it. "Ninety six. Or ninety seven. Now that's old."

"I told you that before he died, actually many years before that, he wished he would have done things differently."

"I know, dear, we all would have. But it is what it is. Isn't it? And it was so many years ago…"

It is what it is. I hated that saying, but sometimes it just fit.

When we hung up, I told my husband William called and that I should now be referred to as *Andrew*.

Not surprisingly, that night, I dreamed about David. Dreams are always so funny; sometimes they can make no sense at all, but they seem so real. This one was sharp as ever.

David actually came to me and wanted me back. We'd been divorced for almost forty years. I was seventy, and he was eighty-five. He didn't look it; he was still fit and distinguished looking. He'd never grayed, except for his mustache.

He never apologized for seeing someone else while we were married, but he assumed enough time had passed that it didn't really make any difference now. I hated to admit that I was still fond of him, that there had always been a place in my heart for him. And in the dream, I remembered he'd come back to me on more than one occasion, and for some reason, I always took him back.

"You'll have to stay at home this time," I said, and he looked at me quizzically. "Oh, you can work in the garage, but you can't stay away whenever you feel like it."

I drew my eyebrows together in thought, and then said, "And we'll have to figure out our finances." I didn't feel it was fair that what was mine would now be his. And then I thought about sex; I hadn't been happy so many years ago, and I wondered if he still had it in him to even *have* sex.

"I'll try to lose a few pounds." I remembered he never liked it when I gained weight, and I was still plump.

Then it woke me. I never knew my decision, whether or not I took him back. And even though I knew it was just a dream, it stayed with me all that day, like some dreams do.

I tried to recall if I'd had that dream before.

Even as I sat down to write, my attention drifted as little thoughts niggled into my consciousness. I tried to remember how I'd felt so many years ago, and I had a hard time. But I'd discovered my notion of being married forever was just an illusion. And I think that's what devastated me the most...the romantic fool that I was.

I thought back to when we split up; moving through the silence of our house as we made our lists of what we each wanted to keep. I refused to break down; I could have, I was so angry...but I was also sad that a portion of my life was coming to an end.

I must have dozed in my desk chair; not an easy feat, for I was suddenly aware of my surroundings.

Now, where was I?

Where We Left Off...

CHAPTER ONE

1981

It was my second year up in the mountains, and I couldn't believe how quickly it'd become the end of February. I was hoping the new year and the rest of winter would bring us only a pocket full of challenges since the previous year had presented us with many. Just to tease me, a gust of ice cold wind blew my sweater open, and I pulled it tight around me. We'd just come off an unusually heavy snowfall, and all the roads were piled high with berms that would keep some homeowners locked down until they could get a snowplow to dig them out.

This latest storm downed power lines in various communities, which left those of us without generators, without power.

"I don't remember that from last year," I said.

"Well, it probably happened, but it didn't last long. It happens regularly," Sam said. "Sometimes we're down for twenty minutes, and sometimes a day. The good news is you can always store your refrigerated foods outdoors in winter."

If we could make it through the rest of this winter without too many repairs, the next thing on my list was to get some pricing to install a generator large enough to run all the cabins if need be.

Thankfully, we were between guests, so it spared us having to creatively heat and light the cabins. That night, Noah and I bundled up and sat in front of his fireplace; the glow of the fire lit his whiskered face and when I reached out to touch him, he took my hand and kissed my palm. We slept cuddled on the sofa, surrounded by the dogs, and I stirred when he got up to add more logs early that next morning. Ginny stayed with Sam and the cats so he could remain on the property in case of an emergency.

The next morning, as I looked out to the tree just outside the French doors, I saw a squirrel sitting on one of the large, low branches. His coat was covered in snowflakes, his eyes were closed, and he was concentrating on eating whatever morsel his little paws held.

I quickly turned to call to Noah so he could witness this sight, and unfortunately, he wasn't as quiet as he could have been. I turned as the squirrel heard us break the silence, and he scampered off before Noah could see him.

"Darn it," I said.

"Sorry," Noah grimaced.

I loved driving the snowy mountain roads once they were cleared, appreciating the snow-covered trees, and one of my favorite roads was the one into Blue Jay. It was a two-lane highway, most of it under trees that formed a canopy, arching so you felt like you were driving through a tall tunnel. There were a couple of icy spots on the road, so even the most seasoned mountain drivers kept to the speed limit. Old cabins lined the road, some with parked cars covered so deeply, it would take forever to clear.

Just when our power was restored, a large tree fell across the highway in front of the cabins and created the worst jam-up I'd ever witnessed. It would be another day before the highway maintenance men finished cutting the tree up and hauling it away. In the meantime, before they could get down the highway enough to make a difference with the street closure signs, cars were pulling into our parking area to turn around. Sam and I alternated guiding people in and out, keeping them from damaging our trees by accidentally bumping into them. I wouldn't know until the snow melted just how badly our landscaping had fared.

"The only good news," Noah said once he could finally get through, "is that we have power."

I'd bought the cabins from Sam Jackson, who'd been up here for years, and he'd stayed on and helped me run the rentals. He'd lost his wife some time back, and we were kind of good for each other, as he'd told me; I came into *his* life helping fill a void and he came into mine when I was starting my divorce.

I'd just discovered my husband had been seeing someone else, and had come up to the mountains for a change of scenery. Once I reconciled to the humiliation of it all, I found I struggled with constant mental conversations and inner conflict. I alternately blamed him and then me for the failure of our marriage. I'd hoped the emotional roller coaster would come to an end, if not slow down, and eventually it had. And having the opportunity to buy the cabins had given me the determination I needed to start over.

I now went into the office to warm up by the fire, and our two camp cats, Jezebel and Socks, greeted me, letting me know in no uncertain terms they missed me and were unhappy with all the noise. Jezebel circled my legs as I turned, and I accidentally kicked Socks.

"Sorry, girl," I said.

I missed them terribly too, but I knew if I took them to Noah's, they'd have to get used to the dogs and the new surroundings, and Sam would be without his two furry friends. Cats were so different from dogs; you could take a dog with you anywhere and they'd quickly feel at home. Cats, on the other hand, got stressed just looking at their carriers, and spent hours slinking around their new surroundings before they could relax.

I decided to make my time in the lobby worthwhile, so I dusted the counter, furniture and tables, and then rearranged magazines and local maps. I took the last of our cabin brochures out of their box and set those out, too. If I needed them for gift basket donations, I'd know where they were, and I took a quick minute to see if there was anything I needed to update before I had more printed.

My dear old friend Sarah had designed them for me, and I wondered how she was doing. If it was cold and snowy here, it had to be worse in Las Vegas. Was it my turn to call her? As I read through the brochure, I didn't see any changes, so I called our local printer to order another box along with business cards.

The next day, Sarah must have sensed I'd been thinking about her, for she called.

We'd been very close throughout school, and she'd moved away the day we graduated. She became a graphic designer, and while we spoke regularly, I hadn't seen her in over three years. I'd been in the mountains for a little over a year and a half, and she'd helped me with my marketing materials for the cabins.

"I'm going to stop and see my mom," she said. "And I'd love to come up and see you and these cabins," she'd said. "I need to rethink my life."

"It's a great place to do it," I said. "Just let me know when. If it's soon, dress warmly. We still have a little snow."

Something was going on, and I figured I'd find out, eventually.

"I was hoping it could be next week?"

I'd seen her before, standing near a group of kids, observing as a boy entertained his friends by calling me names. But the first time I actually met Sarah was when the boy did it again, and she flattened him for laughing at me. When the young man started to cry, his friends were no longer interested in me, but started laughing at him instead.

"Crybaby," they called as they turned to leave him.

"Well, that should be the end of that," Sarah said, wiping her hands in triumph.

And it was.

We were five.

My mother was born and raised in California, and my father in Taiwan. He came here as a student and stayed when he married my mother. I looked more like her, with her German heritage, but there was always something about me, something that made people look at me, as if baffled. While I never felt that way, my first husband, David, called me exotic.

My mother worked in the school lunch program, so I'd see her in the cafeteria when Sarah and I came in for lunch. Unless there was something special on the menu, my mother usually packed lunch for both of us. I think she was afraid Sarah would starve since we'd never seen her bring anything to eat, or have any money to buy lunch with.

I told no one but Sarah about being teased before, but I knew my older sister Loni had had the same problem. I'd also told her that I hated it when anyone met my mother, and she was introduced as Mrs. Chang. She looked like most of the other moms, but our surname didn't match us; it set us apart.

So Sarah started to call her 'Mrs. C', and soon that nickname stuck.

"Just call me Mrs. C," my mother began saying to anyone new, usually with a smile meant just for me.

True to her promise, a week later, Sarah pulled into our parking area. She did the same thing I'd done when I first came up; she stretched her arms high above her head, took a deep breath and said, "It's so peaceful here."

I'd lit a fire in what was to be her cabin, and smoke spiraled up the fireplace. The air smelled like burning pine.

"It is. That's why I stayed. Let me help you with your things," I said, and then looked into the back seat of her car. It was filled with boxes and tied up trash bags.

She saw the look on my face and said, "Most of it can stay in Las Vegas. This is all I kept. My suitcases are in the trunk."

"Let's get you settled. I have you in Cedar Lodge Cabin."

When I opened the door to cabin number three, Sarah held her breath and said, "Wow."

"So far, two of the cabins have histories we've learned about. A woman, Elizabeth, and her husband Thomas stayed in this cabin for three months in the early 1930s while they were finishing their lake house cabin up here. Actually, it's a huge, wonderful old home, and not a cabin at all. People up here call their homes cabins.

"After her grandmother died, I worked with the granddaughter, Carrie, to bring their house up to date. Both the house and Carrie were an interior designer's dream to work with. It turns out her grandmother knew Bugsy Siegel. In fact, I've had professional photos taken of the finished project, and I'd love to have you add them to my portfolio."

I realized I'd been doing all the talking while Sarah looked around the cabin, taking in all the details; the painting over the fireplace, the updated bathroom and kitchenette.

"Sorry, I've hogged the conversation," I said.

"No, Annie, I could tell by the photos you sent you've done a wonderful job. I knew you were good, and you should be really proud of your work," she said, unlocking her suitcase.

"Can I get you anything?" I asked. "Water, cookies? Do you need some time to rest after your drive?"

"I'd love all the above," Sarah said, putting her folded clothing in a dresser drawer. "Let me just have a few minutes, and I'll come get you. Are you hungry?"

"Always. I think it's the altitude. Oh, and you'll need to drink plenty of water up here. It can make you light-headed. Do you want me to leave the fire on?"

"No, it's so beautiful out, and I'm not the least bit cold."

"Okay, you might be when we get back. I'm in cabin one, so come get me when you're ready."

We went to our old standby, Ginny's.

"Wow, you're famous," Sarah said as I greeted the locals.

"It doesn't take long to get to know most of the people up here," I said, leading her to an empty booth.

"So, how's your mom?" I asked, splitting our sandwich when it came.

"Nothing's changed. Once I got there, I could hardly wait to leave."

"I'm sorry," I said, and I genuinely was. Time apparently hadn't helped their relationship. She didn't elaborate, and I was okay with that. I knew eventually I'd hear everything she wanted to share with me.

It was cooling down, so when we got back we brought blankets out and sat in the Adirondack chairs in front of her cabin. The cats seized the opportunity for warm laps and snuggled under the blankets. I knew Sarah was exhausted, and I quickly realized I could use a nap too, and within moments, we were both out. I awoke before Sarah did, and I watched my friend sleep. I wanted to reach out and touch her hand, to show her I was there for her, but I didn't want to wake her. Instead, I closed my eyes again and let the sound of the wind rustling through the pine trees lull me back to sleep.

"Show me around," Sarah said when she woke.

"We do still have some daylight left...are you sure you don't want to put your things away?"

"I can do that when we're done."

"Okay then. We'll start with my cabin first."

"The photos make me feel like I'd love to stay here, but they don't do the place justice," she said. "Each cabin is perfect. I love the names you've given them, and I love the mix of old and new. And I can't think of anything more original to say than I love them all." She gave me a big hug.

"I wanted to save the most dramatic for last," I said, opening the door to cabin number five, the Pinecone Cabin.

I told her how Alyce Murphy came up to see where her father hung himself after he killed his business partner and his family. This was before Sam bought the cabins, and other than speculation in the newspaper stories, there was no definitive answer as to why he'd done it.

"They'd used the cabin as storage for over twenty years, and Alyce came up while we were clearing it out for restoration. Unfortunately, there wasn't anything in there to give us any insight about what happened.

"About three weeks after she left, I found a note tucked away in an old clock Sam wanted to clean up and use on the counter in the office. It said something like, 'I'm a monster and I'm sorry for destroying my family.' I wasn't sure the note would add anything but more disappointment because it didn't unearth the real reason for her father killing his partner. I was tempted to keep the note to myself and just put it in the trinket box where we keep mementos our guests have left behind, like movie theater stubs, old menus, and used ski lift tickets. Both Sam and Noah thought I should send the note, and in the end, I sent it with a letter telling her I hoped she was doing okay. She'd never know why he did what he did, and by hiding the note in the clock, it's a wonder it ever got found."

At lunch, I told Sarah I'd met someone up here, and that we were living together, but I hadn't told her yet about my recklessness with my biggest design client, Grayson Underwood. I wanted to give Noah more respect than to cram the details into our first few hours together, so I filled her in a little more on the drive to meet Noah and his friend Josh at the Cowboy Bar.

We got there first, so we ordered our wine, and talked about sharing the rib eye and fries since we were both still a little full from lunch. When Noah and Josh got there, they ordered their beers from the bar and then joined us.

I assumed Sarah wasn't interested in meeting someone, because I knew she was still married, but I saw a glimpse of a smile when she saw Josh coming towards us. His eyebrows lifted slightly as he sat down.

"Sarah, this is Josh," I said.

"Hey there," he said.

Noah and I exchanged glances.

Made in the USA
Middletown, DE
06 January 2023

18228810R00158